THE GHO

Mike Jefferies was born in Kent and spent several
years in Australia. He studied at St Martin's School
of Art and then taught art in schools and prisons.
A keen rider, he was selected in 1980 to ride for
Britain in the Belgian Three Day Event. He now
lives in Norfolk with his wife, Sheila, working as
a full-time writer and illustrator.

Voyager

MIKE JEFFERIES

The Ghosts of
Candleford

HarperCollins*Publishers*

Voyager
An Imprint of HarperCollins*Publishers*
77–85 Fulham Palace Road,
Hammersmith, London W6 8JB

A Paperback Original 1999
1 3 5 7 9 8 6 4 2

ISBN 0 00 648208 2

Typeset in Goudy Old Style by
Palimpsest Book Production Limited,
Polmont, Stirlingshire

Printed and bound in Great Britain by
Caledonian International Book Manufacturing Ltd, Glasgow

To my wife, Sheila,
who heard the muffled footpads beyond the door
and always knew there was a grain of truth
in the myths and legends we heard whispered in the dark.

1

December 11th 1942

My Darling Ellen,

Yes, it's me, and I've arrived safely in England at last. Say 'Hi' to the kids for me will you and give them both a big hug.

You wouldn't believe how lousy the crossing was or how bitterly cold it can get in these draughty transport planes high up over the North Atlantic. Everybody in the outfit was huddled together trying to keep warm. Oh yes, I almost forgot, tell the kids I'm sure we saw at least two polar bears on an ice floe when we flew over. I guess they must have been watching out for submarines!

Ellen, were we glad to get out of that aircraft when it eventually landed somewhere in the north of Scotland. The Scotch people are really swell and they have gone out of their way to make us feel welcome, but the tea they drink takes a lot of getting used to. It's so strong, I swear they must use it to oil their guns. Their scotch drink is much better, but it's in very short supply.

Our transit camp is in complete chaos, nobody knows what's going on. We've hardly got our feet on the ground and we've just been given our orders to move south. I'll finish this letter after we arrive wherever they're sending us.

3

When the smoke from the air raids clears you can see that England is really beautiful. Everything is so neat, the fields are laid out like a patchwork quilt and the tiny villages we have passed through are so picturesque with their inns and rows of whitewashed, thatched cottages. Sometimes I have to pinch myself because it's just like being inside a picture book.

We finally arrived in ■ ■ ■ ■ this afternoon and I've been billeted at an old coaching inn called the Black Shuck, it's in the centre of a village called ■ ■ ■ ■ ■ ■. It's right on the edge of the Fens and only a short ride from the airfield we are to fly from. The village is the quaintest place you can imagine, with its rows of pink and white houses and a handful of old-fashioned shops surrounding the village green which has two ponds. There is an enormous church, more like a cathedral, right next door to where I'm staying. There are two other inns, or pubs as the locals call them, on the green; one is called the Rose and Crown, the name has something to do with the English Civil War, the other one has the strangest name, no one can explain it, it's called the Louse and Rag. The Black Shuck is by far the oldest in the village, the name refers to some old legend about a demon dog that is meant to roam the Fens. The landlord told me that there are records in the church stating that the owner of the inn was paid one shilling in 1650 for killing sparrows! Don't ask me why they got paid for killing sparrows – and I can't figure out their money yet, they have a Godawful system here and it's going to take some getting used to.

Ellen, you would just love the inn with its low, blackened, beamed ceilings. They're hung with the strangest collection of curios, old tools, lamps, and ancient figures, dolls, made out of straw and grasses. Before I forget, there is a 'snug' bar, the cosiest room, with a huge fireplace that takes up the whole of one wall, it's called an inglenook. You can actually sit in it on old oak benches around the fire grate. There is a wonderful collection of copper pots and pans hanging up in the chimney that are still used to cook our food. The stone flagged floors are swept and sprinkled with sawdust every morning. There is just so much to see here and it's all so old. They even draw their water from a well in the yard!

The rest of the pub is a warren of gloomy corridors and narrow, winding stairways. I keep getting lost trying to find the attic room where I live even though there are numbers on all the doors. They don't help much because they don't follow any order as far as I can work out and I've already walked into the wrong room twice.

The locals here in the village are much more reserved than the Scotch people we met when we first landed. Sometimes it feels almost as if they don't want us here at all. They're secretive and it's difficult to understand their dialect. Not at all the English we were expecting. I'll write more about that later.

The Fenland countryside is desolate and it has hardly any trees, it's so flat all you can see are miles of swaying reed beds and the occasional stretch of water. You feel as though you're standing in the sky. But it can all change dramatically without a moment's warning and the land and the sky will merge together and enfold you in a silent shroud of cloud. We've been warned not to wander too far into the Fens without a guide so I'll try to find one tomorrow because I can't wait to explore it and take some photographs. It looks so mysterious from my attic window. I'll take some pictures of the setting winter sun reflecting on the ice that covers the deep drainage ditches and dykes that vanish away across the Fens.

I might have trouble getting film for my camera over here. Because of the war there's virtually nothing in the shops. Could you send me a couple of rolls, some stamps and some airmail stationery?

I'll write again soon, all my love to the three of you.

Merris.

Hollis Calvin frowned and carefully laid the fragile, yellowing letter from his grandfather to one side of the desk. His father's death had been unexpected and he was feeling quite numb with shock when he sat down to sort through his personal effects. He had never expected to find this small bundle of letters and photographs. He had known about his grandfather's mysterious disappearance in England during the war almost fifty years ago, but the why and the how of it had never been something that was openly discussed. Merris Calvin had always been an elusive, distant figure, a faded image staring vacantly out of an old photograph on the mantelpiece. Reading through his letters, looking at the photographs he had taken, was like putting flesh on to varnished bones. Hollis shuffled through the letters and wondered about the man. Then he began to read another.

My Darling Ellen,

I hope that the parcel I sent back with Chuck on one of the returning transporters reached you in time for Christmas. Chuck promised to mail it on to you the moment they landed in Boston. I'm sorry there wasn't much in the parcel for the kids but everything's in such short supply over here. Believe me it's no picnic, the people have to queue for even the most basic things. Tell the kids that those two little straw dolls are called straw 'dollies'. They were made by one of the locals from last year's corn harvest, or it may have been from the year before, and they have been hung up in the inn for good luck. It's got something to do with an ancient farming ritual but the landlord has assured me that there's nothing sinister about them. Although he was very reluctant to let me have them until I produced a couple of packs of cigarettes and a large bar of candy. Tell the kids I'll make it up to them once this war's over and I get home.

We had a heavy snowfall on Christmas Eve which has temporarily grounded the squadron and given us a welcome break from those long-range bombing raids over Germany. The village church looked beautiful, it was decorated with holly and mistletoe and lit by hundreds of candles that cast a shimmering glow through the frost-covered, stained glass windows out onto the deep drifts of snow outside. I stood there singing 'Silent Night' , thinking of the three of you and how much I missed you. I had tears streaming down my face.

I have palled up with a local farmer who I met one

night in the snug bar. His name is Dennis Skinner. He's a great guy, really friendly, but he doesn't seem to get on with some of the regulars though. So far he's taken me on two short expeditions into the Fens – you just wouldn't believe the wildlife that thrives inside that wilderness. I was surprised to find that there are even people who live out there and scratch a meagre living cutting sedge and peat in the marshes. How these guys know their way through those mires and bogs beats me. I'd hate to get lost on my own out there. Dennis has promised to take me duck shooting soon.

I've also met up with a friend of Dennis', a really swell guy called Douglas Reeve who owns the village drug store – over here they call it a chemist shop. He's a real expert on ornithology and came with us on our second trip into the Fens. Doug was fascinated by my new camera, he thinks he might be able to get me some film through a friend of his in ■ ■ ■ ■.

A really weird thing happened the other night. Do you remember me telling you how easy it is to get lost in this inn? Well, on New Year's Eve I was a little the worse for wear owing to the strength of this warm English beer I'm afraid, and I accidentally barged into the wrong room on the way to bed. I disturbed some private fancy dress party that was going on. You wouldn't believe the strange costumes and bright flowers they were wearing. Some of them had on horned head-dresses and they were shouting as they walked around the room carrying lighted candles. I tell you it was the weirdest thing I've ever seen. They shouted at me and one of them pushed me out of the room. They were real angry that I saw them. I told you the locals were none too friendly.

Later that night everyone in our attic was woken up by an eerie, howling noise. We looked out of the small window and we could see a procession of lights moving slowly out across the marshes. The next morning I asked the landlord what was with all the lights and noise but he said I must have been dreaming. He said neither he nor any of his staff had heard or seen anything unusual. He didn't seem to like answering my questions. There was definitely quite an atmosphere there and then everyone went very quiet when we came in after our mission in the evening too. It's probably nothing to worry about, just the effects of tension and tiredness after all these long-range bombing missions.

Love to the three of you,

Merris

Hollis dropped the letter onto the pile he had already read and unfolded another dated January 18th. He was getting used to skipping over the words the censor had blocked out and was inventing names for the places they had removed in the interest of National Security. He paused for a moment to wonder how his grandfather, or any of the other guys who had enlisted and gone away to fight, had felt about the censors going through their mail. It was such an invasion of privacy; despite the security issue he felt sure he would have hated it.

The next letter didn't tell him much about the village or the people who had lived there. It seemed that the freezing weather had finally broken and they had been flying missions every day after that. Merris had complained about the atrocious wet weather, and the countryside that was continually enveloped in a dreary, grey shroud of mist and rain that often made finding the airfield difficult on their return. He complained that their clothes were constantly damp and he reckoned that the planes would fall apart with rust long before the Germans could get them. There was a long piece about a trip to London that he had taken on a three-day pass with the rest of the unit, and a vivid description of the devastation they had seen.

> . . . the people in London are real friendly, they call us 'crazy Yanks' wherever we go. Believe me, Ellen, they're the crazy ones, to stick around after the terrible beating they're taking in these air raids. You've really got to admire them.

Hollis was about to fold the letter and put it away when he noticed a small postscript on the back.

> . . . we had been told before arriving in England not to upset the local people but it really took the biscuit the other night when the locals blamed me personally for a lone German bomber dropping a stick of incendiary bombs on the village. It killed two cows and an old woman. I don't know why they singled me out and decided it was my fault but a mob of villagers hounded me out of the snug and up to my room in the attic. I had to barricade myself in until they went away. That's the thanks I get for risking my life every day for them! Dennis and Doug took a very dim view of their behaviour and they have warned me not to go out on my own after dark.

But things seem to be settling down again now, thank goodness. This rain is so monotonous, the mud seems to get everywhere, even in the food.

Love to all three of you, miss you,

Merris

Hollis noticed the date as he put the letter in with the others and realized that it had been written only a couple of days before his grandfather's sudden and unexplained disappearance. There were three official letters still in their original envelopes bundled together with a decaying rubber band that broke the moment he touched it. One was a short, but sympathetic, letter from his grandfather's Commanding Officer dated shortly after he went missing and informing his wife of his disappearance. The letter stated that he was a most exemplary officer held in high esteem by everyone he served with, and he assured her that everything possible was being done to trace his whereabouts. The second letter officially reported him missing on active service in East Anglia and there was a paragraph informing Ellen that the local constabulary were investigating his disappearance. The third letter was from the Pentagon dated some nine months later that stated that the investigation into the disappearance of Lieutenant Merris Calvin, Army no. 733726, had proved inconclusive. It stated that the file would remain open recording Merris Calvin missing on active service.

Hollis sighed. That last letter had seemed a cold, abrupt way to end his grandfather's life. He began to shuffle the letters and photographs back into a neat bundle ready to put them away in the bureau when he noticed a letter he had missed. A single photograph fell out as he unfolded the crumpled piece of paper and it fluttered to the floor between his feet. At a glance he could see that the letter was unfinished, a page of

11

hastily scrawled lines, but what quickened Hollis' interest was that it was written on the day before he had disappeared.

February 14th 1943

My Darling Ellen,

Suddenly it has stopped being fun over here. A sinister feeling has taken over quaint old England and the atmosphere in this village has definitely changed since that damn raid. The locals have become sullen, they turn away in the street and make some peculiar sign in the air as I walk past. They go quiet whenever I go into any of the bars in the Black Shuck. I have this feeling that they're watching me, waiting for something to happen, and it's giving me the creeps. Dennis and Doug have tried to laugh it off, they say I'm imagining it, but I can tell they're worried. I overheard Dennis saying to Doug that he didn't hold with the Lanterns – whatever that means. They have both warned me to lock my door at night.

On a brighter note I got Chuck to take a picture of the three of us so you could see what Dennis and Doug look like. We're sitting in front of the inglenook in the snug.

We almost went duck shooting late this afternoon. I was really looking forward to getting away with just the two guys but then the strangest thing happened. We were just rowing out from the jetty when I happened to glance down into the water and I saw lights. It must have been a trick of the light but it looked like queer shapes were rising out of the weeds beneath the boat. I called to the others to draw their attention to what I had seen and they both took one look down and rowed furiously back to the bank. They almost rowed us up onto dry land. Doug shouted something about the Lanterns and then dragged me away from there at a run. They wouldn't explain why. I don't know what it was all about but clearly something had terrified them.

There's so much going on, the atmosphere in the inn seems electric. When we returned everyone in the snug seemed to be sitting on the edge of their seats as if they were surprised to see us or something. It's making my spine tingle just writing about it. I'll finish the letter tomorrow and tell you about a trip we're planning to take up country next week. I'll feel better in the daylight. I just wish –

Hollis bent down and retrieved the photograph, intrigued to see what his grandfather's friends had looked like. A cold rush of shock ran up his spine. He had been expecting to see a picture of his grandfather and his two English friends, and yet he was staring at a yellowing jumble of figures including *himself* with two complete strangers: a pretty blonde woman and a dark, thick-set, serious looking guy standing in the foreground. Both of them were about his age but as if that wasn't weird enough Hollis' father was in the picture standing directly behind him with two other people he had never seen before – and behind *them* his grandfather and his friends posed linking arms in front of an enormous fireplace which was cluttered with old-fashioned pots and pans exactly like the one he had described in his letter. The photograph was badly stained as if it had been left lying in water for a long time.

Hollis tried to swallow but his throat had dried up. He blinked and looked at the picture again, unable to comprehend what he was seeing. 'I've got to be dreaming, this isn't real – it can't be!'

He rubbed his thumb firmly across the surface of the print. He wasn't sure why he did it, perhaps half hoping it would erase the impossible image, but it didn't. His smiling face and shock of unruly hair were still there surrounded by the other ghostly images staring out at him. He could even remember buying the sweatshirt he was wearing in the photograph. It was the distinctive Red Sox shirt he had bought recently. He stared at the picture trying desperately to think of a plausible explanation. The normal, everyday sounds, the shouts of children playing in the street outside, the engine noise of a passing car, all melted into a stifling, enveloping silence. Somehow two different images had superimposed themselves onto the original photograph – but how? He didn't even know the other two people in it. He had never been in a room with a fireplace like that. He knew he had never posed for it and as far as he knew his father had never even been to England. This picture couldn't exist!

He cautiously turned it over and caught sight of faded handwriting on the back. Peering closer he recognized his grandmother's distinctive, spiky script. 'This must be Dennis and Douglas, the two Englishmen Merris wrote me about.' It was dated soon after he had been born.

Hollis felt his blood run cold as he realized that a photograph of him, the one in his hand, had existed in 1970. His grandmother's writing proved that. But how could it be? How could he be in a picture taken years before he was born? It wasn't possible. Hollis suddenly shivered, dropping the picture. There was something sinister and unnatural about it. What the hell had his grandfather stumbled into in that remote village – could it have caused his sudden disappearance?

Hollis was barely aware of the telephone ringing in the kitchen or of his mother's voice answering it, but the sound of her footsteps behind him broke through his concentration, making him jump. It made him realize how engrossed he had become with his grandfather's wartime letters and the photograph he had just discovered. He turned round quickly and found his mother standing in the doorway. There was a lost, bewildered vacancy in her eyes, her lips were trembling slightly and her fingers were repeatedly twisting and pinching at the edges of one of his father's white handkerchiefs, unconsciously teasing loose a stray thread from its hem. She seemed reluctant to cross the threshold of the study, afraid to explore the emptiness that she knew would now always inhabit the room. The doctor had warned Hollis that it would take some time for his mother to get over the shock of her husband's sudden death and that she shouldn't be left on her own for too long.

'I'm sorry, mom, I got sidetracked. I found a bundle of old letters and photographs that grandfather wrote during the war. Don't worry, I'll get those bills sorted out later this morning.'

He put his arm around her, remembering that he'd left her in the kitchen worrying over a handful of final demands that had arrived in the morning mail. He had promised her that it wouldn't take a minute to find the paperwork in the study and get it all straightened out. His father's death had left so many loose ends to tie up, things they had always taken for granted until two weeks ago.

'Who was that on the telephone?' he asked, guiding his mother gently back to the kitchen.

'Telephone?' She frowned. 'Oh, yes, it was your Uncle Joseph. He wants me to go away with them for a while, they're going to stay in that cabin they have on Lake Dillon. But I don't know ... I'm not sure. He's coming over to speak with you.' She answered in a flat monotone as she

15

found herself a chair and sat staring at a cup of coffee grown cold.

It suddenly occurred to Hollis that his mother might have seen that weird picture he had found of himself. He wondered what she had made of it. He returned thoughtfully to the study and picked it up, but then paused. Perhaps he had imagined it. Perhaps because of the shock of his father's death, the funeral and everything, perhaps because he had so much on his mind, he had superimposed his own image onto the picture. There was no point in bothering his mother with an old photograph at a time like this. But he had to make sure first. He took the picture to the window and re-examined it, tilting it slightly to let the light flood across its dull, mottled, water-stained surface. There was no mistaking what he saw. He was still there, smiling out from between those two complete strangers. And something even stranger had happened to it since he'd last looked – the image of his father had faded a little more. A shudder of apprehension rippled up his spine. He would have to ask his mother if she had ever seen the picture before.

He went back into the kitchen to find her lost in her own grief, staring vacantly into the middle distance. 'Mom,' he spoke softly to get her attention. 'Mom, I've found this really odd photograph amongst grandfather's letters. I can't make it out. Have you seen it before?'

She barely blinked or shifted her gaze as he propped the photograph against her coffee cup. Her empty eyes gradually focused on it, her fingers ceased to pinch and pull at the handkerchief and she stared. Seeing that photograph tugged at memories, things George had told her about, things about his childhood. She remembered him telling her about the day that roll of film had been developed, long after the war was over, and the surprise of seeing himself in it.

'Yes, I remember.' Her voice was bleak; looking up at him

16

she intoned, 'It was a mistake, just an over-exposed snap. I told him to throw it away.' And she shrugged, dismissing the picture from her mind as her eyes clouded over and her gaze drifted out across the yard.

'But it's more than a simple over-exposure, mom. Look at it again. Can you explain how I can be in that picture with dad and grandfather – look, there I am, large as life standing between two strangers. Who are those other two? You can't just shrug it off.'

There was an urgency in Hollis' voice that cut right through Helen's grief. She let the crumpled handkerchief drop into her lap and reached for the photograph. A cold wave of uncertainty swept through her as she studied the picture more closely. Yes, it was that same old photograph, the one that had given her the creeps when she had first seen it. Only now there was Hollis in it as well, and two more people, strangers, one of them a pretty young woman. She didn't understand.

The sound of a car pulling up onto the driveway and the squeal of its brakes brought her abruptly back into the present. She shook her head and let the photo fall back amongst the coffee cups on the table. 'I don't know what to make of it,' she said, her fingers reuniting with the handkerchief, pinching it and twisting it reassuringly as it lay in her lap.

The pain of her present loss was so acute that there was no room inside her to worry about an old photograph, and one that should have been destroyed years ago. 'It's probably something to do with the chemicals used to develop it but I can't think about it now, Hollis,' she muttered, dismissing the matter and pushing it to the back of her mind. She glanced up to the door to see the familiar, balding, bulky figure of her husband's brother opening the screen and hurrying into the kitchen.

'Ask Joe,' she added as an afterthought. 'He was the one

who found the roll of film amongst your grandfather's things. Ask him.' Helen's smile of recognition clouded over and her gaze slid past Joe and rested on something in the middle distance.

Joe caught the tail end of her sentence. 'Ask me what? If it's about the trip to Lake Dillon everything's arranged. We'll pick you both up in the morning. The doctor said it would be best for you to get away for a while.'

Helen shrugged and continued to gaze out into the yard. Hollis nodded with concern as he watched her stare blankly out of the window. 'Yeah, I think it is a good idea for mom to get away for a while but we weren't talking about that. I was asking her about that old photograph I've just found. Look, it's there on the table in front of her.'

'What photograph?' His uncle carefully put down the collection of condolence cards and letters that he'd collected from the funeral home and walked over to pick up the print. 'Oh, yeah, I remember the day that bunch of pictures was developed. It's almost like it were yesterday. Your grandmother was quite upset, I guess she was just getting used to not having your grandfather around. I can tell you she was none too pleased with me for finding that roll of film amongst the stuff the War Office sent back from England, but I had no idea any of these photographs were still around. Where did you find it?' Joe gave the yellowing print a brief, perfunctory glance before dropping it back onto the table.

Hollis was disappointed by his uncle's reaction but he wasn't prepared to let it go at that. 'It was in amongst a bundle of old letters at the back of dad's desk. But don't you think there's something really odd about that photograph? Has it changed at all since you last saw it?'

'What do you mean?' Joe frowned and looked down again, then he let out a low gasp of surprise and rubbed his thumb across its grainy surface. 'How the hell did you get into this picture?' he asked sharply, looking hard at Hollis.

Hollis shrugged. 'I don't know, I've only just found it, it's really weird.'

His mother's fingers became agitated and they worked faster and faster on the handkerchief, tearing free the stray threads as his voice rose.

'Let's go into the study,' Joe murmured softly as he picked up the photograph. 'We won't be a moment, Helen,' he said, as he smiled reassuringly at his sister-in-law. 'There are a few things to sort out for the trip.'

Joe quietly closed the door of the study and took a deep breath before turning angrily on his nephew. 'What's all this crap about? What is it about that old photograph – don't you think your mother's suffering enough at the moment? What's gotten into you, Hollis?'

'I'm ... I'm ... I'm sorry, I had no idea that showing her that picture would upset her,' Hollis stuttered defensively. 'But wouldn't you be a little surprised if you found a photograph of yourself tucked away in your grandfather's letters? A photograph of yourself you couldn't possibly be in. Wouldn't it make you a little curious? Go on ... look at it again and tell me I'm making it all up. Tell me the guy in the foreground isn't me, tell me the image of my father isn't getting fainter. Give me some sort of explanation. You must have seen the picture before, you must have thought that it was pretty crazy then.'

Joe frowned. He hadn't expected this. 'Now hold on ...' he began, his words blurring into a whistle of surprise as he stared at the print. 'You're right, we did think it was pretty odd and we tried to explain it away as an over-exposure, just a mess up with the developing. Your father said he was going to destroy it.'

'But he didn't, did he? Look again, the picture has changed, hasn't it?'

Joe nodded bleakly.

'So why didn't you do something about it when you first got it developed? Didn't it seem strange to you – having two complete strangers standing with my father? Didn't it seem just a little curious?'

Joe shook his head slowly. 'Those cameras were different back then, people used to forget to wind them on, pictures did come out double exposed when they were developed. Remember England was a foreign place, it was a long way off. Most of the things we saw in those photographs and on the newsreels looked odd to us. Your grandmother was upset when she saw the picture was messed up, after all it was the last one ever taken of your grandfather. But . . .' He paused and sat down heavily in the leather swivel chair at the desk. His skin paled and a faint sheen of perspiration formed on his forehead, catching the light from the window. Joe seemed to shiver and a haunted look invaded his eyes as he let the picture fall amongst the litter of papers on the desk top before pushing it all away from him.

'I don't know what to say to you, Hollis. I can't explain why you are in that picture now but seeing it again has given me the creeps.'

He hesitated and rummaged in his jacket pocket for a wad of crumpled tissues to wipe his forehead. 'We tried to convince ourselves that it wasn't your father at all, standing there in front of your grandfather, smiling away with those two strangers. We tried to tell ourselves it was just a double exposure but I always had my misgivings about it.'

'What misgivings? Tell me what you thought about it, tell me exactly what you felt?'

Joe thought for a moment and mopped at his forehead. 'I

don't know . . . it's difficult to remember. I've never tried to put it into words before. I suppose . . . but this is going to sound really crazy . . . I suppose it's as though those three figures are meant to be there, as though they are trying to tell us something.'

He sat and thought about it some more. 'It's as though they are there for a purpose, they belong to that picture, but why you have suddenly appeared there as well is beyond me. I don't like it, Hollis, I don't like it at all.'

Joe fell silent and looked at the picture for a long time. 'Hollis, I want you to forget you ever found that old photograph. It's obviously upset your mother seeing it again today. Why, if I'd had the slightest idea it was still around I would have made your father get rid of it.'

Joe shifted his bulk in the chair, making it swivel slightly and lean to one side as he felt in his jacket pocket for his lighter. Hollis saw the flash of sunlight reflect on the smooth gunmetal case between his fingers as his uncle withdrew it from his pocket. Hollis was mesmerized, rooted to the spot. He couldn't believe that his uncle would wantonly destroy the photograph.

'It's for the best, Hollis,' Joe murmured. In one, slow, deliberate movement he snapped his lighter open, releasing a pale blue flame. With his other hand he reached across the desk for the photograph and, bringing them together, ran the flickering flame along the bottom, curling the edge of the print.

'No! No, stop it!' Hollis cried, making a sudden lunge for the photograph as it caught alight, knocking the lighter out from his uncle's hand as he snatched the picture from him. He quickly punched out the flames and crushed the smouldering edge between his fingers. 'You've got no right to do that, none at all. It isn't just a picture from your past, it's my picture as well. I'm in it. I'm a part of it now and I want to know why. I *have* to know why.'

Joe stared up at Hollis' angry face, startled by his outburst. He had always been a quiet, well-mannered boy; this anger shocked him. He began to shake his head as he got up out of the chair to retrieve his lighter but before he could say anything Hollis added softly, 'I must have appeared in that picture for a reason. You've got to help me. Tell me anybody you can think of who might give me some way to begin to unravel this mystery.'

Joe slumped back in the swivel chair and mopped at the cold trickles of perspiration that were creeping down his temples. 'Okay, okay, something odd did happen after your grandfather disappeared. Your father began to have real bad nightmares. I guess you do have the right to know about it all.'

'Nightmares? What's so special about having nightmares? His father had just gone missing, most kids would have nightmares.'

'Well, you listen and then you tell me if they were just normal dreams.'

Hollis leaned heavily on the desk as he listened, and the back of his neck went cold as his uncle described the dark, sinister shapes that had infested his father's sleeping hours, the moving lights beneath the murky waters of the marshes, the tread of approaching footsteps on the stairs and the sense of something closing in, of whispers in the thickening gloom. Hollis could almost see the claustrophobic shadows closing in around his father as his uncle's voice continued.

'There was a recurring pattern to these dreams. They terri-fied your father, he felt as though he was trapped, as though he was drowning and all he could feel was black silence.'

A door slammed somewhere in the house and made them both jump. Hollis blinked and tried to swallow but his throat had gone dry. He had once had the exact same dream and it had terrified him. He could understand now why his uncle had been so reluctant to talk about them.

'Were there any other strange or unusual pictures from that roll of film? Can you remember if any of these came from that batch?'

Hollis started to separate about a dozen old photographs from the bundle of Merris' letters and passed them across the desk.

'There was only that one picture on the roll of film, the rest had been spoilt by the light getting in. All these others were taken earlier,' Joe said as he looked slowly through the pile of faded prints. 'Ah yes, there was this one, and this one, I remember thinking how bleak and desolate the Fens looked when I first saw them.'

He passed over two pictures of the marshes in winter; flat, barren stretches of frozen mud and reeds with tangled, stunted undergrowth beneath an ominously dark sky. 'Oh, yeah, there were a couple of the village where your grandfather was billeted. These, I think, but I remember how most of the rest were blurred and out of focus.'

Joe paused as he went through the rest of the pictures, stopping to single one out and examine it more closely.

'Do you know I don't think I've ever really looked at these pictures before. I mean really looked to see what's in them. I suppose you don't when you're a kid. Take this one, for instance, on the surface it's just another snapshot of an anonymous English village. Dad took so many pictures of everything; everywhere he went he took photographs. We used to have whole books of them. Because the censor erased the names of the places in all dad's letters, and the signposts were taken down to confuse the Germans if they ever invaded, we never knew where he'd taken them. On

23

the face of it it's merely a row of cottages, a church and an old-fashioned inn bordering on a village green that has two ponds. All slightly out of focus. But now I wonder . . . you don't have a magnifying glass do you?'

Hollis rummaged around in the desk drawer. He was sure his father had kept one and eventually he found it and passed it across to his uncle.

'Yes, I thought so,' Joe murmured after a moment, and he grinned as he passed the picture over to Hollis to inspect through the glass.

'You know, one thing we never did find out from his letters – and the War Office never told us. All we knew was that he went missing whilst on active service in East Anglia. Well now, at least, we know the name of the inn even if we still don't know the name of the village. I guess it must have had something to do with dogs.'

Hollis slowly moved the magnifying glass across the faded print. It was amazing to see how much was hidden, blurred and out of focus. At last he found the gallows sign in front of the inn, displaying the black silhouette of a dog amongst tall reeds.

Joe sighed and shuffled the papers together before passing them back to Hollis. 'It's brought back a lot of old memories seeing those pictures again.'

He stood up and straightened the crumpled sleeves of his jacket. 'But that's it. There's nothing more to tell you and I'm afraid it doesn't explain how you got into that old photograph, does it? Nothing will, it's going to have to remain a mystery. Shall I take that bundle of letters and throw them away before we leave for Lake Dillon?'

'No!' Hollis said emphatically, shaking his head as he crossed to the window. 'I'm going to need them, especially the ones of the village . . .' His voice trailed off as he sorted out the one of himself with the two strangers and brushed away the charred crumbs of paper from its edge.

'You're absolutely sure there is nothing else you can tell me?' he asked, glancing up at his uncle who was standing with his hand on the door handle. 'Oh, I'm not coming with you to Lake Dillon by the way.'

The implication that lay behind what his nephew had just told him struck Joe like a bucket of cold water. His mouth dropped open as he stared at Hollis. 'You're going to England, aren't you?'

His words seemed to hang in the silence almost like an accusation. Hollis nodded slowly. He didn't have any other choice, he couldn't accept the picture and just leave it as an unsolved mystery. He *had* to chase it down, at least to find the place where it had been taken. After that who knew what might happen.

'I'm going to find the other people in that picture and see if they know anything.'

'But that's crazy, that photograph was taken fifty years ago, they'd be at least seventy years old by now – or older – and that's if they're still alive. You'll never recognize them after all this time.'

'*I'm* not seventy. Who knows how old the other two will be? The first thing I'll do is try and find that village. It must have all started around there, that's where the picture was taken.'

'But what about that research job in Delaware – I thought you had just accepted it?' Joe protested.

Hollis shrugged. 'I did, but I'll take a short sabbatical first. They told me I could take some time to sort out my father's affairs. I'll write to them this afternoon.'

'But this is the craziest thing I ever heard . . .' Joe paused, distracted by a noise in the hallway. He could hear the muffled thump of something heavy on the stairs. 'Helen?' he called, pulling open the study door and hurrying out into the hallway.

'Helen, what on earth are you doing?' He caught sight of her attempting to drag a heavy, over-packed bag down the stairs. Loose garments, a woollen wrap and the sleeves of her dressing gown trailed haphazardly from the half-open zip, threatening to entangle themselves with her feet at each tread.

'I've decided you're right, Joe. It would be better for me to get away for a while, there are too many memories here.'

Helen's eyes were brimming with tears and her voice snagged with emotion as she struggled with her luggage.

'Leave your things where they are, I'll bring them down for you in a minute. Go and get your coat on, we're almost done here, then we'll get going.' Joe's voice was gentle.

Hollis approached the door, anxious to hear the sound of distress in his mom's voice.

'Wait in here,' Joe muttered, stopping him in his tracks. 'Your mother's upset enough already.'

He left the study and moved quickly over to the bottom of the stairs as he coaxed his sister-in-law safely back into the kitchen. He returned a moment later, his bulky shape filling the open doorway. His eyes trailed slowly over his nephew and the bundle of letters and photographs Hollis was clutching in his hand. 'I think it would be best if your mom stayed with us tonight, don't you?'

Joe spoke quickly but his voice didn't disguise his worry about the whole affair. 'And don't tell her about going to England, it will only upset her.'

Hollis sighed and shrugged his shoulders. His uncle was probably right, there was no point in upsetting her any further.

'Are you all right for money? Your passport up to date?

Have you given any thought to where you're going to be staying once you get to England? How long are you likely to be there?'

His uncle's questions caught Hollis completely by surprise. He hadn't even begun to work out the details yet; the idea of going, of trying to trace the origins of that picture were still formulating in his head.

'I . . . I . . . I don't know . . .' he stuttered. 'The money's not a problem, I can draw money over there. I know my passport's up to date, but I haven't given a thought to what I'll do once I land . . .'

He paused to rummage through the desk drawer. He was sure his father had a map of Europe somewhere. He sighed and gave up the search. 'Well, I'll probably hire a car and drive up to . . . East Anglia . . . that's what they call that part of England, isn't it? It can't be that difficult to find, can it? England always looks so small on the map.'

Joe smiled but there was a shadow of real concern in his voice as he replied. 'Don't be so sure, remember it's a very old country and from what I've heard they've squeezed a whole lot of history into a very small space over there. We may seem very similar on the surface but we're not, we may even seem to speak the same language but first impressions can be very deceiving.'

'I'll be okay, really, you don't need to worry. All I want to do is to find that village, and then I'll find . . .' Hollis' voice trailed off as his mother, wandering vacantly along the hallway, stopped in the open doorway of the study and stood behind Joe.

Joe sensed her presence and turned quickly, his face immediately breaking into a smile. 'We've just finished sorting everything out. Come on, let's get you settled into the car.'

27

'Hollis is coming with us, isn't he?' she asked, resisting Joe's arm as he put it gently around her shoulders and began shepherding her along the corridor.

'He'll be coming along later. There's a couple of things he has to sort out first, but I'm sure he'll be seeing you in a few days.'

'But we shouldn't leave without him should we?'

Hollis heard his mother's vague protest followed by Joe's even, reassuring voice and then the clatter of the screen door as he ushered her out into the car. He took a step to follow and say goodbye but hesitated, overcome and wretched, knowing that his presence would only compound the pain and agony of her loss. He knew he wouldn't be able to stop himself from revealing what he was about to do; he had never been able to keep secrets from her. Joe reappeared in the study doorway, his balding head prickled with perspiration. He was breathing heavily from the climb up the stairs to collect Helen's suitcase.

'You needn't worry, son, we'll look after her. The break at Lake Dillon is probably the best thing. Are you sure you really have to go to England? There's nothing I can do to change your mind?'

Hollis smiled and shook his head. 'I know you'll look after mom and I'll be okay, don't you worry about me.' He reached out to grip his uncle's hand.

'Hollis, wait, I've just thought of something.'

Joe broke free and delved inside his jacket, pulling out his filofax. Flicking through it he found what he was looking for and quickly wrote the name and address of his cabin at the lake on the notepad on the desk. He tore off the top sheet and handed it to Hollis.

'That's where we'll be staying. Call me as soon as you can, just to let me know you're all right. Give me an address or

28

phone number where we can contact you. Now come and say goodbye to your mother, but don't breathe a word about what you're going to do.'

Hollis nodded and followed his uncle out into the yard. Brushing his lips against his mother's cheek, he whispered her name as he held her fragile hand in his, releasing it finger by finger as the car slowly pulled away stirring up the deep drifts of leaves that carpeted the driveway. He stood there for a long time after the car had vanished, oblivious to the autumnal chill and the faint, sooty scent of early snow on the wind. So many questions were squeezing and scratching painfully at the inside of his skull. Why was he in that weird photograph? Why was it only now that he had discovered it? What could it mean? There was a power in that picture: already it had pushed aside his plans and called him towards England. The frightening thing was why?

Hollis hunched his shoulders against the wind and desolately kicked up the leaves as he returned to the house. There was a whole crowd of people he needed to phone. But at least he knew the first step, he had to book a flight to England and arrange to draw some money. The clatter of the screen door slamming shut behind him echoed through the empty house, intensifying the silence which seemed to close in around him. Hollis shivered and had to glance repeatedly over his shoulder. Then gradually his perception of the space around him, the light and shadow, began to change. He was sensing a presence. There was something there with him in the room, it was there but just on the edge of sight. Something he couldn't quite see, or touch, or hear, but it was there, it was most definitely there.

'Jesus Christ, what have I stirred up – what happened to me when I found that picture?'

He was almost glad of the sound of his own voice as he

looked for the travel agent's number in the phone book. Yet even the tone of the telephone seemed to have a hollow, whispering echo to it. It was as though he was hearing the sound of a drowned voice.

'Yeah, hi, I'd like to book a flight to England. Yes, Gatwick will be fine. No, I don't know when I'll be coming back, could you make it open-ended? Yes, that's right, charge it to my card. Whichever flight is the earliest will be fine. Yeah, that would be just perfect. Thank you, thank you very much.'

Thoughtfully, Hollis replaced the telephone, and turned to confront the silent, empty house.

2

HOLLIS YAWNED and dropped his suitcase onto the floor, letting the door of his hotel room swing shut behind him. Uncle Joe had been right, everything over here was different. Perhaps he shouldn't have been so impulsive, he should have made some preparations. Perhaps it wasn't such a good idea to have loose plans – but at least he was here, and he was no longer utterly lost, he was in a hotel near the airport. A sudden roar of noise from overhead engulfed him; it made him start and look up to the ceiling of his small, featureless room. He expected the plaster to fracture and crumble before falling on top of him. It took him a few, disoriented moments to realize that the earsplitting sound, the vibrating, rattling glass on the wash-basin and the trembling of the lampshade was caused by the accelerating thunder of a transatlantic jet departing from Gatwick airport as it climbed away on full power directly over the hotel.

'Jesus, I didn't realize the hotel would be this close to the runway!' he exclaimed as he tossed his travel bag onto the bed and the keys to his hired car onto the bedside table. Driving around lost for an hour hadn't got him very far.

His original intention, after the seemingly endless, slow shuffle through immigration and customs, was to hire a car and drive a good part of the way north towards East Anglia before stopping for the night in a motel. But what had seemed a very straightforward idea while sitting on the plane and watching the glistening, rainswept reflections on the runway

33

as they had taxied into the North Terminal dissolved as he had become bewilderingly lost somewhere beyond the second roundabout after leaving the car hire depot. It wasn't just the driving on the left and sitting on the wrong side of the car that had foxed him, or even having to re-think the concepts of driving at each junction to overcome the urge to steer into the oncoming traffic – it was the whole road system, even the street signs were completely different. There was no grid system: the roads seemed to have been built in a completely arbitrary fashion. It was after he had passed the Skyways Hotel for the third time that he recognized that he should give up and check in. Perhaps in daylight and armed with a proper map it would be easier to unravel the mysteries of the English road system.

Hollis flinched instinctively, his mind snapping back, over-whelmed by the noise, his eyes drawn upwards by the swaying shadows thrown by the lampshade as another jet climbed away over the hotel. He pressed his hands over his ears. It was going to be impossible to catch a moment's sleep with that racket going on every five or ten minutes. He was surprised he couldn't hear the pilots talking to the control tower.

'This is a crazy place,' he muttered to himself, scooping up the car keys from where he had thrown them but he was unresolved about what to do. If he checked out could he find somewhere quieter or would he just get lost again and be inex-plicably drawn back to this echo box of a hotel? Undecided, he crossed to the window and rubbed his fingertips over the thin haze of condensation that had misted the glass.

'What the hell should I do?' he murmured, peering out through the rivers of raindrops that were running down the window pane. He pressed his forehead against its coldness as he watched the shimmering, anonymous stream of car headlamps appear and then pass the hotel, stroking through

34

the darkness on the road below. The steady, swirling drift of wet autumn leaves scattering across the car park and the occasional, hunched and hurrying pedestrian, clutching an umbrella, made up his mind for him. It was better to stay where he was for the night, at least he was dry and warm even if the room was the size of a cupboard.

Sighing, he drew the curtains shut and turned away from the inhospitable night. He was probably tired enough to sleep through anything, even the noise of the planes. Yawning, he kicked off his shoes and pulled off his jacket before taking the bundle of his grandfather's letters out of the bag. He lay down on the bed, pulling the quilt up over him. He thought he would rest for half an hour while he went through the letters again before going down to find something to eat.

Hollis read through the letters slowly, carefully studying the ones his grandfather had written early in January. There was something about the description of that fancy dress party that Merris had accidentally blundered into that bothered him. There was nothing he could actually put his finger on but the more he thought about that procession of strangely robed figures carrying lighted candles and chanting around that room in the inn, and then the lights that Merris had seen disappearing across the marsh later that same night, the more it seemed to Hollis that it was all part of some pagan ritual. Logic told him that it was absurd, that he was letting his imagination run away with him, perhaps even coming here to find out about that old photograph was ridiculous, but still . . .

He yawned again as waves of drowsiness folded over him. But what, he wondered, clinging to wakefulness, had his grandfather seen beneath the water? What was it that his English friends had been so frightened of – so frightened that they had abandoned their duck shoot? What were the Lanterns that they had warned him about? The sudden, swelling

35

thunder of jet engines rattled the glass on the wash-stand and grew louder and louder, sharpening his senses and making him blink and stare around the room. There was the briefest impression of something, another presence, in the room. Yet it melted into the background as soon as he became aware of it. It was the same presence that he had sensed in his father's study after discovering his grandfather's things. Hollis held his breath as the aircraft passed slowly overhead and then he listened as it receded and left a mumbling silence. He strained his ears, watching, waiting for that presence to reappear, but all he could hear was the distant swish of car tyres through the puddles on the road outside and the soft patter of the rain on the window pane. He shivered and settled back into the warmth of the quilt. He was dog tired, that was why he was imagining there was something in the room with him. He felt safe under the quilt, he would be okay after half an hour's sleep. He reached out to flick off the light switch.

Instantly the silence seemed to intensify and burrow inside his head. It expanded and filled his mind with vivid images of water, reeds and a low sun reflecting blood-red across the ice. He could hear urgent, whispering voices calling out his name. The sound mingled with the haunting cry of eider duck and water rail; he could feel the crackle of frost. Reality blurred into dreamscapes, and then there was someone there with him, someone beside the bed. A voice seemed to whisper his name and a hand reached out to touch his sleeping form. But it melted, dissolving into the shadows as it passed through the quilt. Hollis' eyelids flickered and his lips moved, stirred only slightly by the whispers as he slept. The images in his dreams changed: now he was sitting in an old flat-bottomed wooden boat and drifting aimlessly through a maze of narrow, swampy channels. It was growing dark and the only sound was the soft lap of water breaking against the blunt bow of the vessel which cut sluggish, molten ripples through the surface of the peaty water. His feet felt cold, ice cold, and he looked down. Panic invaded his mind as he realized that the boat was leaking, silently filling with swampy water. He had to get out. He had to find dry land or he would drown. But he couldn't move. He couldn't lift his hands to reach for the paddle that lay on the seat beside him. He couldn't even cry out for help.

Suddenly, without warning, three figures wreathed in shadows began to materialize beside him, rising up out of the reeds. The tallest of them started to move, sinking with each wading stride as it came towards him. It was clothed in sodden, rotting rags, its face and hands interwoven with strands of weed, its body tangled with roots of bladderwort. Marsh orchids and broken reed stems clung to its matted hair. Hollis tried desperately to move, to try and escape the approaching figure but he was paralysed. His arms felt as heavy as lead. In horror he saw that his fingers were growing into the wooden planks of the boat – he was becoming part of it. The sinking vessel rocked violently, filling with even more water as the sinister figure gripped the gunwale and climbed in, bringing with it the reek of rotting vegetation and stagnant mud. Droplets of brackish water and tentacles of slime splattered Hollis' face as the figure reached out to clutch at his arms. It tried to speak to him but the words came out as a bubbling, choking cry. It gesticulated, waving its dripping, weed-entangled arms in the air, pointing repeatedly at the two other figures in the reeds. Its gestures encompassed the darkening sky and silent, swampy landscape. Suddenly there was another sound, the distant chant of voices, and Hollis saw lights moving through the reeds towards the boat.

The apparition clutched at Hollis' arm and paused, half-turning as it lifted its head towards the approaching lights.

In that instant Hollis saw it silhouetted against the light, saw its blackened skin stretched tightly across its skull, saw its tufts of matted hair and petrified, wrinkled flesh, saw the bone and sinew, the empty eye sockets. There was something about the profile that touched a hidden chord, stirred up a memory of a face. This was somebody who –

The figure turned back to him, frantic. It grabbed at his arms, engulfing him in a hideous stench, in a desperate effort to make him understand something, but its gurgling voice meant nothing. The two figures in the reeds began to sink out of sight. Hollis recoiled with horror as the figure crowded closer. The boat rocked violently and the water surged up all around him. The images began to darken and he was sinking, drowning, turning over and over, unable to breathe. He awoke with a start, gasping for air as he sat bolt upright, bathed in sweat. The dream had been so real, so vivid.

The echo of the images stayed with him, haunting the silent darkness of his hotel room. The pungent smell of peat and trampled reeds, the stench of decay, seemed to linger, waiting to be inhaled with each shallow, frightened breath. Hollis remembered sensing a presence in the room as he fell asleep and his skin prickled as he frantically searched the darkness, but it had gone. He was totally alone. Gradually, as his racing heartbeats slowed, he tried to remember what had terrified him the most. He tried to piece his dream together, to reach back and explore those swampy channels, to remember the details and find out why – what had it meant? He tried to grasp more firmly at the feeling of impending danger that the dream had portrayed, to rationalize and understand his sense of loss, of uneasiness, that was creeping up on him. He tried to remember what that looming apparition had looked like but the memories of the dream shrank back into his subconscious as soon as he tried to touch them, scattering into fragments, leaving him with only the vaguest impression of sky and water – and whispering, threatening voices in the wind.

Hollis shivered and used his sleeve to rub at the cold trickle of perspiration on his forehead before he sank back against the pillows and fell asleep. He didn't want to shut his eyes again, he was afraid of what might be waiting for him in his dreams. He glanced at the luminous dial of his watch, it was a quarter after three, much too late to get a bite to eat. He knew he should get up and take off the rest of his clothes but he was warm beneath the quilt and he yawned as he reluctantly closed his eyes while he listened to the soft, rhythmical patter of the rain on the window. Perhaps if he concentrated his mind on ordinary things, perhaps if he thought about the job that was waiting for him in Delaware, or on the new car that he was going to buy, or how his team were making out in the World Series then he could avoid returning to the nightmare. Then reality gradually blurred again and he could hear the rattle of the rain and the sound of the wind in the trees; he was standing in an expanse of grass surrounded by old-fashioned houses. A cart loaded with barrels and drawn by two horses was slowly approaching him along a dusty road.

The picture changed and now he was in a crowded, unfamiliar street surrounded by tall buildings. The whine of sirens hurt his ears, people were shouting, scattering, jostling and pushing him out of their way as they tried to escape from the rumble of explosions that were drawing closer and closer. He tried to follow the running crowds but his feet kept getting stuck to the ground. He couldn't keep up, and the terror of being left behind overwhelmed him. Clouds of black smoke rolled over him and now it was pitch dark and stiflingly hot. There was a crush of bodies and all around was the reek of sweat, children were crying and voices were calling out. He could hear the sound of water dripping as the crowd surged backwards and forwards, and there was a second echo as though he was in a tunnel. He worked his hand free and reached up, inches above his head he felt the rough, wet texture of bricks. He was trapped, entombed, there was no escape.

The rumble of thunder grew ever closer, he could feel it through the bricks, feel the mortar crumble and sprinkle down upon his head. He had to get out, he couldn't breathe. The noise was getting louder. Abruptly the picture changed and he found himself standing on a windy airstrip with the low, winter sun riding the horizon; only the roar of thunder had followed him. The sound of it made him spin round. He ducked, throwing himself to the ground as three huge aircraft skimmed overhead, their prop wash tumbling him over and over. He awoke with a cry, his hands pressed against the sides of his head, as the thunder of the third early morning jet climbed away from Gatwick airport assaulting his ears.

It took Hollis a moment to separate the dream from reality and to work out where he was. He shook his head until the noise of the plane's engines had faded and then he threw back the quilt and got out of bed. It was six-thirty, he wasn't going to get back to sleep now. He opened the curtain to be greeted by a grey, wet morning.

'Perhaps it will be better in East Anglia,' he muttered to himself as he opened his suitcase and sorted out a change of clothes.

The English road system didn't give up its secrets easily, despite a detailed list of directions that he had been given by the desk clerk, and that should have taken him directly to East Anglia. The weather had also conspired against him. His grandfather had been right when he had described the English rain in his letters: it fell in a grey, unrelenting curtain

40

that mixed with the blinding clouds of spray thrown up by the constant stream of heavy traffic and reduced visibility to only a few yards. It made reading the road signs almost impossible.

Hollis suffered a string of false starts as he threaded his way through the intricacies of the M23, the London orbital route around the M25 and its eventual intersection with the M11. He breathed a sigh of relief when he passed a sign headed 'M11 – East Anglia' which, he felt, must show that he was on the right road at last. But he didn't dare relax his concentration, the intersection of the M25 had merged and funnelled him into the fast lane of the M11. Driving in England was terrifying, as frightening as any Californian, white-knuckle ride. Everybody drove so fast and so close to one another. There were moments of near panic when, without warning, people seemed to change lanes simply for the hell of it, and his head ached from the tension of keeping alert and out of everyone's way. Cautiously he changed lanes, slotting his hired Honda into a gap in the slow lane and managed to relax his grip on the steering wheel a little.

The traffic thinned out after he passed the Bishops Stortford intersection and he had time to catch more than a glimpse of the low, rolling fields that had been ploughed umber, bare and ready for the winter with dark, conspiratorial clumps of trees on the headlands, standing in their rain-soaked nakedness on either side of the motorway. England was different, the colours, the shapes, the textures of the earth – and the sky, the sky was very different.

Hollis eased his foot off the accelerator pedal to allow the gap to widen between the hood of his car and the truck in front which was kicking up clouds of spray ten yards ahead. Getting on the right road was only the first obstacle, he had no idea where to start looking for that inn with the sign of the large black dog. He didn't even know if it still existed, or if the village with its rows of cottages and its two ponds still looked anything like the photograph. He had shown these pictures to the desk clerk while he was taking down the directions but he had merely given them a cursory glance, shrugging them aside as he swept his hand vaguely over the map. From what he said he remembered from his history lessons, there had been a rash of wartime airfields in East Anglia – those pictures could have been taken anywhere, and fifty years was a long time. Anything could have happened to the village since then. Most of that wartime landscape had probably vanished under the plough or been used for new urban developments. He had suggested that Hollis could either start in Cambridge and then work in an arc through Huntingdon, Peterborough and Lincoln or leave the M11 motorway at exit 9 and drive up through Newmarket, Fordham, Soham and from there cut across the heart of the Fens towards Norwich. But whether he would find that village was anybody's guess.

Hollis glanced down at the open map. It was a meaningless tapestry of coloured lines and names – Upware, Witchford, Adventurers Fen, Freckenham – he was spoiled for choice. Something, a flicker of red lights, made him look up and an instinct for survival made him stamp savagely on the brakes as the tailboard of the truck ahead loomed close, filling his windscreen. The stream of traffic was coming to a sudden, unexplained halt. The car slewed and juddered, skidding sideways, sending up a fine shower of spray and rubber as it stalled only inches from the back of the truck. Hollis sat staring at the mud and water dripping off the tailgate of the lorry. He was so close he could see the individual raindrops. His fingers were clamped on the steering wheel and his breaths were coming in short, ragged gasps of shock. Another couple of inches and he could have been underneath it. Squalls of weather buffeted the car, hitting the windscreen and covering it with rain, blurring and obliterating the huge bulk of the vehicle that almost filled his vision. Hollis glanced out at the lines of other stationary cars and fired up the engine, waving shamefaced to the guy in the van behind him and trying to apologize to the driver of the car he had almost collided with beside him. He carefully manoeuvred the car, straightening it up amongst the waiting traffic.

'Now what?' he thought to himself, looking out through the measured swish of the wiper blades at the continuous line of red brake lights that snaked away into the distance. He yawned and stretched his arms, pressing the palms of his hands onto the padded roof of the car above his head. Driving under these conditions in a strange country, on roads that were completely unfamiliar, was exhausting.

He glanced down at the map and worked out that the next junction was exit 9, the one that would take him to Newmarket. He decided he would turn off there and find somewhere to rest. He would then start asking if anybody recognized the places in his photographs. As he sat back to listen idly to the rain while it drummed against the roof of the car fragments of the previous night's dream began to break through the surface of his mind. They were disquieting, disjointed images that he didn't understand, things he had never imagined or seen which kept crowding forwards. He could see hideous, half-submerged figures drowned in mud, claustrophobic crowds smothering him in a subterranean cellar. There was a sense of being lost, utterly and hopelessly lost, a feeling of even doubting his own identity. He shook his head and rubbed his hand over his eyes in an effort to disperse the images but he couldn't quite shake off the uneasy sense of apprehension that they had seeded into his consciousness. He began to realize, to half guess, that the dreams, the sense of uneasiness, was connected to that weird photograph, the one he had found amongst his grandfather's things.

But why? Why was he having these dreams, and why had he been dragged halfway across the world?

With these unsettling thoughts working themselves endlessly around in his head, Hollis grimly continued his journey towards where he hoped he would find some answers.

3

Black Shuck

HOLLIS' CONCENTRATION was failing. The print was beginning to blur as dream images began to form, encouraged by the soft patter of rain on the small window of the room he had checked into in the King's Head in the village of Wicken. His head nodded forwards and the small book about the inn's history that he had borrowed from the landlord slipped through his fingers and fell with a thump onto the floor beside the bed, waking him with a jolt. He blinked and tried to catch at the elusive threads of his dream. He had been running, he was sure of that, he still felt out of breath. He had been running along a narrow, muddy path between tall reed stems. There had been somebody with him, maybe two other people, he couldn't be sure, and something had been chasing them. There had been lights in the reeds: they were moving, drawing closer, he had caught a glimpse of their reflections in the black, peaty water. But there was something wrong, something wrong with the reflections. They seemed to be under the water, their faces were underneath the water all around them.

The sound of a car swishing through the puddles in the street outside fractured the memory – the dream – and sent the images into retreat leaving only the gnawing sense of pursuit. Hollis shivered despite the warmth of the low-beamed room and swung his legs off the bed before standing up, stretching and straightening his clothes. It felt like midnight but a quick glance at his watch, and at the piece of gloomy, grey sky he could see between the glistening, wet rooftops of the village, told him that it was only quarter after four in the afternoon.

'I hate jet lag!' he moaned to himself as he turned on the bedside lamp. 'If I sleep now I'll be awake half the night.'

He retrieved the booklet and placed it on the bedside table before he crossed to the window to take in a last look outside before it got too dark. He wondered if it was ever going to stop raining. The huddle of old, weather-streaked houses around the village green and the bleak, Fenland landscape that hemmed them in looked so inhospitable through the persistent, drifting curtain of rain. His grandfather had been right when he had said that it was sometimes impossible to see where the sky ended and the land began. It had been the strangest sensation entering the Fens and driving along the straight, narrow roads that were bordered on each side by enormous drainage dykes. The landscape had seemed to swallow him up, water and earth blended together in a vast well of silence. The only signs of habitation had been the single power line that followed the road and veered off at intervals to an isolated farmhouse, and the freshly cut plough furrows carved in a vanishing perspective into the black, peaty fields. Glistening, petrified ridges of turned earth that he imagined would have dissolved into sludgy ripples at the slightest touch of the wind. He'd been told by the desk clerk that East Anglia had been literally carpeted with airfields during the war but he shuddered at the thought of trying to find anywhere to land a plane in the countryside he was driving through.

A sudden squall of raindrops hit the window panes, cutting through his thoughts, and he noticed that lights were coming on in the village houses and a large bus had pulled up on the far side of the green disgorging noisy school children who began to hurry away from it under a canopy of bright umbrellas. He wondered why so many people lived here, there couldn't be much in the way of employment for miles.

Hollis laid his spoon on the plate beside his half-eaten mound of spotted dog and congealing custard. He couldn't eat another mouthful. The name of the dessert had intrigued him and the landlord's description of the pudding had tempted him to give it a try, but the taste was very different from the one he had anticipated; it had a heavy texture and a strong flavour of suet that left a fatty taste on the roof of his mouth that he couldn't get rid of despite swallowing almost two glasses of the local ale. The beer was a tepid, cloudy liquid with a frothy head on it that he had immediately taken a liking to, and he was about to order another glass when he realized that he was feeling light-headed. Obviously it was much stronger than he was used to and he decided to wait a while before ordering another.

Pushing his plate away he sat back and surveyed the straggle of drinkers. Apart from the people sitting at the bar there was a noisy group playing darts on the far side of the room and two old men engrossed in a game of dominoes at a table close to the fire. He listened to the soft hum of conversation around him and just managed to pick out the odd, familiar word. He felt very much like a foreigner and he wondered if he could find the courage to approach any of them with his photographs. He had shown the pictures to the landlord before ordering his supper and explained that he was trying to find the village where his grandfather had been stationed during the war but the landlord had merely shaken his head and passed them back to him, giving them no more than a casual glance. He had only taken over the licence of the King's Head four years before and he hadn't the time to explore much beyond the boundaries of Wicken. He barely knew any of the surrounding villages, but he did suggest to Hollis that he should ask some of the locals, especially Tom Watts or Maurice Flower who were from two families who had lived around Wicken for years. They would be sure to know where the village was – if anybody did.

But as he sat watching the men playing dominoes he hesitated. He didn't want to interrupt their game as they sat huddled by the fire. Anyway, what on earth would he say to them? He wasn't even sure that the two men were Maurice Flower and Tom Watts. He thought he would wait a while, see if the bar filled up, perhaps he wouldn't feel so obvious if there was a crowd. Hollis let his gaze wander across the interior of the inn. How many footsteps, he wondered, had it taken to wear the flagstones in the fire hearth? He noticed the collection of fire-irons stacked carelessly to one side of the chimney, the blackened trammel and the bunches of yellow flag and bladderwort that had been hung there to dry in the sooty draught. He looked at the dozens of faded photographs, paintings, engravings and mezzotints that crowded the yellowing, stud and plaster walls. They showed serious, frock-coated Victorians, bearded entomologists, navigators in their narrow, flat-bottomed boats, turf cutters sitting outside their hovels. Every one of them, he was sure, charted some small part of the long conquest of the Fens.

A forest of blackened beams spanned the sagging ceiling and were hung with the most curious collection of wooden turf-cutting spades, scoop shovels, beckets, foot-irons and creepers. Everything looked so old, so interesting. He half-rose from his seat as he tried to read the faded label on a long-handled turf-cutting knife that was hanging from a beam above his head. He didn't notice the conversation at the bar begin to die away as heads turned towards him. Gradually he sensed he was being watched and the colour rushed hotly into his cheeks. He sat down abruptly.

'Hey, you're American ain't you, young fella?' One of the domino players stopped playing to look up and ask in a crackling, dry voice as he pointed the stem of his smouldering pipe directly at Hollis' chest while inspecting him with a critical, watery gaze. 'You've come at the wrong time, Yank, most of the Fens are about to close for the winter. Ask Tom here if you don't believe me.'

He turned back to inspect the dominoes that had been placed in front of him.

'No, no, I haven't just come over here to visit the Fens. I am looking for a village . . .' he stammered, trying to keep the old man's attention but losing it fast.

He rose quickly to his feet and crossed to their table, fumbling in his jacket pocket for the bundle of photographs. 'I'm trying to find the village where my grandfather was stationed before he disappeared during the war. All I've got to go on are these old photographs. You wouldn't happen to recognize where they were taken would you?' He held out the pictures towards them.

'Yanks! Of course I remember the Yanks. I remember them as if it was yesterday. Don't you remember them, Maurice?'

Tom laughed, draining the dregs from his glass and putting it down heavily on the brass-topped table.

'Yes, I remember them. What did we used to say – overpaid, oversexed and over here!' Maurice roared with laughter, his toothless mouth splitting into a wide grin as he licked at the froth on his yellowing moustache and put his empty glass purposefully beside the other.

Hollis took a startled step backwards. He hadn't expected these insults. Old Tom Watts saw the hurt and discomfort in the boy's eyes and the laughter faded abruptly as he leaned forwards, suddenly serious, to catch at Hollis' sleeve. 'Now don't you go getting us wrong, young fella, we don't mean no disrespect to your grandfather. I met a lot of Americans during the war and they fought better than most.'

'And it wasn't really their war but they still came over and did their bit,' added Maurice hotly.

Tom smiled and settled back into his chair. 'They certainly did that, and more besides. Why, I remember the day Ed Kransky breezed in here with a Jeep full of Yanks – larger than life they were – they were supposed to be at an airfield north of Peterborough but they had lost their way. They drank this place dry in less than an hour and were banging on the bar for more . . .'

Maurice coughed and moved his empty beer mug, tipping it and peering hopefully into the bottom of the glass. 'I don't think it's stories of the war the boy's after – perhaps we had better have a look at his pictures.'

'Pictures? Oh yes, mind you it's thirsty work looking at pictures,' Tom mumbled as he picked them up and shuffled through them. Hollis suddenly caught on to the broad hints they were both throwing his way and he quickly offered them another drink. They were obviously the two characters the landlord had suggested he ask and their faces broke into wide smiles as he took their glasses up to the bar. He glanced across while he waited for their pints to be pulled and he saw that the dominoes had been swept away and put back into their wooden box as both of them were poring over the photographs now laid out on the table.

'Well?' he asked hopefully as he put their drinks down on an adjacent table and looked over their shoulders at the spread of photographs in front of them. 'Have you recognized which village it is? Is it anywhere near here?'

Maurice shook his head slowly and sat back, wetting his lips in anticipation as he reached for his drink. 'No, I can't say as we have. There must be dozens of villages that look something like these pictures, but I wouldn't like to say exactly which one this is. They've all got ponds, churches and a village green.'

'My grandfather wrote in one of his letters that the airfield he flew from was only a short ride from the village. Does that help?'

Tom laughed, the sound crackled in his throat as he slapped his thigh. The draught scattered some of the pictures and they fell over the edge of the table. 'Well that narrows it down, doesn't it!'

Maurice grinned as he answered, but Hollis was unable to decipher what he said. Frowning he crouched down and gathered up the fallen pictures from the floor.

'That village wouldn't be anywhere around here, young fella,' Maurice smiled at him as he straightened up. 'You see they didn't build any American airfields for miles around here because of the Fens. The ground's far too wet and marshy.'

'Your best bet is to go and look further east, round where the ground is higher. They built lots of airfields that way.' Tom reached for his glass. 'Or to the west,' he added, after a moment's thought. 'There were plenty of air bases between Cambridge and Peterborough and all the way up to Lincoln.'

'No, not that far north, the houses are all wrong, I'd try further east if I were you.'

'Surely there must be something in the pictures to give you a clue where the village is? What about the sign on the inn? Or how about the church? It looks very imposing.' Hollis tried shuffling through the photographs for the best ones that his grandfather had taken of the village.

For a moment the two old men pored over the photographs again. Tom was the first to look up, pointing with the stem of his pipe to the picture of the church. 'Nearly every village has got a church and they all look alike to me – I'm not much of a one for churches, I only seem to get into them these days to see my mates off and I reckon my turn will be coming up pretty soon.'

'It's fairly easy to tell you what one of the pubs was called.' Maurice pointed at a photograph. 'I'd say that the first one, the one with the roses twisting up around a crown, was obviously called the Rose and Crown, which probably refers to the Civil War. But I don't know about this second one,' and he returned his attention to the first one he had been looking at.

He concentrated hard. There was something about the dark form on the gallows sign in the faded photograph that sent a shiver down his spine. He pulled out his spectacles and put them on before peering even more closely at the picture. The huge, black, menacing shape of a dog with yellow eyes leapt into focus on the inn sign. Maurice inhaled a shallow breath and quickly put the picture down as if it had burned his fingers. Tom looked across at him curiously and then picked up the same photograph.

'What's up? What's the matter? What have you seen?' Hollis asked, leaning forwards and trying to see what they were looking at.

Tom laughed and passed it across. 'It's nothing, just a picture of a black dog on that inn sign, that's all.'

'It's Black Shuck. It's the demon dog.'

'I don't know what he's making a fuss about, I've heard about inns named after him before, but I've never seen a picture of one.'

'So why does it bother you? What's so awful about a pub being named after a dog?' Hollis asked, taking a closer look at the picture.

'It's no good asking him.' Tom cackled sarcastically. 'Maurice believes in all that stuff and nonsense about ghosts and fairies and the like. He'll have you dancing with your own shadow if you listen to him long enough.'

'It's easy for you to talk, you haven't seen half the things . . .' Maurice paused and wiped his hand across his mouth with an angry gesture.

'No, don't stop, tell me who is Black Shuck? I really want to know,' Hollis urged, trying to regain the old man's attention.

'He is the Devil's dog. He's huge, a terrifying creature, he has paws bigger than my hands, long, wet fangs and yellow staring eyes that can hypnotize you and lure you into the marshes. He is not easy to see because his coat is as black as ebony but you can always hear him when he's padding up after you in the dark. And when he's in pursuit of his quarry his howls can be heard above the shrieks of the wildest gale. He haunts the Fens looking out for lonely travellers, he prowls through the villages in the dead of night –'

'It's all stuff and nonsense, old wives' tales – take no notice . . .' Tom tried to interrupt but Maurice hushed him into silence, pausing only to glance anxiously behind him at the rain battering on the window panes and to listen for a moment to the wind roaring in the chimney before lowering his voice even further as he continued.

'Believe me, young fella, there's more than old wives' tales in this. Black Shuck has haunted the Fens for over a thousand years, plenty of people have caught a glimpse of him loping along the top of the dykes or leaping over churchyard walls to worry the bones of the dead. Why, only recently a motorist swerved and went into a dyke – he told the police that he was trying to avoid what looked like a monstrous hell-hound crossing the road. Black Shuck's real enough, believe me!'

'But if people fear this creature so much why do they name an inn after him?'

'To attract the tourists of course, why else?' Tom muttered, only to be glared into silence by Maurice before he continued.

'There are a dozen different stories told across the Fens about the demon dog and in most of them he is a creature people dread. At the turn of the century I believe it was quite common to name an inn after him, especially if he frequented the village and terrorized the inhabitants. They tried to appease him and make him go away. I have heard stories, though I don't know how true they are, but it is said that some folks went as far as dabbling in Black Magic and ancient rituals to try and drive the demon away from an area.'

'Magic? Whatever will you come up with next? What are you trying to do, frighten this young man out of his wits?' Tom muttered crossly, getting up from his chair and stalking off towards the toilets in a cloud of tobacco smoke.

Maurice sighed and shook his head as he watched his friend go. He turned back to Hollis and leaned close to him, dropping his voice to barely above a whisper. 'Tom knows there's too much evidence pointing to Black Shuck's existence for him to really dismiss these stories, that's what's frightening him so much. It makes him pretend that he doesn't believe it but inside he's even more afraid of the beast than I am.'

For a few moments he seemed to be lost in his own thoughts, his lips moving silently, his eyes rolling back slightly as though he was combing through his memories in search of something. Suddenly he sat bolt upright and grabbed at Hollis' wrist. 'Now you listen carefully, young fella, and remember what I tell you. If you go off searching for that village which I know you've set your heart on finding, just remember this dog may still be haunting it. Yes, he may suddenly appear especially on a wild night like this. Never, never look back at him across your shoulder, if you hear him padding along in the darkness behind you just you look directly ahead. Never stop or turn around, do you hear? And never open a door if he's on the other side of it. Even if you feel his icy breath on the back of your neck don't you look round, because to stare into his eyes will mean your certain death. There is a saying among the Fen people: "Beware the black dog on your heels!"'

There was an urgency, a real sense of fear in the old man, and it sent a shiver down Hollis' spine. 'Surely there must be somewhere that's safe from this creature?'

'Safe? I wish there was,' Maurice said with a hollow laugh as he pushed the rest of the photographs towards Hollis. 'There's nowhere, not even the church, that's safe – and I should know. When I was a lad I went on a visit to Blythburgh Church with the school and I saw the claw marks that he had gouged on the doors.'

'My God! What on earth happened?'

Old Maurice shrugged and glanced anxiously towards the rain-swept windows again. He felt he had already said too much and it was a long walk home beside the dyke in the dark. 'I don't know,' he answered reluctantly. 'It all happened hundreds of years ago but the marks are still there. If you don't believe me you can go and see them for yourself. Mind you, it's a long way away, it's over on the coast near Southwold.'

Tom Watts appeared and sat down moodily in his chair. 'Have you finished with all that nonsense yet? All that talk about dogs and demons makes me sick,' he grumbled, fidgeting with the dominoes box and removing its lid to tip the contents out onto the table.

Maurice nodded silently and drank deeply from his glass. Hollis caught the broad hint and knew it was time for him to leave their table so he smiled and rose to his feet, pushing the bundle of photographs back into his pocket. 'Well, thanks, what you've told me was really interesting. I'll certainly bear it in mind if I ever find that pub.'

'You'll be lucky if even one of the pubs in those pictures still exist. The breweries have closed down so many of their tithe houses over the last fifty years, I doubt your grandfather would recognize the place now. Sometimes you have to drive for miles before you can get a drink. But try looking further east for that village, that's where most of the American bases were sited.' Tom offered this last piece of information without even looking up from the game they were about to start.

'Thank you very much, thanks,' Hollis murmured, returning to where he had originally been sitting.

The crowd at the bar had thinned out and the fire in the grate was beginning to burn down as he glanced at his watch to discover that it was already a quarter after ten. He blinked and rubbed his eyes. They felt heavy and sore; he wasn't sure if it was the jet lag and the long drive up from Gatwick catching up with him, or maybe it was the rich dessert, or, more probably, the local brew he had been drinking in the unfamiliar, smoky atmosphere of the old pub. Whatever it was he suddenly felt very tired. The conversation at the bar seemed to wash over him, the words and laughter merged together and the soft East Anglian dialect blurred in his head. The sense of history that stared at him from the pictures on the wall and had so intrigued him earlier now seemed to close in oppressively, cocooning him in images of the Fens. He seemed to catch whispers in the wind, rustling in the reeds, he thought he could hear the slap of water on the wooden hull of a flat-bottomed boat. In the background there was the persistent cry of water-rail and eider duck, and the far-off song of the skylarks seemed to stroke the summer sky.

Somebody called out goodnight and the outer door slammed shut. Hollis jumped slightly and inhaled as the dream was broken. He was abruptly aware of the smell of stale tobacco smoke and beer ingrained in the walls and ceiling of the low-beamed room. He looked around him and that first impression it had given him seemed to take on a tarnished, faded look. He reached for his glass to finish it but hesitated, his head ached and he felt slightly dizzy, he had already had enough to drink. Stifling a yawn behind his hand he decided it was time to turn in and he climbed to his feet slowly, acknowledging the landlord before making his way back up to his room.

He couldn't get old Maurice's story of the black demon dog out of his mind as he got ready for bed. What if the story of that spectral hound was really true, what if – somehow – on a night like this it was out there, silently crossing the Fens, hunting some lonely traveller down? Hollis shook his head. Tom Watts was right, Maurice would have him dancing with his own shadow, or at least jumping with fright if he let his imagination run wild. He had almost brought out the letter that his grandfather had written describing those strange lights he had seen while travelling across the marshes. He had almost asked Maurice what the term 'Lanterns' meant and whose dead faces his grandfather might have glimpsed beneath the surface of the water. But he had thought better of it and instead he had listened to the story of the demon dog. It was bad enough discovering that the inn where his grandfather had been billeted was tied up with ancient legends, he didn't want to hear anything worse. No, he had to concentrate on finding the village first. He had to hold onto what was real – what he could touch. Or was any of this real? He hadn't forgotten that it was something far more weird than the story of Black Shuck or lights vanishing across the marshes that had brought him here in the first place.

Hesitantly he reached into the inside pocket of his jacket where he had hung it on the chair beside his bed. He pulled out the crumpled envelope that contained that single, impossible photograph of himself and the group of strangers. Even looking at it sent a shiver up his spine and he tentatively rubbed his thumb across its grainy, wet-looking surface. The picture seemed almost more real, more three-dimensional now and yet the image of his father seemed to have grown slightly fainter. Staring at it seemed to open up something in him, seemed to release images from his subconscious that had been buried a long, long time. He knew the room where it had been taken, he could somehow hear the laughter and listen to the conversation, he could smell the tobacco smoke and hear the clink of the glasses. Shadowy, indistinct figures were moving in and out of focus, somebody called out and then, with a sharp click, the images vanished.

Hollis suddenly felt very cold and very alone. He threw the duvet back and prepared to jump into bed but the sound of the wind moaning beneath the eaves of the old building, rattling the shutters as the rain beat on his window, drew him across to press his nose against the cold pane of glass. He looked out through the rivulets of raindrops that were running down, beyond the small huddle of village lights to the inhospitable marshlands merged with the limitless sky until it was all one, vast, black landscape where only a handful of pinpoints of light showed the few isolated homesteads that rode the precarious, invisible horizon. It made the story Maurice had just told him, and all those other, half-guessed, legends he had hinted about, seem all the more real. Hollis shivered and quickly drew the curtains to shut out the dark. He jumped into the bed and pulled the duvet up around his ears, blocking out the wild night that was battering on his window.

But sleep did not come easily. Images of that monstrous hell-hound seemed to rush at him from across the room with each shrieking whistle of wind that found its way through the age-warped window frame. In that half-world between waking and sleeping his mind was drawn back to explore the photograph, to reach inside it and see the frost on the window-panes, to smell the hot bread rising from the bake ovens that were set inside the inglenook. He tried to look at the figures that filled the room, to catch more than the blurred impression of uniforms and men in cloth caps and heavy farm clothing. He felt as though somebody was standing very close to him in that sepia room; somebody who was trying to catch his attention. He felt an urgency in their touch.

A very English voice close to his ear whispered, 'You have to get as far away from here as you possibly can. The Lanterns you are searching for . . .'

The howl of the wind and the sound of the rain beating on the window drowned out the rest of the words. Hollis turned his head on the pillow and covered his ears to block out the noise of the storm. He concentrated on reaching deeper into the photograph. A young face came into focus, a ruddy, wind-scalded face with thick reddish hair and pale eyes. He could see him quite distinctly, his eyes kept shifting as though he was anxiously searching the room for somebody he didn't want to see. Suddenly Hollis felt a light touch on his leg through the duvet. It scattered the images conjured up from the photograph instantly, making him jump as panic tightened in his throat and the hair prickled on the nape of his neck. He went cold all over.

He could see nobody and yet he knew he had not imagined it. There was somebody in the room with him. His senses screamed out at him telling him to shout, to raise the alarm. He reached out for something to throw and made a grab at the light switch. He wanted to do something to scare it away and yet he lay there, paralysed. His heart was pounding in his chest and he was too terrified to move. He started to smell the odour of stagnant water, mud and slime and it was getting stronger as the presence moved closer. He had to open his eyes, he had to confront it, whatever it was, before it touched him again. The smell was beginning to trigger memories of a dream, something he almost remembered that had woken him up that morning. It had troubled him then but he had forgotten about it on the journey up. He recalled how he had been trapped in a flat-bottomed boat. It was all rushing back to him now. He could feel the fear of drowning as the boat began to fill up with water. Three figures had risen up out of the reeds. Three ghastly, decaying apparitions. It was the same smell, it was here in his room with him. He had to open his eyes. He had to see what it was.

A car drove past noisily and the spell was broken. Hollis managed to force his eyes open as the glare from the headlights flooded through the narrow gap above the curtains and slowly tracked across the ceiling. He caught his breath and shrank back in terror as the soft light picked out the silhouette of a tall figure standing close to the bed. It took a faltering step towards him and reached out a trembling, blackened hand that dripped with mud and slime, dirtying the bed clothes. It called out Hollis' name in a muffled, drowned, gurgling voice but as the hand touched his arm the figure dissolved. It vanished into the gathering darkness as the lights from the car faded. The last momentary glimpse of the sodden, rotting rags it wore, its blackened, decaying face and hands, its matted hair interwoven with weeds and broken reed stems, would stay with him for ever, engraved into his memory.

It wasn't a dream. Hollis knew he was awake. He reached out for the bedside lamp and turned it on. He sat up in bed carefully and searched the bed clothes for traces of slime and mud; he looked across the floor for pools of water. The figure had been real, it had stood there, touched him, but there was nothing to see, no water, no mud. He frowned and shook his head. It was one of the three figures in the boat, the ones who had appeared out of the reeds in his dream the previous night. It was the tallest one, the one who had tried to climb into the boat, he was sure of it. But this time it was more than a dream, much more. The figure had actually stood there in his room. Jesus! It had even tried to speak his name, he was sure of it. It was nobody he had ever seen before, nobody he could recognize. None of this made any sense and it was beginning to frighten him.

He shivered and pulled the duvet around his chin. He really wished he had stayed at home. His grandfather had died fifty years before, what did it matter now? He glanced across at the bedside table, undecided about turning off the light, and the picture caught his eyes. He picked it up and studied the faces of the other people in it. It was impossible to see if either of them resembled the one he had imagined and he sighed before putting it down. It was a pity it wasn't in colour. Gradually his heartbeat calmed down but he was still afraid to shut his eyes, instead he began to go over everything he had experienced since finding that impossible picture. He had to try to put his thoughts into some sort of order.

As a child Hollis had never suffered from nightmares. He was normally a very good sleeper who rarely remembered his dreams beyond that first cup of morning coffee. Now that had all changed, he was being caught up in something he didn't understand. He had never been one to take notice of ghost stories or to believe in the supernatural, none of that stuff really existed for him beyond dressing up for Halloween. It all belonged to the world of make-believe and legend – or did it? After that figure appeared beside his bed he wasn't at all sure.

Something – a shadow, a movement of the curtains, maybe a cold draught of air, he wasn't sure – made him glance around the room, his skin tingling coldly. The ghost may have vanished from his sight but it was still there. He could feel its presence in the room quite distinctly. It wasn't threatening him, it was just very close. It made him think back over the last few days and he realized that it had been in the background ever since he had discovered that photograph of himself amongst his grandfather's letters. But why should it haunt him now after all this time? What had he triggered by finding that picture?

The dreams of those ghostly figures seemed to have come as a warning of some sort leaving him with a gnawing sense of anxiety and a fear that he was being pursued. But it was all wrong. It was Hollis himself who was trying to find the source of the picture, it was he who was doing the pursuing. It just didn't make any sense. He was far too afraid to close his eyes and try to sleep while he knew the presence was still in the room. He stifled a yawn and reached for the bundle of pictures that his grandfather had taken of the other men in his unit, the planes that he had flown and the village and countryside where he had been stationed. He had left them on the table beside the bed. An idea suddenly occurred to him and he looked through them slowly. Gradually his fingers stopped trembling as he held one of them up for closer inspection. He could almost smell the cut bank of pungent peat and he knew exactly how it felt to sit in the flat-bottomed boat that was tied up to the small, wooden jetty, almost hidden amongst the tall reeds where it rode the sluggish, stagnant water in the narrow channel. The low, winter sun, the stunted blackthorn tree – everything in the picture was the same as in his dream. But was it because he had already glanced through these pictures a dozen times when he had first found them, had that painted the images in his head, perhaps unconsciously? Could he find other pictures from his dreams if he looked hard enough?

He sighed and laid the picture down on the crumpled duvet. Maybe he had just remembered the picture but that didn't explain why the dream filled him with such anxiety. It didn't explain why even looking at it sent a cold shiver through him, and he hastily pushed it in amongst the others. He picked up another of a group of young men posing with linked arms on the front steps of the inn where his grandfather had been billeted. Unfortunately that picture was blurred but he could still see that some of the men were in uniform. The face of the stoutish figure in the middle right of the group caught his eyes. It could have been the same face, the one with the reddish hair, the one his imagination had already conjured up. But it was much too out of focus to be sure. Hollis settled back, determined to stay awake as he listened to the wind and rain, and tried to put the fragments of his dreams together. He had to find out what it was that kept drawing him back to that stagnant channel in the reeds.

He was warm beneath the duvet and gradually, despite his determination, sleep crept up on him. His concentration kept slipping in and out of focus, the smell of the marshes seemed to have grown stronger but the images of water, reeds and sky dissolved as his eyelids grew heavy. The persistent sound of the wind and rain began to merge and blend in with the vivid dreamscape that was unfolding in his head. The room grew cold and heavy with the odour of weeds and decay as the presence Hollis had sensed gradually reappeared, a blackened, decomposing silhouette standing out against the curtains.

It took a slow, hesitant step towards him raising its drip-ping arms, it drowned voice gurgled softly as it chanted wordlessly.

Hollis mumbled and stirred fitfully, the dream broken, and he began to wake. The figure shrank back and started to melt, its voice dying away slowly. Hollis half-turned and sank deeper into sleep as the translucent silhouette of the figure moved back close to him. The dreamscape returned. He could smell the thick, smoky atmosphere of the inn and hear the murmuring voices laughing and talking all around him. Abruptly the atmosphere changed, it became dark and threatening, the voices grew harsh and seemed to be gnawing painfully at the inside of his head. He tried to reach out, to hold onto them but they suddenly weren't there. He was alone, or should have been, but he had the prickling sensation that there was something lurking in the shadows, that something was pursuing him. He had to escape. The next thing he knew he was climbing up an endless, twisting flight of stairs and he was gasping for breath. His feet were pounding on the treads but he wasn't getting anywhere. The sound of his pursuer was getting closer and closer, he could hear its padding footsteps and feel the growling snarl of its breath on the back of his neck. It was right behind him now and he couldn't escape. He tried to turn, to raise his arms and fend off the looming shadow that was engulfing him but his screams and shouts were stuck in his throat, they were choking him. He felt as though he was drowning, he couldn't breathe. He was underwater, mud and slime were filling his mouth and throat, he was sinking down . . . down . . . down . . .

Hollis shivered violently and fought against the bedclothes, his mouth open and gasping for air. His eyelids twitched as the nightmare tightened its grip, suffocating him. The translucent figure stooped to bend protectively over him, reaching out with a blackened, decaying hand. Two cold, wet, shrivelled and skeletal fingers touched his forehead, brushing it as lightly as eider featherdown over his eyelids. The drowned voice was filled with a gurgling urgency as it repeated its incoherent chanting.

Hollis took a deep breath and his back arched as his hands trembled where they gripped the duvet. The apparition touched his forehead again and his eyelids stopped twitching, he expelled his breath in a long, mumbling groan as the nightmare shrank away into black emptiness. He stretched and moved his head on the pillow as a new dream began to unfold. The streets of the village were carpeted with fresh snow, there were lights and singing coming from the church as he walked towards it. He knew it was late, very late, and bitterly cold, but as he reached the building he found it dark and empty. Hollis suddenly realized that he was on his own in the churchyard. An eerie howl broke the silence and he glimpsed something moving through the gravestones in the glittering frost. It was an enormous, black dog that seemed to glide effortlessly over the snow. Suddenly it rushed at him and he turned to run, only the snow was as heavy as wet concrete and he sank deeper and deeper with each footstep. The beast was gaining on him, he could feel its claws on his back as he fell forwards and he felt its weight on his back as he hit the snow. At that moment the dream fractured and he suddenly found himself in a small attic room looking out across the moonlit Fens. A low ground mist was swirling and drifting through the reeds, smothering everything in a white shroud. Hollis yawned and was about to turn away when he saw a procession of lights moving towards him, crossing the marshes in a straight, impossible line.

Suddenly the room began to shrink and tighten in around him. The window frame warped and twisted out of shape, the small panes of dirty glass trembled and wobbled as softly as the membranes of soap bubbles. The dry, crumbling lathe and plaster walls started to bulge and sag, taking on the dull, wet sheen of soft putty. Instinctively he raised his hands to protect himself but where he touched the wall the surface rippled, rupturing into gaping mouths and lips that cursed and snapped at his fingers, making him snatch them away. Voices began to whisper and call to him through the molten walls, getting louder and louder, fingers and hands began to push their way through the wet plaster, grasping at his clothing. Heavy footsteps creaked on the stair treads outside the attic door, making the floorboards buckle and sway beneath his feet. It was getting blindingly bright and hot in the room. The lights crossing the marsh were rising out of the mist, metamorphosing into monstrous, winged insects that flew against the window, popping the trembling panes of glass one by one. Hollis tried to cover his head and scream but he found he couldn't move or make a sound. Somebody was trying to get into his room. They were rattling the door handle and hammering and banging so violently on the door that it was splintering and falling apart. Slowly it began to tip and fall in towards him. There were lights, dozens of white lights, painted faces, heads with horns. Their voices rose to screaming shouts as they crowded in the room and came towards him . . .

Hollis awoke with a jolt and sat bolt upright in his bed. He was soaked with sweat and staring wildly around the room, throwing up his arms as though to fend off attackers. Everything was blurred, out of focus, and he blinked to clear his vision. The phantoms of his nightmare began to shrink and the claustrophobic walls melt back into his subconscious, but the memory of the dream stayed with him, etched in vivid detail. The lights in the marsh, that attic room – for some inexplicable reason they were familiar to him. The noise of something hammering and banging persisted and there were voices calling, shouting. They were coming from somewhere just outside his room. He threw off the duvet and turned anxiously towards the door only to freeze and catch his breath as something moved on the edge of his vision, vanishing before he could get a proper look at it, blending back into the shadows as though it had never been.

'What the hell?' he hissed, going suddenly cold as he remembered the ghostly figure that had appeared in the room beside his bed as he was drifting off to sleep. He remembered trying to stay awake because he had sensed it was still there, even though it had hidden from sight. He shivered as he realized that he had actually slept with the thing right there in the room with him.

'Jesus Christ – this ought to get rid of you!' he growled, more with fear than with anger as he crossed to the window in three steps and threw back the curtains.

The bright morning sunlight that streamed into the room made him blink and shield his eyes. He fiddled with the window catch and opened it. The sound of banging that had awoken him grew louder. Standing on tiptoe to look down into the road below, Hollis saw that a brewery lorry was parked immediately below his window and that two men were unloading barrels and rolling them noisily down the chute into the cellar of the inn.

'Well, at least that explains away a part of my nightmare!' he murmured as he turned back and pulled on his dressing gown before crossing the corridor to the bathroom. But he paused, his hand still on the door handle. It wasn't so easy to find an explanation for the rest of his dream. The vividness was beginning to fade but it left him with the nagging question, were the dreams he was having something to do with his grandfather and his sudden, unexplained disappearance? If only he could understand what they meant. He sensed that the ghost, or whatever he had glimpsed in the night, was still there in his room. He couldn't see it now but he could still smell the faint, clinging odour of decay and stagnant water even with the window open. Shivering slightly he showered and dressed before going downstairs for breakfast.

'Ghosts? Well of course we do have a couple . . .' the landlord exclaimed, pausing at Hollis' table after he had told him about the apparition he had seen in the night. 'East Anglia's full of ghosts, but I didn't think we had one in that room. We've got old Betty, the parlour maid, she mainly hangs around down here though – and, yes, I mustn't forget that disgruntled peat-digger from about a hundred and fifty years ago – I wouldn't be surprised if you had told me you had seen *him* in the bar, he haunts the place on wild, stormy nights, sits all hunched up in that old wing-backed chair by the fire. I'm not much of one for ghosts myself, I haven't actually seen him, but by all accounts he's a small fella, wears a long, buttoned coat with a high collar. His face is supposed to be all shrunken, wrinkled and brown like old leather, but he doesn't bother people much, as long as they don't sit in his chair. Story is he died in it!'

The landlord coughed and cleared his throat, glancing up at the stairs. 'But I don't remember anyone reporting him haunting the bedrooms. Well, not since I've been here anyway.'

'No, no, it wasn't him.' Hollis shook his head. 'Whoever I saw didn't look like that at all. I'll try and describe him to you.'

Hollis toyed with a strip of bacon that was congealing in the grease on his plate as he tried to remember exactly what the apparition looked like. 'He was tall, a tall thin man who appeared to be soaking wet. Yes, I remember, there were broken reeds and weeds hanging from his clothing and caught in his hair, and his hands and face were blackened and decayed. The skin, or what was left of it, looked as though it had been immersed in water for a very long time. I even remember looking down at the bedclothes and the floor to see if he had left any traces of mud or water on them after he vanished. When he tried to speak his voice gurgled weirdly, it sounded almost as though he had been drowned.'

'You must have been really frightened, seeing something like that suddenly appear in your room. We can't have our guests being terrified like that, it won't do at all.' The agitated landlord began to clear the table as he apologized.

'It did scare the hell out of me the way it suddenly appeared like that, standing beside the bed, and I'm sure I wasn't dreaming – how could you dream up something that looked so real, so horrible, with all that slime and water trickling down its face and oozing out of its rotting clothing. But oddly enough, come to think of it there wasn't anything menacing about it . . .'

'Nothing menacing? I should think that seeing something like that would be quite enough to give anybody a heart attack!' the landlord interrupted.

'No, no, that's just it, it wasn't. In a strange way I almost felt as though it belonged to me – no, that's not right, I'm not explaining this all that well. It's as if it was there to warn me, to tell me something, only I couldn't understand . . .'

Hollis let his voice trail off, the sentence unfinished. There was a hostile, guarded look developing in the landlord's eyes. Obviously he didn't think much of the visitors who brought their own ghosts with them to haunt the bedrooms.

'Perhaps I did dream it after all. That spotted dog I had

for dessert last night was pretty rich wasn't it!' Hollis tried to laugh.

'Nobody else has complained,' the landlord muttered testily.

'Oh no, I wasn't complaining, it tasted very good.'

Hollis blushed as he pushed away the empty coffee cup and glanced out of the window at the pale blue, rain-washed sky speckled with ragged, wispy clouds that were chasing their shadows over the flat, featureless expanse of Fenland that he could see beyond the village. 'Looks as though it's going to be a great day,' he added quickly, trying to change the subject.

The landlord nodded without enthusiasm before asking Hollis whether he would be staying another night.

'No, I don't think so, I'll be moving on right after breakfast. Those two guys playing dominoes you pointed out to me last night suggested that I should try further east for that village where my grandfather was stationed. Do you remember, I showed you the photographs?'

Hollis pulled the bundle out of his pocket and removed the rubber band that held them together. He quickly shuffled through for the ones that showed the village at its best but he came to a startled stop when he reached the one slightly out of focus, the one of the group standing in front of the inn. He remembered singling out that same picture the night before while he was in bed. He looked at it again and wondered; the thick-set figure towards the right of the group could well be the same one he had dreamed about, the one with the English accent and the reddish hair, but this time it was the tall, thin, uniformed figure in the centre of the picture who caught his attention, the one he had assumed was his grandfather.

'No, it can't be!' He stared at the picture for a moment and then half-closed his eyes and slowly rubbed his thumb backwards and forwards across the blurred image as if to rub

72

the genie alive. A cold shiver of realization touched his spine. There could be no doubt. The slight stoop, the way he stood, it was clear that the apparition that had appeared in his room the previous night had to be his grandfather.

'Hey, look at this, you won't believe it . . .' he began, glancing up to where the landlord had been standing close to his table, but he had moved away, gone back to stand behind the bar where he was checking the pumps and racking up the glasses for lunch time.

Hollis looked hard at the old photograph and his skin prickled. He pushed the picture back amongst the others and slipped them into his pocket before standing up in a hurry. If that apparition was the ghost of his grandfather why was his skin decomposing? He had always imagined that ghosts were supposed to be images of the living person, frozen at the moment of their death, always remaining the same, never growing any older. But whatever he had seen in his bedroom had existed beyond death. Worse than that, it had a future. It was a presence that existed into this dimension. It seemed so absurd but it appeared that this ghost was growing older, or rather decomposing almost on the edge of his consciousness. Somehow, he guessed, it had been waiting for him to discover that photograph – but why?

'I think I had better check out now,' he called over to the landlord. 'Thanks for a great evening, I'll be sure to stop in on my way back.'

Hollis grinned and waved as he walked past the landlord who was standing in the doorway, arms folded across his chest. Hollis was sure he had only followed him out to make sure he actually left. He tossed his bag into the trunk of the hire car and slipped into the driver's seat, it still felt very unfamiliar being on the wrong side of the car.

'So now where? Soham, Isleham, Lakenheath, Northwold?'

he recited, firing up the engine and glancing down, undecided as he spread the map out in front of him.

From what he had been told the previous night most of the wartime bases were much further east, at least that meant he didn't have to attempt the narrow, single-tracked roads that dissected the centre of the Fens. On the map they seemed as straight as a ruler for miles and then they took a few unexpected twists and turns before vanishing abruptly in the middle of nowhere.

'Freckenham, Mildenhall then Lakenheath – they sound as though they deserve a look,' he decided, moving the gear shift into drive and pulling out of the car park.

The sudden blare of a horn and a squeal of tyres to his left made him stamp hard on the brake pedal and snap his head around to see an articulated lorry bearing down on him. Its wheels were locked up and it was sliding sideways, churning up clouds of smoky rubber and tarmac. The lorry juddered to a halt only inches from his nearside wing and the driver threw open the cab door, red-faced and swearing, his hand knuckled into a fist.

'I'm sorry . . . I'm really sorry . . . I'm not used to driving on the lefthand side yet,' he called out as an apology before stamping hard on the accelerator.

'Damn Americans!' the driver cursed, but it wasn't only the angry driver who was shaking his fist at the departing car, the landlord was nodding in silent agreement as he stood in his doorway and watched Hollis leave.

Panic had tightened in Hollis' stomach as he had swung his head around at the warning blare of the lorry's horn. In that fleeting moment he had caught a glimpse of something else, a translucent figure, somebody sitting in the back of his car. It was no more than a blink, a shadow on the edge of his sight, but mixed with the sudden reek of the marshes that now filled the car he knew it had to be that same, drowned apparition that had appeared in his room the previous night. His back tingled and a cold sweat broke out on his temples.

'Jesus Christ what have I got to do to get away from you?' he hissed, instinctively stamping down hard on the pedal and hanging on grimly to the steering wheel as the car slewed across the road, mounted the opposite kerb, missed a lamp post by inches before straightening up as he swung the wheel and accelerated out of the village.

Easing his foot off the pedal Hollis took a few deep breaths and sniffed. The smell of the marshes had receded but it was still there in the background. He searched the rear-view mirror and then glanced repeatedly over his shoulder for any sign of the figure, but the car was empty. 'It doesn't make any sense,' he muttered as he pulled over to a lay-by and stopped. He frowned as he opened all the doors, letting the strong morning breezes pass through the car. It ruffled the pages of his map book, scattering the loose newspapers, candy wrappers and petrol bills that he had left over the passenger seat. He began to feel a little silly. Ghosts didn't follow people about, he had to be imagining it. But still he examined the inside of his car before getting back in and restarting the engine.

'People are going to think I've gone stark, staring mad if I carry on like this!' he sighed, slipping the gear stick into drive but as he pulled back onto the road he knew it was still with him. The smell of the marshes was getting stronger, and now it was all around him.

4

The Haunting Strengthens

HOLLIS DREW A COMPLETE BLANK in Freckenham. Everybody he asked or tried to show the pictures to were either too young to remember the war or seemed to have moved into the area recently, but his hopes began to rise as he drove past the American airforce base at Mildenhall. Surely somebody there would be able to tell him where those photographs were taken. There must be records, photographs he could compare them with. The duty sergeant smiled and shook his head as he passed the pictures back. To him one English village looked much like another, and Hollis wasn't the first person he'd had to deal with who was trying to trace relatives who had been lost in the war. Showing Hollis out he explained that everyone who had served in England, especially in East Anglia, had retired a long time before, but he suggested that Hollis try the various memorial museums and he gave him a printed leaflet cataloguing them.

'But you could start by trying the village store. It's just across the street, they seem to know everybody around here and their family has owned it for years.'

'No, I can't say that any of them pictures strikes a chord. That village could be one of a dozen,' the storekeeper replied, refusing to commit himself. The momentary flicker of interest as Hollis spread out the photographs on the counter quickly faded as the bell on the shop door jangled and he focused his attention on a couple who entered the store, moving away to serve them.

'Oh, you could try towards Old Buckenham and Snetterton Heath – there were lots of airfields out that way. Take the A11 towards Thetford and then follow the signs for the motor racing circuit,' he called out after Hollis as he left the store.

'Thetford? Thetford? I wonder . . .' he murmured to himself as he climbed back into the car and consulted the map. Thetford seemed altogether in the wrong direction, away from the Fens, but perhaps somebody out that way might remember, might recognize something in one of those photographs. Another idea suddenly occurred to him and he glanced down at the list of museums the duty sergeant had suggested he visit. The 100th Bomber Group memorial museum at Thorpe Abbotts wasn't too far way from Snetterton Heath. He could easily drive to the museum if he had to.

Hollis caught a movement out of the corner of his eye. It was something that he would have barely blinked at a week ago but now he automatically hunted the rear-view mirror, searching quickly over his shoulder as that tingling coldness crept up his back, past his collar to prickle the hairs on the nape of his neck. That faint but familiar odour of stagnant decay gradually invaded the car. It was still with him, he could smell it, he could sense its unwelcome presence even if he couldn't see it.

'Damn you!' he muttered, as he accelerated the car, more out of shock at its reappearance than in anger. But it took a lot of concentration to keep his attention on the road rather than chasing the half-seen images his imagination began to weave around him as he joined the heavy traffic on the A11. In an odd way the further he drove the car the more agitated the spectre became. It began to fill the car with its presence, as if it didn't want Hollis to go that way.

Anger boiled up inside him. 'Why don't you get the hell out of here and leave me alone!' he shouted, punching the empty air beside him.

The car swerved and veered dangerously across the road towards the oncoming traffic. He had a brief glimpse of headlights flashing at him and the blurred, white face of the driver in the oncoming car as it passed barely inches away from his offside mirror.

'Okay okay, you win!' he muttered, feeling a cold sweat break out on his forehead as he eased his foot off the accelerator and straightened up the car. He had better find that damned village soon and somehow lay this ghost to rest before it killed him. He had already had two near-misses that morning and he didn't want another one.

Ahead of him he saw the signpost to a small, minor road that cut back across Thetford Forest and a quick glance at the map showed him that it would lead him back towards the Fens. The way was narrow and gently undulating, it was like riding over petrified waves, but it was very straight and the trees lining the sides of the single-track road had the unnerving appearance of being hundreds of ancient warriors withered and frozen by time, their feet buried in the banks of nettles and brambles as they waited to be released from some magician's spell that had enchanted them centuries earlier. A straggle of houses began to appear, half-hidden between the branches. A neat row of cottages close to the road and then a shop/post-office/general store, its windows plastered over with advertisements for the local newspaper, stood slightly apart from them. The bell on the door jangled noisily behind him as he closed it and it took him a moment to get his bearings and find the counter amongst the maze of shelves and magazine racks that crowded the tiny shop.

'Yes, young man, can I help you?' A crisp, almost brittle voice called out enquiringly from between the shelves.

'Ah, yes, I was wondering if you could have a look at these photographs and tell me if you recognize the village in them. I am trying to find the place where my grandfather was stationed in the war.'

Hollis pulled out the bundle of pictures as he made his way through to the counter and smiled as he put them down in front of a small, grey-haired woman in thick-rimmed spectacles.

'You have an amazing collection of stuff for sale here.' He looked around at the array of tins, bottles and groceries which were packed neatly on the shelves. There were dozens of cardboard boxes of haberdashery and items of hardware stacked to the ceiling, each one of them carefully labelled in red pen, and sagging rails of stout, practical clothes filled every available gap while the floor beneath each over-flowing shelf was literally carpeted with boots, shoes and wellingtons of every shape and size.

'We carry almost anything you might need. We have to, we are the only shop and post office for miles around here. Go on – ask me for something – I'll bet we have it!' she replied proudly, shaking her head at the photographs while gathering them up ready to hand back. 'I really couldn't begin to guess which village this is, I'm afraid.'

Hollis smiled and slipped them back into his pocket before thanking her and turning towards the door. He was beginning to think that the village had never really existed, that it was as much a freak illusion as that photograph of himself and those other people he had found.

'An umbrella! Have you got an umbrella?' he asked, pausing at the door.

The old woman laughed and clapped her hands with delight. 'That's an easy one! Imagine a shop like this – in England of all places – not having an umbrella for sale!'

'Do you take credit cards?' he asked, returning to the counter and examining the umbrella before fishing for his wallet.

'Why, yes, of course we do. We're thoroughly modern here you know.'

There was almost a note of accusation in her voice as she carefully wrapped the umbrella in brown paper and tied it up with a piece of string. Hollis smiled at her neat grey head of hair as she bent to carefully tie each knot. There was something so charming, so eccentrically English about her.

'You could try at the forge, Edgar's bound to know which village it is in the photographs. His family's been here since Boudica first learned to drive a chariot. Yes, you ask Edgar Stern, he's at the forge at the end of the village on the right. You can't miss him.'

Hollis hesitated at the entrance to the forge, gripping his bundle of photographs. He blinked and wrinkled his nose at the sharp, acrid, hazy smoke and the blast of dusty air that smelled of horses and hot metal that met him as he stepped in over the threshold. Directly ahead of him, half-hidden in the gloomy interior, he could see the red glow of the coals in the fire bordered by the quenching trough. The wall was lined with dozens of pairs of tongs and farriers' tools, rasps and paring knives. Beside the forge, bent over an anvil, the blacksmith, dressed in a leather apron and a dirty yellow vest, was hammering at a horseshoe, his arm and shoulder muscles drenched with sweat. A movement to Hollis' right caught his attention and through the haze he saw a dark grey horse tied

83

by its halter rope to an iron ring set into the wall, and there was the groom, leaning nonchalantly against the wall on the far side smoking a cigarette. He straightened himself up as Hollis entered and called out to the blacksmith to tell him that he had a visitor.

Edgar scowled and glanced up. 'I'll be with you in a minute, son.' Then he returned his attention to the shoe, gripping it with a set of long-handled tongs and pushing it back in amongst the hot coals of the fire.

Hollis let his gaze wander through the forge from the lengths of heavy chain that lay coiled haphazardly to one side of the cobbled floor to the mound of rusty, worn-out horseshoes that were piled up in one corner. He looked across the long, wooden workbenches littered with flatteners, ball hammers, swages, hot punches, callipers, cold chisels and drifts to the rows of ready-forged horseshoes of varying sizes that hung from hooks in the soot-scarred walls. From there he looked up into the steeply-gabled roof where bundles of lengths of iron hung from the rafters. Everything in the forge seemed so old, from the cobbles which were worn smooth beneath his feet to the smoke-kippered beams above his head.

The sudden hiss and splutter of the shoe being plunged into the quenching trough made him look back in time to see the blacksmith, who was already turning, bending down to lift the horse's hind leg and pressing the red-hot shoe into the horn of its hoof. The hiss and smell of the burning hoof almost overwhelmed Hollis as he watched, transfixed, while dense clouds of yellow smoke curled up around the edges of the shoe, enveloping the blacksmith's chest and face.

'Doesn't it hurt?' he asked, taking a tentative step towards the horse as the smoke caught in his throat and made him cough. He had never seen a horse being shod before.

Edgar glanced up at Hollis and laughed. He held the hot shoe to the hoof a moment longer, checking that it had burned evenly before he let go of the horse's leg and tossed the shoe into the quenching trough to cool down thoroughly. He wiped his dirty hands on an old towel and beckoned Hollis over to where he stood.

'Now what can I do for you?' he asked, lifting the dripping shoe out of the water.

'These photographs – I was wondering if you would be able to recognize where they were taken. The lady in the shop thought you might know.' Hollis felt awkward about bothering the blacksmith in the middle of shoeing the horse.

Edgar took the photographs and rifled slowly through them before he scratched his head. 'That's Candleford, or at least that's what it used to look like just after the war. I had a drink or two in the Black Shuck before it closed down. Mind you, it's changed a bit since then, everywhere has, but . . .' Edgar paused and glanced around towards the smoke as it drifted out of the open doorway.

'That's odd, I could have sworn I saw somebody just then. A tall, dishevelled sort of figure. Did you see anyone.'

Hollis shook his head. He had, for a moment, thought he'd glimpsed the apparition standing in the doorway, but he was never going to admit it to this man. Someone else seeing it made it all the more frighteningly real. Edgar walked slowly across to the doorway and crouched down to examine something on the ground.

'That's odd. Look at this. There's a pool of water right there where I thought I saw him. Smell it, it smells of stagnant water.'

Hollis felt a cold shiver of panic knot inside him. This ghost was becoming real, it was breaking into his world.

'Can-Candleford you say. Which way do I go from here?' Hollis stuttered, trying to mask his fear.

'Candleford – now let me think.' It had been a long time since Edgar had last been through that village. Returning to the quenching trough he gathered up the four new-forged shoes and selected a box of shoeing nails before he crossed over to the waiting horse. 'I reckon it must be almost due north of here. Yes, and that village sits so close to the edge of the Fens that its feet virtually dangle in the marsh.'

'I know Candleford,' the groom added, treading on the stub of his cigarette and grinding it into the cobblestone floor. 'Took a horse there once. Was a year or two back. Must be twenty-five, no, nearer thirty mile from here. Best way is to go across country. Take the forest road to Mundford, you'll pass Grimes Graves along the way, when you reach the Swaffham Road follow the Cockley Cley signs and then head towards Beachamwell. You can't miss it after that because the road will run out when it reaches the marsh.'

'Thank you, thank you very much, you've been a great help.' Hollis hurried towards the open doorway of the forge, stuffing the photographs back into his pocket. He had to get to that village fast and jettison the ghost of his grandfather before it materialized again.

'Candleford isn't much of a place. Why are you looking for it anyway?' Edgar stopped him, making him look back.

'My grandfather was stationed there during the war. I just wanted to see where he was billeted before he disappeared.'

'Disappeared you say. Well just you be careful, my son. Candleford's a funny place, all isolated out there on the edge of the Fens.'

Edgar looked concerned before he returned his attention to the shoeing of the horse, picking up a foreleg to carefully rasp the sole of the burned hoof. Hollis watched him test the shoe for a perfect fit before trimming out a small nick in the front of the hoof for the clip. He used one of the nails he had slipped into his mouth to begin to secure the shoe into place.

'Careful? What do I have to be careful about?' Hollis asked, his curiosity pricked.

Edgar paused in his shoeing, his hammer poised ready to tap the third nail into the ready-prepared nail hole. 'I don't rightly know.' He scowled, searching for words to express the uneasiness he felt about the village. 'As George here says,' the blacksmith nodded towards the groom, 'Candleford's a very isolated place stuck out there on the edge of the Fens. They don't get many visitors and they don't like strangers poking their noses into their business. It's best you be careful. Don't you go wandering into the marshes on your own just because you think you're looking for something. Your grandfather wasn't the first person to vanish in Candleford – and I don't suppose he'll be the last either.'

'What? Who else has vanished?' Hollis was shocked, but Edgar merely grunted dismissively and returned to his shoeing. He refused to be drawn further and not another word was said about Candleford.

Hollis climbed shakily back into his car. As he pulled the door shut he was not surprised to see his hands were trembling. It had been quite a shock seeing the ghost appear like that in the doorway of the forge. The way it had left behind a pool of stagnant water left Hollis' stomach knotted up.

'What the hell do you want from me?' he whispered, glancing anxiously around the interior of the car, half expecting the apparition to appear again. But there was not the slightest sense of its presence.

Sighing, Hollis reached for the map, and it didn't take him long to find Candleford. It was perched on the edge of the marshes, surrounded to the west by a network of drains and dykes and what looked like inhospitable Fens. He traced the route the groom had suggested he take and fired up the engine before slipping the car into gear and pulling out of the forecourt in front of the forge and onto the forest road. Suddenly he didn't feel in quite the hurry he had been in earlier – finding out where those photographs had been taken had become almost an obsession but now he felt quite differently about them. The village had a name, a reality, a life of its own. It lived beyond those faded old pictures, and now he knew where it was he wasn't sure what he was supposed to be looking for. His grandfather had vanished there over fifty years ago – what could he possibly find out after all this time? The trail must have gone cold years before he was even born. But there was something else that fuelled his reluctance, something in the blacksmith's veiled warnings about the village that made him hesitate as he eased his foot from the accelerator. There was something sinister, almost threatening in the words he had heard in the forge. They still echoed around in his head.

'Candleford's a very isolated place, they don't like strangers poking their noses into their business.'

No, he would go back home. At least he had found out the name of the village, perhaps that was enough. Hollis braked as he caught sight of a dirt track that led off into the forest on the left. He could pull in and turn round, he would head back immediately. His mind was just about made up, he had even decided which flight he would catch the following day, when the wheel was suddenly wrenched through his hands and the car slewed violently across the track, coming to a juddering halt and sending up a shower of loose earth and stones as the engine stalled.

'What the hell . . . ?'

The air darkened around Hollis and the car filled with the sickening and now familiar, overpowering reek of decay. He tried to reach for the door catch to escape but some invisible force was pinning him down. His arms felt as though they were stuck in treacle and his body was pressed hard into the seat. The darkness thickened and the air became stifling, almost impossible to breathe. The sounds of the birds in the trees that lined the track, and the tick, tick, tick, of the hot metal as the engine cooled and contracted seemed muffled and far away.

The tall figure that was haunting him so persistently began to materialize in the passenger seat beside him – its blackened, decomposing silhouette becoming sharper. It was so close to him by this time that he could see its face in all its revolting detail as it turned to look at him. The shrivelled flesh and sinews stretched like wet leather across its bones, its face had become an animated mask of anatomy as its drowned voice gurgled in its throat and its bony fingers probed and rifled through his pockets.

'You cannot turn back. I will not let you. You must find . . . you must find . . .'

It kept on repeating itself, the words barely audible as they bubbled and frothed in its mouth. Hollis shuddered at the dead, wet touch. He felt violated and helpless but he couldn't resist. He couldn't even cry out as the contents of his pockets were flung carelessly across the car.

'Find . . . find . . . find . . .'

The voice spoke faster, growing more agitated as it found the bundle of photographs and scattered them across its lap, lifting and pressing them across Hollis' face one after the other before letting them fall on the floor.

'Find . . . find . . . find . . .'

Suddenly the figure stopped, its fingers frozen as it held

up the picture that showed Hollis and the two strangers in the front of the inglenook. The impossible, freak photograph that had drawn him to England. A movement in the rear-view mirror, a swirling darkness, made Hollis look up. His eyes widened in horror – there were more of those blackened, decomposing figures in the car. One . . . two . . . he couldn't be sure. They were leaning forwards, gripping the back of his seat, smothering him with their reek of decay, making him giddy. Their drowned voices rose in excited, gurgling sounds as they reached over his head to touch the photograph. Their arms were dripping cold, slimy water onto his neck and shoulders. Everything seemed to swim and grow hazy in front of him as their voices assaulted his ears. Their faces closed in, filling his vision until they were almost touching his. He could feel their cold, wet flesh against his cheeks. Hollis felt as though he were falling, sinking down through the seat, melting into a black well of emptiness as unconsciousness folded over him.

'Must find . . . must find . . . must find . . .'

The echo of their voices faded as the apparitions vanished leaving him slumped in a dead faint over the steering wheel.

Awareness slowly began to return, seeping into his mind in dark, terrifying dreams. The black beast of Hell was mauling him, devouring him, its fetid breath making a white halo, moon-white around its head. He could see its eyes, liquid fire, and he was running, trying to escape from it. Every footstep he took sank into a soft, snowy landscape. Strange and yet familiar faces crowded around him. He was engulfed in the thunderous roar of aero-engines, their propellers scything glittering arcs as they advanced menacingly along the runway. He was running, sinking into the tarmac. He couldn't escape. The B17 metamorphosed into the huge, bounding shape of a black dog. There were rows of lighted candles stretching out across the marshes. He could hear chanting, singing voices converging on him. Their voices seemed to rise into a wailing, persistent cry that cut deep into his soul.

With a jerk and a frightened, disorientated gasp he woke up. He sat back and stared around him. He realized that he must have blacked out and slipped down across the steering wheel, the wailing sound was coming from the car horn where his elbow had caught the central hub. He wiped the back of his hand across his forehead, it was soaking wet. As he moved he realized that his jacket, shirt and trousers were damp and crumpled. They seemed to have the faint smell of stagnant marshes about them. He caught sight of the photographs and the contents of his pockets scattered on the floor and all over the seats of the car. He glanced frantically in the rear-view mirror and the seat beside him, searching and yet terrified at the thought of finding. The awful reality of what had happened to him came flooding back. He could not turn back. He reached for the door handle expecting something dreadful to happen but instead the door catch released to his touch and he tumbled out, breathing in frightened sobs of clean air in short, strangled gasps.

'You cannot turn back. I will not let you. You must find . . . find . . . find . . .'

The drowned words of the ghost of his grandfather were a persistent echo in his head. He took a couple of quick steps away from the car towards the road. A brief idea that he might make a run for it, flag down a passing motorist and escape, didn't last two yards. He sensed somebody behind him, a shadowy figure materializing on the edge of his sight. He could feel the grip of its bony fingers on his arm.

'All right! All right! For Christ's sake, I'll go!'

He turned savagely to confront the apparition that he

knew was behind him only to find nothing there, nothing but the quiet, leafy shadows. Nothing to hear but birdsong in the trees and rustles of wildlife in the undergrowth that bordered on the forest track.

'I'll go to that damn village!' he muttered aloud, getting back into the car. 'But I don't know what the hell you expect me to find after all this time – unless you want me to find those other two . . .'

He frowned as he gathered up the photographs, pausing to study the picture of himself and the two strangers taken in the inglenook. He tidied up his scattered possessions, putting them back into his pockets before he glanced at his watch and fired up the engine. It was getting late and the sun had dropped low in the sky, casting long shadows across the car. He realized that he had been there much longer than he had thought as he pulled the car out onto the road.

As he reached the road to Swaffham he was about to turn towards Cockley Cley when he noticed the lights of an inn or an hotel away to his right just on the main road. Looking around the interior of the car he shouted, 'I'm going to stop there for the night. I'm not trying to run away or anything but I don't want to arrive in Candleford in the dark. I just want to get cleaned up, get the smell of the stinking marshes off my clothes and have some sleep. Is that okay?'

He hadn't realized how tightly he was gripping the steering wheel or that his voice had risen to a high-pitched shout. The sudden blare of a car horn behind him made him nearly jump out of his skin. He glanced into the mirror and saw that two cars had pulled up behind him at the junction and were waiting for him to pull out.

'Okay! Okay! I'm going,' he shouted, turning to the right and pulling across into the car park of the Swan Inn.

*   *   *

The landlord of the Swan frowned and looked Hollis up and down dubiously as he signed the register, wrinkling his nose at the unpleasant odour of stagnant marsh water that seemed to be clinging to his clothes. He was obviously American to judge from his accent, but his clothes indicated that he was neither a rambler nor from one of the airbases. The only explanation the landlord could think of was that he was a birdwatcher, or twitcher. Perhaps he had been in the Fens all day. He used to get quite a few of them stop overnight on their way to the coastal marshes closer to Christmas, and sometimes, if they spent the day in the Great Fen, they would bring that stench of the marshes into the pub with them along with the thick, black mud and slime that would cling to their boots until they traipsed it through to the bar. But he didn't get many Americans, especially at this time of the year.

'If you're one of those twitchers then you're a bit early and too far inland for the oystercatchers or winter waders. They won't be flying in for another month or six weeks at the earliest. Not unless the weather turns bad.'

'Twitchers? What are twitchers?' Hollis asked, his eyebrows raised in curiosity.

'Birdwatchers. I thought you might be one of them birdwatchers. I was going to suggest that you go up to the coastal marshes, try Fosdyke or Holbeach on the edge of the Wash. That's where most twitchers go for the waders.'

'Thanks.' Hollis smiled as he realized what the landlord meant. 'But I have come over to visit Candleford. I've come to see where my grandfather was stationed during the war.'

He paused and glanced at his jacket, catching the stagnant smell each time he moved. 'You couldn't get my jacket and pants cleaned for me, could you? I'd need them in the morning though,' he asked as he followed the landlord up to his room.

93

'No, I'm sorry, we don't do anything like that. My wife could have got one of the girls to run them into Swaffham if you'd been stopping any longer,' he replied, opening the door of the room and passing Hollis the keys before hurrying back to the bar.

Hollis shut the door and tossed his case onto the bed before glancing anxiously around the room. His skin was prickling and it wasn't just the smell on his clothes that suddenly filled the room. He could sense the presence of that apparition, it had followed him to the inn. It was standing so close that, despite its invisibility, he could hear and feel its shallow, gurgling breath on the back of his neck.

'Get out! Get away from me!' he hissed, spinning around, shuddering as the atmosphere in the room became airless and stifling. He flung the window wide open and tore off his jacket and pants, throwing them into the corner.

'Damn you! What have I got to do to make you leave me alone? I promised to go to Candleford, didn't I?' he muttered, running the shower. But it didn't matter how much soap he used he couldn't seem to wash away the odour of stagnant decay. It hadn't only clung to his clothes, it seemed to have become ingrained into his skin.

'I wish I had never come to England! I wish I had let Uncle Joe burn that cursed photograph!' he swore, closing his eyes as he washed the shampoo from his hair.

Suddenly he gasped with revulsion – his hair was full of slimy, matted weeds. His fingers were tangled, trapped. Water was running into his mouth, his nose, he was choking, he couldn't breathe. Stumbling blindly and knocking his elbow on the door of the shower, he leaped out and rubbed frantically at the steamy mirror over the wash-basin to stare at his reflection. There was nothing in his hair, nothing except streaks of shampoo. He frowned and gingerly touched his hair and then bent forwards, cupping his hands to fill them from the tap on the basin to rinse the soap away, and shutting his eyes beneath the soft spray of hot water. He was afraid to step back into the shower. He was afraid of what the ghost would conjure up in his imagination to frighten him with next.

Hollis dressed quickly without drying himself properly. He needed to be surrounded by real, live people; people he could see, people who would bleed if they cut themselves. He hurried down to the bar for a drink before dinner.

'Candleford – yes, I know the village.' The landlord was a little non-committal as he finished pulling Hollis a pint of Abbotts and pushed it across the polished surface of the bar towards him.

'What's it like exactly? How big is it?' Hollis asked, getting the bundle of photographs out of his pocket. 'All I have are these old pictures and some letters that my grandfather wrote before he disappeared. I expect it's changed a lot since then.'

'Changed?' The landlord picked up the photographs, scowling. 'In some ways it's changed a lot, but in others . . .' he stopped shuffling the pictures and passed them back to Hollis before turning away to busy himself drying glasses.

'What sort of changes? Please tell me.' Hollis pressed him for more information as he tentatively sipped at the frothy head of his beer, remembering how it had made him so light-headed the previous night.

The landlord shrugged and turned back. 'Everywhere has to change, doesn't it? Candleford's no different from any other village. I blame it on modern technology: the farms don't need the labour any more, nobody digs the peat in the Fens now, it's protected, no one cuts the sedge – so people move away. They have to, don't they, if there's no work what else can they do? The villages shrink and some of them die. Back in history it used to be things like the Black Death that wiped out a community – now it's your modern technology that does it. Just look at those old photographs hung up around the walls of the bar and you'll see how it's changed here since the turn of the century – and they call it progress!'

'Is that what's happened to Candleford? Has everyone been forced to move away? That's a pity because the village looked so busy in the pictures my grandfather took.'

'People don't leave that village!' The landlord laughed harshly and then leaned closer across the bar. 'Oh yes, it was a busy place before the war, my father knew it well in those days. There were more than six shops, two butchers, they had their own tailor and a harness maker, even a chemist – and three pubs. Mind you, the people there were always closed in, sort of private, they didn't take well to outsiders. I suppose that living out there on the edge of the marshes made them like that. It created a terrible upset when the airfield was built and the Yanks arrived. There was no end of . . .'

The landlord paused, darting a glance around the other customers who had gathered further along the bar and were sitting in the room. It was almost as though he was afraid he might have already said too much.

'There is some mention in my grandfather's letters of the hostility from the villagers. Do you know what happened exactly?' Hollis pressed, raising his voice and making those closest to him turn to stare.

'It was nothing special,' the landlord replied quickly, lowering his voice to barely a whisper. 'The outsiders just upset things with their constant prying into other folks' business, poking their noses in where they weren't wanted. You be careful if you're planning on visiting Candleford tomorrow, young man. You say your grandfather disappeared, well don't be too inquisitive, sometimes the past is best left well alone if you know what's good for you.'

There was a slight sheen of perspiration on the landlord's forehead as he warned Hollis to be careful, but he refused to be drawn any further on the subject of Candleford and he moved away along the bar to join in some noisy local debate. But his eyes kept straying back to Hollis as though there was more he would like to tell him if only he were not so afraid. Hollis indicated to the young waitress that he would eat in the bar and he took a seat at one of the tables near the window. He took out the letters his grandfather had written during the war, smoothing the last, unfinished one on the tablecloth before he read it through again. After the veiled warnings he had just received from the landlord and the one he'd had earlier in the blacksmith's forge he wondered exactly what it was that had made the villagers of Candleford so hostile to the airmen stationed there. What were they trying to hide? Was it something to do with the Lanterns that his grandfather mentioned in his letter? Were they connected to that strange ritual that he had intruded into? Was it to do with the lights and queer, half-seen shapes that he had seen rising up out of the water? His two English friends who had taken him duck shooting had been pretty quick to get out of the marshes – what had they been so frightened of?

Hollis sighed and pushed the letter back in amongst the others as the waitress brought his soup. He realized that he would probably never get to the bottom of this mystery, it had all happened so long ago. Idly toying with his spoon he looked out of the window, letting the hum of the other diners' conversations and the noisy talk and laughter at the bar wash over him. Floodlights illuminating the beer garden cast squat shadows beneath the empty, summer tables, picking out the drifts of fallen leaves that littered the lawn and the bare, black branches of the trees that were ready for winter. The scene gave off a forlorn, melancholy atmosphere and made him wish that he was back home in New England where the aspens on the hills behind his house would still be a riot of colour and he wondered what the hell he was doing there. He couldn't solve something that had happened over fifty years ago. He wouldn't know where to begin. He knew he had to go to that village, he didn't have much choice with that diabolical, decomposing ghost haunting him – but why? What good could he possibly do now?

He caught the aroma of the soup and it made him realize how hungry he was. He tasted it and found it to be delicious, home-made, and he was just leaning slightly forwards to finish the bowl when he remembered those two English friends of his grandfather, the ones he had mentioned in his letters. They might still be alive. They might just be able to throw some light onto what had happened. It shouldn't be too difficult to trace them, their names were in the letters. Surely that, at least, couldn't do any harm.

A spot of dirty water, no larger than a dime, suddenly appeared on the white tablecloth in front of the empty chair opposite him. Then another, and another, and some more slightly to the left in front of the other empty chair. The same thing was happening in front of the chair beside him. Hollis' head snapped up and he took a sharp, startled intake of breath as he let the spoon fall from his fingers into the soup, splattering it all over the tablecloth. He knew the instant that the first spot appeared, even before he looked up, what was happening. His skin was crawling at the now familiar reek of decay. But it wasn't only one ghost who had now appeared, this time there were three, and they were materializing against the flood-lit window. They had to be the same ones who he had seen in the rear-view mirror of his car earlier that afternoon when he had tried to turn around and get as far away from Candleford as possible. They leaned forwards, crowding in around him, their blackened, pitying faces only inches from his. Mud and water was oozing out of their rotting clothes, their voices were gurgling and whispering urgently as though they were trying to tell him something. Their withered, skeletal fingers briefly touched his sleeves and then their images seemed to shimmer and break up, to ripple into nothing the way a reflection fragments when a stone is dropped into a still pool of water.

The sudden shock of seeing the three, revolting, decomposing figures sitting around him made him gasp loud enough to attract the attention of the other diners, and they turned to watch as he dropped his spoon into the soup. The hum of conversation at the bar faltered as some of the evening drinkers turned to stare at him in curiosity. Somebody mentioned something about Americans that Hollis didn't quite catch in the confusion of the moment, and then they all turned back to their drinks with the incident forgotten. The waitress hurried across to his table and began to fuss around him.

'I told you the soup was very hot. You burned your mouth, I expect. Never mind, dear, it won't take me long to clear up the mess. Would you like some more?'

'No, no thanks, I'm sorry I made all this mess, I must have been daydreaming. I was just thinking about something else entirely.' He smiled at her apologetically as she picked up his soup bowl and gathered up the dirty tablecloth.

The waitress paused in the doorway as she went into the kitchen and glanced back to where the young American was sitting on his own close to the window. For a moment there, before he had cried out, she could have sworn that she saw other people sitting with him. But she must have been mistaken. They would have had to have vanished quicker than she could blink. She wasn't even sure how many of them had been there, and she couldn't describe them in any detail, except that they had left her with the distinct impression that there was something very odd about them. It was almost as though they had been wet, very wet. The chef called over to her and she shrugged, dismissing the weird thoughts from her mind as she hurried over into the kitchen, letting the door swing shut behind her.

Seeing those three, ghostly figures had put Hollis completely off his food and he picked at the plate of game pie half-heartedly before pushing it away from him, defeated. He would have gone back up to his room but he was afraid of being on his own, afraid of what they would do to him next. At first it had only been the one ghost, who he guessed probably was his grandfather, but now there were two more and their presences seemed to be growing ever more real, more frightening. They had left drops of water on the tablecloth and faint muddy finger prints on his sleeves where they had touched him. He shuddered and sipped at the remains of his beer, keeping a watchful eye on the space around him, half-expecting them to reappear at any moment.

'Coffee?'

The waitress' voice made him jump.

'Oh, yes please, lots of it – and can I have it strong and black in a large cup?'

Tonight he was afraid of shutting his eyes and he wasn't intending to sleep. Hollis sat alone, cradling his coffee cup in his hands as he watched the floodlit garden and tried to work out what the hell was happening to him. The other diners had left and the crowd at the bar had thinned out to a few serious drinkers as the landlord began to close up for the night. Suddenly it occurred to Hollis why those ghosts had appeared at his table and what their urgent whispering might be all about. It had happened only moments after he had decided to try and find those two English friends of his grandfather's. A cold shiver prickled at his scalp. What if they had disappeared at the same time? There was no reason that his grandmother would have known and his grandfather's commanding officer would have had no reason to connect their disappearances. There had been a war on, plenty of people disappeared. Perhaps their sudden appearance at his table had been a warning that he was to be careful what he said in Candleford. Perhaps there really was something sinister about the whole affair and the villagers were trying to hide it. Could they have been murdered, he wondered?

A slight movement in the garden from amongst the shadows cast by the trees caught his attention. Hollis leaned forwards, his interest sharpening. He picked out one and then two more silhouettes in the undergrowth, tall, weed-entangled figures who were standing statue-still, watching, guarding the inn.

Reluctantly Hollis returned to his room with the dregs of the percolator in his cup as the landlord finished shutting the bar and began to extinguish the lights one by one. 'Don't forget breakfast starts at 7.30am,' he called after him as he switched off the outside floodlights.

Hollis glanced anxiously along the dimly-lit corridor and took a last, quick look down the darkened stairway. There was something about all these old buildings, there was so much history woven into their fabric, all held in place by the masses of blackened beams and thick, stone walls. Every creaking footstep he took on the sloping floor echoed this past and so much of it was trapped in the atmosphere of the building. He locked the door of his room and made sure every light was switched on. Normally the dark didn't bother him much but tonight was different. Those ghosts were getting much too real, too physical, and the thought of spending the rest of the night on his own waiting for them to appear, or of accidentally drifting off to sleep and waking to find them crowding in around him, touching him, was terrifying. His nerves were as taut as piano wire, cold sweat was beginning to bead on his forehead and between his shoulder blades, every sound seemed magnified by his imagination as it heralded their approach. To make it worse the wind was picking up, rattling the old window frames, billowing the curtains and making the inn's gallows sign squeak on its rusty hinges outside his window.

Hollis pulled the curtains aside and pressed his nose against the cold glass as he searched for the figures in the garden but it was pitch black outside. He could barely see the outline of the trees against the sky. Faintly, from far in the distance, he could hear a car approach from the direction of the Swaffham road. He waited, holding his breath, only letting it escape in a sigh of relief as he saw the silhouettes of those three diabolical figures standing in the gravelled car park below his window as the car's headlamps stroked through the darkness, briefly illuminating them as it swept past. At least while they were out there he knew where they were – but how long would they remain there?

He sat down on his bed and began to think. Was he trying to create a connection between the three of them that didn't exist? Who else could they be? They had to be his grandfather's friends, it was the most logical explanation. If they were not then who were they? Perhaps if he tried to look past their grotesque, shrunken, decomposing flesh and concentrate on their height, the way they stood, or their clothes he would get a clue. He went back to the window and concentrated on the other two weed-entangled figures as the headlamps of the next couple of cars thundered past but then he gave up and sat on the bed, shuffling through the bundle of photographs again. Waves of tiredness were washing over him as he looked but he was determined to stay awake. One thing he was certain of was that their rotting clothes were not military uniforms and they were both a lot shorter than the ghost of his grandfather. One of them was much stockier. But even if he had been able to match either of the men to the ones in the pictures it wouldn't have helped him much. There wasn't anything written on the back to indicate who they were.

Then he remembered the impossible photograph. The one he kept separate from the others, the one of himself and two strangers taken years before he was born. It hadn't been developed until much later and his grandmother had written something on the back of it. He got it out of his inside jacket pocket and studied it carefully. The young man in the picture was definitely shorter than him, and thick-set, but that was where any similarity to either of the ghostly figures ended. Nor did the young woman fit in. He turned the picture over and read what his grandmother had written again.

'This must be Dennis and Douglas, the two English men who Merris wrote me about before he disappeared.'

It was dated 1970, a few years before she died.

Hollis turned the photograph over and slowly smoothed his thumb across the three faces that stared back at him and a crazy idea began to form in his mind. This was meant to be the photograph of his grandfather and his two English friends taken just before he had disappeared only the negative, for some reason, had stayed in a state of flux until the roll of film had been processed. Their sudden deaths had somehow altered the negative – but how? How could it portray a person who hadn't even been born when the picture was taken? Perhaps the others in the photograph were only his age too.

What sort of magic or supernatural power could have reached that far into the future?

Hollis frowned and shook his head. The whole idea of that picture wasn't only ridiculous it was terrifying. Photography was a chemical process, the film was light sensitive, it recorded whatever the camera lens was pointed at. And it recorded it the instant the shutter was clicked open and shut. The image that was encapsulated was that moment in time held forever. But the images had not been fixed on that day, had they?

Hollis yawned again and let his head fall back into the soft, downy pillows. Despite his determination to stay awake sleep was creeping up on him. He blinked and tried to focus on the picture. The image of his father had almost completely disappeared and now the thick-set guy standing in the foreground seemed to be fading. What the hell was going on? His mind began to wander and he mumbled sleepily, his jaw going slack just before he drifted off into a deep, dreamless sleep despite his efforts to stay awake. He didn't hear the distant cry of the monstrous hell hound hunting through the dark marshes, or sense the presence of the three, dripping figures closing in protectively around him, guarding him, watching him as he slept through the long, dead hours of the night.

5

THE ROAD SIGNED TO CANDLEFORD narrowed rapidly as it followed the double line of power cables out across the Fenland. Clumps of weeds and grasses grew along the centre and its surface was fractured with potholes of neglect. Hollis slowed the car, aware of the deep drainage ditches on either side of the road that were choked and overgrown with reeds, brambles and banks of nettles. The wind was blustery as it sent low rain clouds scudding across the desolate, flat, featureless countryside. Everywhere he looked there was a glint of weak sunlight and shadow on stretches of water partially hidden by tall reeds and tangled undergrowth. Occasionally he caught a glimpse of vast ploughed fields between the dykes as he crossed small, hump-backed bridges. The black earth seemed to glisten in frozen waves that vanished towards the low horizon. The further he drove the less he liked it but he knew he could not turn back. He could sense the three, ghostly figures and the car was full of that smell of stagnant decay despite having all the windows open. He couldn't see them, although he frequently risked glancing behind him and was always looking for them in the rear-view mirror. But they were there, he knew they were there. The tension in the car was becoming electric the closer they got to Candleford.

For a while he had been able to see the church tower and the red pantiled roofs of the villages in the distance, the only splash of colour in that flat, dreary landscape of black, liquid earth and water. But there was no warmth or welcome coming from it. He found it hard to keep his attention focused on the driving, there was something so familiar about the tall, swaying reeds as they bent in the wind, the cry of the invisible water rail and the spreading ripples in the dark, peaty water channels. He cursed. It stirred up memories of those recent nightmares that had etched themselves into his consciousness. He felt his eyes drawn into the maze of drainage channels and meres that he knew must lay beyond the roadside undergrowth. He found himself searching for that special, secret place where the rotting, submerged skeleton of a boat might lay hidden between the reeds.

Hollis was unaware that he had let the car gradually veer across the road as he stared out over the marshes and the atmosphere in the car suddenly became agitated as the gurgling voices cried out to him. He jumped and slammed on the brakes, causing the car to come skidding to a halt, the front wheels only inches from the offside ditch. He swore under his breath, angry with himself for letting his concentration wander before he drove slowly on. The road seemed to rise gently after a few hundred yards giving him a view across the Fens which stretched for miles. The village was very close now and beyond it there was nothing but dark, inhospitable marshes for as far as he could see. Immediately in front of him to his right he could see what must be the remains of an airfield.

The drainage ditches gave way to a low straggle of blackthorn hedges and elderflower bushes with an old, rusty, chain-linked perimeter fence that still clung in place to pitted concrete stanchions that leaned at drunken angles amongst the wild grasses and weeds. Beyond the fence he could just see a small cluster of derelict, concrete buildings covered in tangled undergrowth, their windows smashed and their roofs collapsed, opening them up to the weather.

The sudden blare of a car horn from the road behind him made Hollis instinctively clamp his fingers tighter on the steering wheel as he searched his rear-view mirror. The road had been so empty he had believed himself to be totally alone, so the other car took him completely by surprise. A small, bright, metallic blue sports car was rapidly catching up with him, its headlamps flashing, its alloy wheels stirring up a gale of leaves and dust from the narrow marsh road behind it.

'Impatient bastard!' he cursed angrily, but he looked ahead for somewhere to pull off the road. He didn't want some lunatic hanging onto his tail lights as he drove into the village which was no more than half a mile ahead.

Twenty yards away he saw what looked like the main entrance to the old airfield and he pulled off the road between the broken gates, stopping to let the car go past. He had the briefest glimpse of a pale, female face, dark sun-glasses and long, blonde hair streaming out in the car's slipstream as it roared throatily past. A hand waved in thanks and a moment later the car decelerated, the engine note changing abruptly as its driver worked it through the gears. The brake lights flickered on and off before the car suddenly turned off the road less than a quarter of a mile away, close to the boundary fence of the airfield, with its tyres squealing in protest.

Hollis followed the sound of its engine as it accelerated along the hidden track and he spotted the red roof of a large house and some farm buildings some distance away, partially screened by a dense copse of oak and elm trees. He hadn't remembered passing any proper roads, only rutted tracks that led off the road he was on and it came as a surprise as he looked at the area around the edge of the village that there were quite a few houses on its outskirts. He had imagined, quite wrongly, from the descriptions that he had heard that the Fens came right up to the back doors of the houses of the village and that beyond it was all mud, reeds and water. He could see now how wrong he was, quite a lot of the Fens were farmed. It did look desolate and bleak but it wasn't half as wild as he had been led to expect.

'I would need to know these narrow roads better than the back of my hand to drive that fast – crazy fool!' he muttered to himself before returning his attention to the overgrown entrance of the American airbase.

He felt an overwhelming urge to walk out onto the airfield, to try and capture what his grandfather must have felt as he'd arrived in that cramped, draughty transport plane over fifty years ago. Getting out of the car he turned up his collar against the raw, autumn wind and thrust his hands deep into his pockets. One glance back at his car was enough to tell him that his three ghostly chaperones weren't coming with him. He could see their dark silhouettes crowded in the back seat, their eyes watching him suspiciously.

'Please yourselves, I can't go very far can I!' he muttered, but there was an edge of relief in his voice. He was glad of a few moments without them breathing down his neck.

The hangars and control tower had long since vanished and all that was left now was a small cluster of single-storey buildings. Hollis walked slowly between them, forcing a path through the undergrowth that had grown up to mask their dereliction. He trampled down the nettles to peer in through the broken windows, wrinkling his nose at the stale, airless smell of neglect from their gloomy interiors. He could hear the soft rustle of vermin as they scuttled through the debris and rubbish that had accumulated over the years. After a while he left the buildings behind him to walk out across an area of rough grass to where he thought the runway must have been. He found the curved taxi way and followed it for about six hundred yards, deep in thought. Weeds and countless severe frosts had lifted and fractured the concrete slabs in many places making walking over it difficult, eventually he reached the main runway and turned onto it, and then stopped in amazement. The concrete was clean and well-kept, there wasn't a stone or a pebble in sight. No weeds had been allowed to grow in it and bulky night-landing lights lined the left hand side. The ground on either side was planted with neat rows of sugar beet for as far as he could see. He hadn't felt anything except a faint echo of sadness when he had looked into the old wartime huts but when he saw the runway so well kept and obviously still in use it had surprised him. He had not expected that at all, it was almost as though nothing had changed since the war.

Standing there staring into the distance he noticed a large, prefabricated, green building close to the end of the runway which he felt must be the hangar. He was wondering who would use such a remote airfield on the edge of the Fens when he heard the sound of a diesel engine behind him and tyres crunching over the rough, broken concrete of the taxi way. He turned to see an old, green, mud-splattered farm truck come to a stop only a few yards away. The driver's door was flung open and a short, thick-set man with a ruddy face jumped out. He was wearing a patched tweed jacket and threadbare cords with a flat cap that had definitely seen better days, but despite his worn-out work clothes there was an air of authority about the man as he strode purposefully towards him, and his anger showed. A large, ferocious looking dog with the face and muscular shoulders of a pit bull terrier leapt out of the cab and ran past its owner towards him, barking and with its fangs bared. Hollis froze as the dog circled, its ears flattened against the side of its head and saliva drooling from its growling mouth. There seemed to be a murderous, wild look in its eyes and the closer it got to him the more obvious it became.

'You're trespassing! You're on private property! The sign on the gate says "Private – Keep Out!" Can't you read?'

The man was shouting angrily, his fists clenched to his sides and the broken veins in his cheeks were darkening as he came closer.

'I-I'm sorry, I must have missed the sign when I pulled over to let a car go past. I-I didn't mean to trespass. This is Candleford Airfield isn't it?' Hollis was breathless as he apologized, trying to keep the fear of the dog from his voice.

'Yes, yes, this used to be Candleford Airfield but it's private property now, and you are trespassing. I'll set the dog on you if you don't get going and get out of here!' the man snapped angrily.

The dog crouched in front of Hollis, its hackles raised as he responded to the anger in its master's voice. It began to edge forwards, snarling, its lips curled back to expose its fangs. Hollis swallowed and began to back away, a cold sweat prickling his forehead and dampening the palms of his hands.

'I . . . I said I was sorry. I honestly didn't see any signs. I only came in here to take a look, to see where my grandfather was stationed during the war. I'm really sorry.'

He struggled to keep his voice calm as he tried to placate the farmer. The dog made to leap up at him and Hollis instinctively raised his arm to shield his face but the animal suddenly howled mid-leap and seemed to convulse. It rolled over and over on the concrete and then scrabbled to its feet before fleeing, its tail between its legs. Hollis could hear it yelping and howling in the undergrowth around the old huts.

'What the blazes? Culloden – come back here! Come back at once, you mangy cur!' The farmer began shouting after the dog, turning back to eye Hollis suspiciously as he retreated back to his car.

'Hey you! Wait a minute! What have you done to my dog?'

Hollis opened the car door and slipped into the driving seat as he suppressed a smile. 'No, I won't wait, thanks all the same, I had better be going. I don't know what's wrong with your dog, sir, and I'm sorry I trespassed. I won't do it again.'

He grinned to himself as he pulled back onto the road. He knew exactly what had happened to the dog back there. In the moment when it had seemed as though it was going to attack he had caught that familiar reek of stagnant decay and he had glimpsed a shadowy, weed-entangled figure, no more substantial than the shadow of a cloud briefly crossing the sun, move between him and the dog. He had seen the hands grab at the creature, its blackened, dripping, skeletal fingers wrenching the poor dog's head back, almost snapping its jaws as it was thrown over and chased into the undergrowth. Hollis' grin widened, those ghostly chaperones obviously had their uses.

He glanced back to see the man crouching down on the runway. He seemed to be examining the globules of muddy water that were scattered on the ground. The dog had crept out of the undergrowth but was refusing to go anywhere near the spot. The farmer seemed to be frowning darkly and mouthing words at him as he drove away but Hollis was far enough away now not to feel threatened.

Beyond the boundary fence and the white gates of Sparrow Hall, where the blue sports car had turned in with such a violent screech of tyres, a straggle of small cottages with neat, well-kept gardens began to appear on either side of the road. Hollis passed a large village sign, beautifully carved and painted to depict a group of sedge cutters from the turn

113

of the century cutting and tying the sedge into bundles using long-handled scythes. The church and village had been carefully painted into the background and the whole scene was encircled with an inscription. He only had a quick glance but he guessed it was in Latin or medieval English. He eased his foot off the accelerator as he entered the village, following the one road around the first of the two ponds past what looked like a disused Methodist chapel and then the post office before he started to look for somewhere to park. Ahead on his left, opposite the other pond, he saw the Louse and Rag Inn with its brightly-coloured gallows sign and rows of coloured light bulbs strung beneath the eaves to illuminate it at night. Hollis pulled into a parking space in front of the pub, cut the engine and looked slowly at the scene that surrounded him.

The village of Candleford was as pretty as a picture postcard, not at all the dismal place he had expected, and as he thumbed quickly through the photographs that his grandfather had taken he saw that it was still much as he had described it. There were more ornamental trees and shrubs around the two ponds but the ducks and moorhens still paddled in and out of the reeds and thick clumps of bulrush stems that grew along their banks. The rows of neatly kept, colour-washed houses that bordered the green hadn't changed very much from the old pictures but the one road and the small tracks had been covered by tarmac and there were a number of parked cars on the grass. There was the occasional addition of garages and modern doors and windows, and, of course, a forest of television aerials, otherwise time seemed to have passed the village by, leaving it almost untouched. Looking carefully at the pictures Hollis could see that only two of the shops had survived, a general grocery store and the post office that he had passed as he drove into the village. It was easy to pick out the building that had once been the Rose and

Crown, the architecture of these old inns was so distinctive. The gallows sign had gone and there were brightly coloured curtains at the windows so he had to assume that it had been converted into a private house.

All the time he had been comparing the houses that bordered the village green with his grandfather's photographs he had become increasingly aware of the church on the far side of the pond, seeing it just out of the corner of his eye. It seemed to squat squarely between its ancient flying buttresses on a small hillock, surrounded by serrated rows of broken, bone-white, eroded tombstones and long-forgotten, overgrown, monumental sculptures that stood penned in behind the low churchyard wall that had long ago been built out of flint and stone. It seemed to huddle in conspiratorial silence. Huge, olivaceous yew trees partly screened the church adding to its mystery, the obvious age of them suggesting to Hollis that it was probably the site of some pagan worship long before the church itself was built. He remembered a passage from the letter that his grandfather had written when he had first arrived in Candleford, '. . . there is an enormous church, more like a cathedral.' Later he'd written: 'Its central presence seems to dominate its surroundings with a brooding intensity.'

But it was the smaller building next to it, the other old inn that dwelt in its shadow, that really caught Hollis' attention. That must have been where his grandfather had been billeted. It was by far the oldest of the three inns in the village. The ridge boards of its vast, pantiled roof had warped and sagged and the brick arches over three of its four upper windows had collapsed, pressing down crookedly on its window frames. The Black Shuck Inn looked forlorn and deserted, a remnant from a lost age, a beggar beside the road. Weeds and nettles grew up against it from cracks in the pavement, the wrought iron

115

handrail that had once led up the outside edge of the front steps was rusty and bent, the cream colour wash was flaking off its brickwork and all the lower windows were shuttered and bolted. A 'For Sale or Rent' sign had been nailed onto the peeling paint work of the front door and had been partially obscured by grime.

Hollis sighed. He hadn't given much thought as to what he intended to do once he had found the village. 'Okay, now what?' he murmured, striking the steering wheel lightly with the heels of his hands as he waited for an answer.

He glanced around to where he half-expected to see the three shadowy figures in the back of his car. He sniffed and frowned, searching the back seat more thoroughly. They were gone, vanished, evaporated into thin air. There wasn't the slightest trace of them, not even a hint of that now familiar, yet still disgusting, odour that clung to them. He slowly opened the car door and climbed out, at a loss about what to do next. He was sure that he couldn't just get back into the car and drive away, no matter how much he may want to they would never allow him to do that, not after the way they forcibly stopped him from turning the car around when he was on the road through Thetford Forest. So why had they abandoned him now?

Hollis sucked in a shallow, indecisive breath and reached into the car for his coat and then pulled it on slowly before buttoning it up against the raw wind. Since he had arrived in England he had become convinced that something terrible must have happened to his grandfather and, perhaps, now it seemed also to his two English friends. Something had happened that was so violent, so unnatural and so evil that their spirits were calling to him by altering the picture and drawing him all the way to this tiny village that sat on the edge of the Fens. But how was he ever going to find out what had really happened? He wasn't a detective, he hadn't got the faintest idea where to begin an investigation. He couldn't just go up to people, stop them in the street, and ask them about something that had happened over fifty years ago. Anyway, apart from a couple of people walking their dogs on the green and two men fishing in the pond, hunched against the weather behind large umbrellas, the place looked deserted. But he couldn't just stand there staring into space all day, he would have to try and do something. Perhaps if he walked around the village, looked at the houses, visited the church, he would ask about the wartime airfield in the shop or post office, an idea might come to him. He would have a drink in the pub, maybe somebody there would remember the American airmen and would talk to him about them.

He locked the car and walked slowly around the village green. The damp, springy turf soon soaked through the soles of his shoes and wet the bottom of his jeans. He nodded to the fishermen and called out a greeting but only received the briefest acknowledgement. The people walking their dogs were too far away for him to accost without it looking as though he were chasing after them and instead he studied the neat rows of cottages that surrounded the green, whose front doors and windows opened straight out onto the narrow pavement. Curiosity got the better of him and he tried to peer in through the windows, to see past the bric-a-brac of ornaments on the window sills and examine how the people of Candleford lived, what kind of books they read, what choice of furniture they crowded into their tiny front parlours and what kind of pictures they hung from their walls as he walked slowly past. But he quickly averted his eyes, his cheeks flushed with embarrassment as he caught sight of their faces behind the net curtains staring suspiciously back at him. They were watching him. They were studying him.

Hurrying on he came to the handful of shops that had been converted into private houses and this time he looked at the architecture rather than risk being caught prying again. There was nothing special about them except for a few old, hand-painted metal signs from the early nineteen-thirties advertising coal tar soap or chocolate clinging precariously to the colour-washed walls. Spreading rust spots had eaten away at the paint until they almost obliterated the messages they had once told so boldly. Hollis was about to move on to the village store when he noticed that he could see the faint outline of the name of the shop he was walking past through the colour that had been painted over it. Carefully standing so the light helped rather than hindered him he read, 'Chemist, proprietor Mr. D. Reeve.' The name struck a chord, that was the name of one of his grandfather's friends – Douglas Reeve – he must have been the chemist who had got him the film for his camera.

Hollis saw the curtains that partially covered the large picture window move and he realized that he was being watched again. He hurried on, a little unnerved by being the object of so much silent attention.

Entering the village store, he found it was very much like the one he had stopped at in Thetford Forest only much smaller and darker. Everything in it seemed to be crowded together, competing for space.

'Yes, young man, can I help you?'

The storekeeper's voice made Hollis look round to the counter which was set well to one side of the doorway. Four or five people were standing there with baskets of groceries, staring at him with unashamed curiosity.

'Oh yes, sure you can, do you do sandwiches or rolls or something?'

The storekeeper frowned and shook his head as he pointed

to the section of shelving filled with bread, cakes and biscuits. 'No, I'm sorry, we don't do anything like that, but you could buy some ham or cheese and make your own. Mind you, if you are still in the village in an hour or so you could go across to the pub. The Louse and Rag does excellent bar snacks.'

Hollis thanked him and turned towards the door. He wasn't really very hungry but he hesitated, his hand upon the latch. The question he wanted so much to ask was on the tip of his tongue.

'You're American, aren't you?' one of the women in the queue suddenly asked, staring at him as she clutched her basket of shopping defensively to her chest.

'Yes, that's right,' he answered quickly, smiling and snatching at the unexpected opening. 'My grandfather was stationed here during the war and he wrote home what a beautiful village it was here and said how he had made friends with a couple of local people so I thought while I was on holiday I would come over and see it for myself, take a few pictures for the family album. I'm intending to look up Dennis Skinner and Douglas Reeve to see if they're still alive, see if they remember him.'

'Americans! I thought we'd had enough of them sticking their noses in where they weren't wanted during the war. We don't want them back! Those times are gone and best forgotten!'

An old man leaning heavily on a walking stick and wearing a greasy, threadbare raincoat and flat cap was talking in a thick Norfolk accent that Hollis couldn't quite decipher, and he was about to ask him to repeat what he had said when a plump, dark-haired woman turned sharply on him.

'Now there's no need to be so rude to strangers, Walter, the young man's probably come a long way to be here.'

She turned back to smile at Hollis. 'I'm sure he didn't

119

mean no harm, dear, running on like that. But I'm afraid there are a lot of folks who live around here who don't take too kindly to strangers. They're not used to them, see, living out here on the edge of the Fens. It's very isolated you know, especially in winter. You're looking for the Skinners you said? Well they farm out by the old airfield, you must have passed the entrance to Sparrow Hall on your way into the village. But I don't think any of the Reeves still live in the village, not after young Richard's accident . . .' She hesitated and glanced nervously at the shopkeeper.

'My grandfather was billeted at the Black Shuck Inn –' Hollis began, trying to fill the awkward silence as the store-keeper glared at the plump woman.

'That pub's been closed down for years,' he interrupted. 'You won't find anybody who'll remember your grandfather, or any of the others who were stationed here for that matter. It was too long ago, they've all been forgotten.'

There was an air of finality and dismissal in his voice as he returned his attention to serving the line of customers waiting at his counter. Hollis stood there for a moment, baffled by the sudden coldness, the quick, furtive glances from the customers. That blacksmith was right, they really didn't like strangers in Candleford.

'Thanks anyway, you've been very helpful.' He tried to smile as he left the shop.

It was beginning to rain and he turned up his collar and hunched his shoulders while he hurried across the green towards the post office. He had got the distinct impression that the storekeeper had something he wanted to hide, or certainly something about the American airmen he didn't want to talk about, and it couldn't have been specifically about his grandfather or his sudden disappearance, he hadn't even wanted to know his name. And it was very strange the way everybody in the shop had clammed up. He had sensed the atmosphere becoming tense when that woman had mentioned Richard Reeve's accident, but why? He hadn't asked about him, he didn't even have a clue who he was except that he must have been a relative of Douglas Reeve, who he was going to look up. Hollis paused outside the post office and glanced back at the huddle of villagers leaving the general store. Surely everyone couldn't have something to hide, that was crazy! At least he had got one thing sorted out in the store, Dennis Skinner couldn't have been murdered, and he couldn't have disappeared with his grandfather. The woman had said that he farmed the land around the old airfield. He remembered seeing the entrance to Sparrow Hall and he made up his mind to call in there on his way back. Dennis Skinner could probably clear the whole mystery up in a few minutes. But first he had to finish exploring the village and he intended to have a drink and a bite to eat in the Louse and Rag. There had to be somebody who remembered the war years and who had a few tales they wouldn't mind telling.

6

THE WOMAN SERVING BEHIND THE COUNTER of the post office was guarded and cautious in her answers as she kept reminding him that she had only been a child at the time and her most vivid memories of the war years were the sweet rationing and the planes thundering over the village in formation, waking everybody up at all hours. He thanked her and pulled the door of the shop shut behind him before walking across towards the church with very little to add to what he already knew from his grandfather's letters and the two picture postcards of the village he had bought, supposedly to post home.

Hollis sensed a change in the atmosphere as he went through the arched gates into the churchyard and walked between the enormous, dripping yew trees that guarded the entrance and lined the gravel drive to the porch. The sound of the rain seemed softer and streaks of water drifted across the rows of leaning headstones, glistening on the top of the broken, monumental sculptures that lay scattered and half-hidden in the undergrowth. Hollis felt himself drawn off the path by curiosity as he tried to read the carved names that time and weather had almost obliterated in the crumbling stone. There were Chubbs and Pigges, a family of Blythes, Stebbings, Sillus and others that stretched as far as he could see beneath the ancient yew trees.

The rain was getting heavier and Hollis retreated into the church through a tiny arched chancel door that stood ajar.

The click of the iron latch sounded louder than a pistol shot in the oppressive silence of the austere, white-washed interior as he pushed it shut behind him. Immediately to his right the high altar was a blaze of golden colour, gold leaf overlaid upon an intricate wood carving of the annunciation made out of lime wood and oak. Hollis paused, admiring the beauty and workmanship of the altar, before turning and walking slowly down the aisle between the rows of massive, ornately carved, dark oak pews that had been there since the fifteenth century. He ran his fingers over the glass-smooth, polished figureheads that surmounted the end panels and marvelled at the detail. The walls of the church must have been almost a yard thick and were rough rendered and white-washed without any form of decoration except for a few memorial brass plaques and two painted shields so aged that the blue dye that had been used had turned black. Below the brass plaques, set on its own, he saw a much more recent memorial to the men of the Eighth Airforce. Searching through the names he found his grandfather's mentioned as one of the men who didn't make it home. He moved on and stopped near the bell tower where an old Victorian bier, partly hidden by a screen, caught his eye. Its perambulator wheels and long, wooden handle with its decorative scrollwork looked so out of place amongst all that simple medieval architecture that it surprised him. He glanced up to the wooden, vaulted roof supported by the stout columns of stone with its host of grinning gargoyles on every capital and listened to the rain drumming on the slates and gurgling in the gutter spouts. There was a sense of ageless peace, of sanctuary, in the soft, gloomy light and shadow and he remembered that letter from his grandfather in which he had described it in the candlelight on Christmas Eve. He could imagine the rich, dark colours of the bunches of holly and mistletoe and the frost sparkling on the stained glass windows above the altar. A slight sound broke through his dreams, no more than a whisper in the brooding silence, but it seemed so out of place that it made the hairs on the nape of his neck prickle as he strained his ears to try and catch it again.

Instinctively he sniffed and caught the faintest odour of the marshes. He spun round – sitting in the darkest corner of the church on a broken, neglected pew, he thought he caught a glimpse of three weed-entangled figures. He knuckled his fist and took a step towards them, angry that they had violated the sense of peace, the feeling of sanctuary that the old church had given him. But they vanished before he could confront them, melting so quickly into the shadows that he bent to feel the dry, dusty surface of the broken pew for the tell-tale drops of dirty, slimy water they seemed to leave wherever they appeared. But there was no trace. He began to doubt that they had manifested themselves in the church at all, his imagination must have conjured them up because he thought he had heard something. They were in his mind all the time dwelling in his subconscious, increasingly playing tricks with his grasp on reality.

Hollis let out a pent-up breath and looked carefully around where he stood just to make sure that he was really alone. Tentatively he sniffed again, hunting for that reek of decay, double-checking his senses, but all he could smell was the faint, timeless, sweet scent of incense and dust mingled with the rich odour of beeswax that had been polished into the pews for centuries, darkening the oak and giving it that glassy, hard surface. The only sound that invaded the silence was the muffled, monotonous drumming of the rain upon the roof. He relaxed and listened for a while, letting his mind wander again, imagining the sounds that must have filled the church for hundreds of years, the weddings, the funerals, midnight masses and harvest festivals. He could almost hear the echo of the hymns and the thunder of the organ in the candlelight of Christmas Eve.

He blinked and glanced at his watch. The time had raced by while he had been looking around, daydreaming, and it was getting late. He hadn't meant to stay so long, the last thing he wanted was to spend the night in Candleford. One quick drink and a sandwich in the pub and then he would head back towards Swaffham and find somewhere to stay in Thetford Forest. He would rather not drive along that marsh road in the dark. He would finish his journey back to Gatwick the next day, or perhaps the day after that. He had kept his promise to that grotesque, decomposing figure that he believed must be his grandfather. He had come to the village and asked around, he couldn't force the people to talk to him, could he? He would call in at Sparrow Hall on his way out of the village and ask Dennis Skinner what everybody was so frightened of. He would have one last go at finding out what had happened to his grandfather and that would be the end of it.

He retraced his footsteps along the aisle, lightly touching the carved figureheads on the end of the pews on the right hand side until he reached the choir stalls and the chancel door. Something made him stop and look back into the deepening gloom of the church and his hand tightened on the latch. His skin felt cold as he caught that sound again, the one he had heard earlier, only this time it sounded much clearer. He realized that it had been there all the time, faint, in the background, but imagining that he could see those ghosts had distracted him. Now as he listened it became a distinct beat, a pulse, he could feel it in the floor beneath his feet and as a slight vibration in the iron latch he was holding. It was most definitely not the sound of the rain or anything to do with the ghostly figures that were haunting him. It was more vital, more real, almost as though the ancient building itself were alive. It was as though he was feeling its heartbeat.

The sound receded and he was left in utter silence. It was so quiet it unnerved him and sent icy shivers down his spine. He could hear his own blood pounding in his ears and he could sense the building listening to it. Wrenching open the door he ran out into the pouring rain, only stopping to look back when he reached the gateway in the low flint wall.

'You are going crazy! If you're not careful you'll get yourself locked up,' he muttered to himself crossly, brushing away the raindrops that were trickling down his forehead.

The coloured lights on the front of the Louse and Rag had been switched on. He would welcome a pint of beer and a sandwich so that he could be on his way out of Candleford, and he was about to hurry across the green towards the pub when he paused and felt himself drawn, no – compelled – to walk in the opposite direction. He splashed through the puddles that had formed on the uneven pavement and found himself on the front steps of the deserted, shuttered inn where his grandfather had been billeted. He stood on tiptoe and tried to peer in through the dirty glass and the cracks between the shutters, but it was too dark inside to see more than the vague outline of broken chairs and upturned tables that littered the floor. He went through the side gate and the weedy, overgrown back yard to find himself looking in the tumbledown cart sheds and outhouses that were strewn with broken beer crates and old, rotten barrels with missing staves. There were cracked, dirty ale jugs and rusty, bottomless coal scuttles with countless other implements and pieces of furniture all half-buried beneath years of neglect. A rat squealed and ran between his feet from the opening of an old earth closet that had long ago lost its door and was now choked and overgrown with nettles.

Hollis shuddered as he listened to it burrowing beneath the rubbish in another shed.

He hated rats and quickly stepped backwards to get away from the outhouses and move closer to the main building but in doing so he almost tripped over the sharp, unseen lower edge of the sloping trap doors that concealed the barrel roll down into the cellars. The sound of the rainwater spilling out of the broken guttering above his head and the sudden cascade of icy water down the back of his neck made him jump forwards and gasp in shock. He shivered, shaking his head and wiping the back of his neck with his hand as he looked up to the broken gutters. One glance was enough to show him that the back of the old inn was in a much worse state of dereliction than the front which faced onto the street. Here there had been no pretence at keeping up appearances. The brickwork was spalled and bulged dangerously in places and was streaked with dark, glistening, mossy stains where the water leaked from the broken gutters and, missing the downpipes, ran down the bricks, washing away the white lime mortar. Almost all the paint had flaked off the rotting window frames and many of the upper windows, including the ones in the three dormers set high in the sagging roof, were missing panes of glass and were boarded up with strips of wood and hardboard, nailed roughly across them.

The rain was getting heavier and it was beginning to soak through his coat. Hollis tightened his collar and took a last, cursory look through the rear shuttered windows on the ground floor into the gloomy interior of the inn. He couldn't see much more than he had through those cracks between the shutters on the front, except he noticed masses of dead flies and curled, blackened wasps. Their carcasses littered the window-sills and were caught suspended in the thick shroud of cobwebs that nature and time had drawn across the dirty window panes. It didn't look as though anybody had been in there for years. He tried the handle on the back door, turning it and giving it a rattle, but it was locked, as he had expected. With a slight sense of regret he turned away and walked out of the side gate. He would have liked to have taken a look inside and tried to find the room his grandfather had slept in and looked out of his window across the marshes – it had to be one of the dormer windows, but they were boarded up anyway so what the hell.

He crossed the green, hunched against the weather, and skirted the pond with its tall reed stems bent beneath the persistent downpour. The gunmetal grey surface of the water was now deserted by the ducks and moorhens and the deepening gloom of the pond was mottled and broken by the rain. He hurried past his car, half-expecting to catch a glimpse of the three ghostly figures through the pattern of raindrops on the windscreen but the car was empty. He glanced up at the lighted windows of the Louse and Rag as he climbed the three, worn, stone steps to its entrance. Two, maybe three, faces were pressed against the window panes watching him, but they vanished from sight as he pushed open the heavy wooden door with its frosted panes of engraved and bevelled glass.

Stepping in over the threshold and shaking the water from his hair he let the door swing shut with a click behind him and smiled to himself. He inhaled the smoky, slightly beery, atmosphere and let his eyes travel around the cluttered, dimly-lit, low-beamed room with its yellowing ceiling and cosy, secretive alcoves furnished with high-backed, old-fashioned leather seats and copper-topped tables. There was a log fire in the grate that reflected warmly in the long-handled brass warming pans, kettles and pot-bellied saucepans that filled the hearth. Bundles of dried, smoke-blackened hops and a string of old, brittle corn dollies hung from the chimney beam while

131

a clutter of rusting gin traps, turfing irons, wooden spades and beckets lined the walls between a collection of mezzotints and paintings. There were about a dozen drinkers standing at the bar or sitting talking close to the fire, their wet coats draped across the backs of their chairs. Two of them were smoking, engrossed in a game of cribbage at one of the tables near the door. Hollis noticed a large clock that was ten minutes fast ticking away noisily on the wall behind the bar partly hidden by a row of spirit bottles and optics. It was exactly as he imagined an English pub would be only much more earthy, more real than the ones he had already visited.

One of the cribbage players looked up at him as he unbuttoned his wet coat and walked towards the bar. He scowled and nudged his partner, 'That's him! That's the stranger I was telling you about.'

He muttered loudly enough to stop the hum of conversation in the room. Hollis smiled uncertainly as everybody seemed to turn towards him and stare, following him with their eyes. In the sudden silence he could hear the flames crackling and spitting in the grate and the clock behind the bar seemed to tick the seconds off noisily. He felt as though he could have cut the unwelcoming atmosphere with a knife. He was beginning to regret stepping in over the threshold and wished he had got straight into the car and driven away instead but he knew he would feel foolish later if he turned on his heel and walked out. He put their stony, staring silence down to them not being used to seeing strangers.

'Your English rain is certainly very wet!' He smiled as he reached the bar, trying to strike up conversation with the barman who, like the others, was staring at him as he automatically wiped and re-wiped the same glass.

'My grandfather was stationed here during the war and he wrote home and told us that it rained a lot – he sure was right.

Can I have a pint of your draught beer, the dark one. Oh, and can I see the menu? The guy in the store across the green said you do great bar snacks. I'm over here on holiday and I thought I would take a look at the village, it's real pretty.'

Hollis paused and delved into his pocket for some money. The barman frowned slightly, shaking his head as he called out something in the thick, Norfolk dialect that Hollis had difficulty understanding. He removed the tea towel from the glass so slowly that, for a moment, Hollis thought he wasn't going to serve him at all.

'Adnams!' he muttered, more as a statement of what he was serving than a question.

Putting the glass beneath the tap he lazily pulled at the pump, staring past Hollis, his eyes focusing on something behind his head as though Hollis himself didn't really exist. The door to the kitchen swung open, wafting the smell of cooking into the bar as a large, pasty-faced man with watery eyes and straggly grey hair appeared. The lower part of his face seemed to have expanded into a sagging, surly mouth and a slack, double chin. Rivulets of sweat matted his hair and trickled down his cheeks to vanish inside the frayed collar of his shirt. He was wearing greasy, shapeless trousers and broken-down carpet slippers beneath a filthy kitchen apron that hadn't seen soap powder for years. The apron ties that had been knotted across his enormous stomach strained and threatened to snap with each ponderous step he took towards Hollis.

'The kitchen's shut. We aren't serving any food tonight.'

The man spoke brusquely, folding his arms and resting them on the swell of his stomach with an air of finality as he stared at Hollis, daring him to contradict him or try to open another line of conversation. Hollis drew breath as if to speak, glancing along the bar to where he had noticed a pile of plates with the remnants of recently eaten food that were still waiting to be taken back to the kitchen, but he thought better of it. Mumbling his thanks for the beer he paid for it and retreated to an empty table by the window. The people of Candleford weren't just unfriendly they were downright rude. He took a sip from the glass and quickly put it down, even the beer had a bitter, peaty taste.

For a moment he looked out across the village. Dusk was falling early beneath the heavy storm clouds, blurring and merging everything into shadow. The church and the empty inn across the way stood out, black and silent silhouettes against the rain-distorted lights of the cottages scattered around the green. The silence surrounding him in the bar was so unnatural he could feel everybody's eyes boring into him. There was something far deeper than just a dislike of strangers in Candleford, something much more sinister. They were trying to hide something, he had sensed it earlier in the village store and the post office, but now that darkness was gathering the feeling was getting stronger and he didn't have any inclination to hang around to find out why.

Swallowing another mouthful of the sour beer he pushed the glass away and got up. 'Thanks,' he smiled, glancing quickly around the silent, hostile figures in the bar.

Nobody seemed to have moved an inch since he had walked in the door. It was almost as though they were all holding their breath, waiting, willing him to go. He left the drink unfinished and hurried out without bothering to button up his coat. It didn't matter anyway, he would be in his car and out of there for ever in five minutes.

Slamming the car door he stabbed the key into the ignition and turned it. Nothing. The starter motor didn't even whine or make any attempt to turn over. He cursed under his breath and tried again. Beads of sweat were forming on his forehead. He glanced up into the rear-view mirror, his guts contracting with panic. He had caught that all too familiar odour of stagnant decay and in the lights from the Louse and Rag he could see those three, shadowy silhouettes in the back of his car.

'Damn you, damn, damn, damn!' he shouted at the three silent figures as he angrily struck the steering wheel and dashboard with his fists.

He twisted the ignition key so savagely that he almost bent it and then sank his head into his hands. There were tears in his eyes, tears of helpless rage, tears of fear. They weren't going to let him escape, he was trapped. Trapped in this Godforsaken village. The only way out of there was to walk along that marsh road in the pitch dark – and he certainly didn't fancy doing that, he wouldn't even want to do it if he had a torch, and he didn't. He sat there for a moment listening to the rain drumming on the roof of the car and he was filled with a sense of panic.

'Why me? I kept my promise, I came to this miserable village, didn't I? Why do you want to keep me here?' he muttered angrily.

'What can I possibly do now, nobody will even talk to me about the war and I don't know what else to talk about. I don't even know where to begin!'

He let his head fall forwards against the rim of the steering wheel in despair. He felt so helpless, so alone and very afraid.

'You must find us. We will not let you escape. We will not allow you to give up now. You must stop the Lanterns . . . must find us . . . must find us . . .'

The car rocked gently and was suddenly filled with the urgent gurgling voice of the tall, decomposing figure. The reek of the marshes grew stronger and he felt the sharp bony touch of skeletal fingers prodding his back, touching his arms through his wet coat. He shuddered in disgust and sat up, twisting round, his face contorted with anger as he

135

confronted the three apparitions who were crowding forwards on the back seat.

'Get back! Get away from me! Don't ever – ever touch me again!' he hissed, inhaling a short, ragged breath as he struggled to control the rage and frustration that he could feel building up inside him. 'You may have some supernatural power to stop me driving this car, even to keep me here against my will tonight, but that's it. I'm walking out of here first thing in the morning and I'm never coming back! You can all rot in hell for the rest of eternity for all I care, do you hear? I've had enough.'

The three ghosts raised their hands as their faces grew taut with dismay and with a gurgling sigh they shrank away, folding in upon themselves as they melted into the fabric of the back seats. Hollis was all alone with the sound of the rain beating on the roof of the car, even the smell of decay had vanished. He sobbed once and swallowed as his anger subsided. He had felt an overwhelming sense of loss, an empty, hollow despair that seemed to fill the three figures while he had shouted and cursed at them, refusing to help. Remorse began to rub against the shoulders of his resolve. How would he feel if it had been him that had mysteriously vanished? How would he feel if his ghost had been condemned to wandering restlessly through this unsociable landscape of mud, water and sky until somebody, somehow solved the mystery and put his remains to rest?

'All right, all right, damn it!' he muttered, reaching out his hand in a gesture of reconciliation towards the empty back seats before letting it drop down beside him. 'I'll go back into that pub again, I'll try to get some information. There isn't anywhere else I can think of asking except down at Sparrow Hall, and I'm not going down there in the dark – but don't blame me if I don't get any proper answers. Here is how it goes from now on – you don't touch me any more and I will try my best. Tomorrow, come what may, I'm out of here. Have we got a deal?'

The shadows in the back of the car stirred and one by one the three figures began to reappear. They didn't say anything or attempt to come any closer but their blind, staring silence quietly convinced him. He flung open the door of the car, jumped out and slammed it shut without bothering to lock it. Anybody who wanted to steal it was welcome, perhaps they would also be lucky enough to take the three apparitions with them. Climbing the steps to the entrance of the Louse and Rag he took a deep breath before pushing open the door. The noisy conversation in the bar died abruptly and the stony, blank stares of earlier were replaced with a brief look of surprise that rapidly darkened into anger. He walked quickly to the bar and spoke to the landlord in the dirty apron.

'My car won't start. The battery seems to have gone dead, it's probably all this rain. Could I rent a room for the night and perhaps telephone a local garage to come out in the morning to get the thing started? Would you have their number?'

The landlord scowled and scratched at an invisible itch beneath his filthy apron before shaking his head. 'We don't rent rooms here. Nobody rents rooms in Candleford. There isn't a local garage, nearest one's Bennets in Crimpsmarsh, that's fifteen miles away.'

'Oh, then I'm stranded. Are you sure there isn't anyone in the village who would rent me a room for the night? Perhaps one of the cottages round the green does bed and breakfast?'

He tried to smile to disguise his nervousness as he glanced anxiously at the people in the bar. They seemed to be edging forwards, closing in around him. A young, thickset youth with his hair shaved close to his scalp who had been playing bar billiards at the far end of the room with two of his friends thrust his way through the other drinkers to confront him.

137

He raised a work-hardened hand and stabbed a dirty fingernail into Hollis' chest.

'He told you, didn't he? Nobody will put you up, we don't like strangers round here. Now get out or do we have to throw you out?'

Hollis swallowed and retreated a step. The threat was real. The thug had a murderous look in his small, mean eyes and the other two were holding their billiard cues in a menacing manner.

'Stop it, Billy, I've already told him he can't stay the night here and there's nowhere else nearby. There's no need to get violent, it won't do any good.'

The landlord's voice from behind the bar made Billy hesitate and before he could do or say anything else the old man who had spoken against Hollis in the shop earlier called out from beside the fireplace. 'I told my Doris last night that a stranger would be coming into the village. When I heard that howling in the Fens I said to her "mark my words, no good will come of it. There'll be a death before morning." Now you see if I'm not right.'

Somebody close to the old man told him to shut up and the lingering silence seemed to fill the room as the locals looked at each other with knowing, secretive glances while they averted their eyes from Hollis.

'If you know what's good for you you'll get out now while you still can.'

The landlord turned away from him and seemed to put him out of his mind for good. Hollis retreated another couple of steps with Billy and his two friends keeping pace with him. He heard the main door open behind him and he could feel the cold, wet, night air as it blew onto his neck. He spun round, expecting to find more of Billy's friends behind him but instead he froze, rooted to the spot. There was a young woman standing in the doorway. It was the same woman who was with him in the photograph he had found with his grandfather's things.

138

7

EMILY SKINNER HAD COME HOME from the University of East Anglia so that she could have a couple of days of peace and quiet to concentrate on finishing her thesis and type it up in the farm office. She was already over two months late in submitting it and her tutor had given her a final warning. She'd only hurried into the village under protest to get some crisps and cigarettes from the pub for her father because he was tied up with some lengthy telephone calls while he organized the beaters for Saturday's shoot. She had not failed to notice the hire car parked outside the pub, they got so few visitors in Candleford even in the holiday season. Pausing to take a good look at it, she wondered if it was the same one that had pulled over to let her past earlier in the day, it certainly seemed to be the same colour. She had caught a momentary glimpse of its driver, a serious looking young man, but she had been in too much of a hurry for a better look. For some strange reason, though, the image of him had stayed with her all day.

Emily sensed the tense, aggressive atmosphere the moment she stepped in over the threshold of the Louse and Rag and almost collided with the stranger. He was the same man who had pulled into the gates of the disused airfield to let her past only now his face was taut with startled surprise and there seemed to be fear and panic in his eyes. Behind him she saw Billy and two of his brain-dead hangers-on holding billiard cues converging on him. She knew all three of them. Billy and one of the others worked on a neighbouring farm and the third

141

one did occasional labouring jobs around the village. Growing up at Sparrow Hall meant that she knew almost everyone who lived in the village by name, but she didn't know any of them very well because she had spent most of her childhood away at school, and now she was at university. They had always treated her with the same guarded respect they showed to her parents and kept her at a polite distance.

The crowd at the bar seemed to have closed in behind Billy and his two accomplices in support but everyone stopped as she entered the room and they seemed to shuffle uncomfortably as they glanced furtively from one to another. It was almost as though she had interrupted something. Billy's anger seemed inflamed, he didn't care, and he merely glanced at her, only briefly intimidated by her presence.

'What the fucking hell do you want – get out! You can get out if you don't want some of what he's going to get!' he snarled at her, knuckling his fists in anger.

Before he could raise a hand or take another step something really strange happened, something that sent an icy shiver through Emily and made the angry crowd cower away. An overpowering stench of stagnant water filled the bar and sparks blazed and crackled in the grate, almost as though water had been splashed over the burning logs. The air in the room became thick and it was difficult to breathe, the lights dimmed and, for an instant, three ghostly, almost transparent figures appeared. One of them seemed to hesitate and turn towards Emily, his blind, imploring look held her frozen as it reached out with trembling fingers. The spell was broken by Billy's scream. The shadowy figures blurred and moved together to send him flying backwards against the bar before he crashed to the floor in a heap. The billiard cues were snatched from the hands of the other two youths and snapped in half before being hurled across the room. It all happened so quickly that

142

it left the crowd staring down at Billy lying in a puddle of dirty water in a stunned silence.

Emily was completely unable to comprehend what she had just witnessed, she seemed to be in shock. Her surroundings had slipped out of focus and she was unaware of the young stranger trying to get her attention. Her mind was full of the image of that ghostly figure that had turned towards her for that second, the shape of him, the rotting clothes, the blackened, decomposing face that had stared, so briefly, in her direction. It had struck a hidden chord in her memory, there was almost something familiar about it. It was impossible but it seemed to be a face from a photograph she had once seen.

Hollis was the first to break the startled silence in the bar. Seeing Emily come in had thrown him into confusion, he had never considered actually meeting either of the other two people from the photograph. The shock of seeing her had thrown the threat from the villagers into insignificance, he just wanted to reach out, touch her, see if she was real. He wanted to make sure he had not invented her but more than that there was something else, something beyond all knowing that warned him not to let her leave without telling her about what had drawn him all the way from America to this remote place on the edge of the Fens. Something inside him knew that he had to talk to her because she was as much a part of this nightmare as he was.

'I-I-I'm really sorry we had to meet like this. I hope the ghosts . . .' He hesitated. What could he possibly say about them that wouldn't frighten her off?

'My name's Hollis, Hollis Calvin.'

He smiled, taking a step towards her and extending his hand in welcome. Emily blinked and reciprocated with the briefest of touches, seeming barely aware of the handshake as she looked past him to Billy who was sprawled out on the floor against the bar. The group of frightened villagers had moved well back and they were all looking at the two broken billiard cues and the small puddles of dirty water all around them. She wasn't sure what she had walked into or even what had happened, it was all so quick.

'My name's Emily, Emily Skinner,' she replied defensively, quickly withdrawing her hand and moving away from him. What was wrong with this man? For some reason he was under the impression that he knew her and he was trying to apologize for meeting her like this – but she had never met him before in her life. She would have remembered, he was fairly good-looking and there was something about his sea-grey eyes, a depth and warmth, a direct way of looking at you that she wouldn't have forgotten in a hurry.

'I'm sorry, you must have made a mistake. I think you have confused me with someone else.'

She smiled as she turned towards the door. Perhaps if she hadn't seen those strange, ghostly figures and felt that hostile atmosphere it might have been nice to get to know him.

'No please, wait, Emily!' he called out after her. 'You must be related to Dennis Skinner – my grandfather knew him during the war. I was going to call in at Sparrow Hall to talk to Dennis only my car won't start, the battery or something. I hoped Dennis might be able to throw some light onto my grandfather's disappearance, it happened while he was stationed here.'

Emily stopped with her hand on the latch. There was a tenuous connection between them then, but her grandfather had died years before she was born, when her own father was only a boy. Surely if their grandfathers had been friends during the war then his family would know that he had died. How could he be under the impression that he was still alive after all this time? She turned back in curiosity as sharp intakes

144

of breaths and hurried whispers rippled through the villagers at the bar. The landlord muttered something to Billy as he reached down to haul him up onto his feet and sent him hurrying through the bar and out of the kitchen door into the night, followed by his two friends. One by one most of the remaining villagers took their coats from the chairs, avoiding going anywhere near Hollis as they shuffled out leaving old Walter sitting on his own by the fire.

Hollis watched as the bar emptied and laughed softly as he turned to Emily. 'This isn't the friendliest of places, is it? Let me get you a drink, please, it's the least I can do – and then I'll try and explain why I'm here.'

'No, I can't stop . . .' she began, shaking her head, but she was intrigued. Then she looked directly at him and changed her mind. 'Oh, yes, all right then, I'll have a gin and tonic, but I haven't got long, my father's expecting me back.'

She moved across to the table by the window, sitting and watching him as he collected the drinks. The landlord was reluctant, almost hostile, and old Walter had begun muttering to himself about having strangers in the village.

'No wonder we don't get many tourists if the village people behave like this towards them,' she thought as Hollis returned and she realized what he had obviously had to put up with on his brief visit.

Hollis put the glass down and slid into the seat opposite her. 'You're not going to believe this but take a look.'

He delved into his jacket pocket and took out his grandfather's bundle of letters and photographs, separating the special picture which he now kept on its own in an envelope. He took another look at it then passed it across the table, holding his breath as he watched her reaction carefully. Emily looked at the faded, yellowing picture and her eyes widened in surprise as she saw her own face smiling back at her. She moved slightly to catch the light from the wall lamp behind her head and examined it more closely and then her eyes contracted into a frown of disbelief. Her lips trembled slightly.

'But this isn't possible!' she murmured. A cold shiver ran up her spine and she put it down as if it had burned her hand. What was going on? Hollis, the young man sitting opposite her was in the centre of the picture, Richard Reeve was standing on one side of him and she was on the other. They were all linking arms and looking as though they were the best of friends, a group of unfamiliar figures who were faded and slightly out of focus. The one behind her could have been her father but she wasn't quite sure, his image seemed to be blurred. They stood in front of an enormous inglenook fireplace that was cluttered with old-fashioned pots and pans, but she didn't recognize the place. She had never met Hollis before this but she was standing there with him in the photograph. The image of Richard was slightly blurred too, but there was no mistaking that dark, serious expression, it was so typical of him. But he was dead. He had drowned just after she went back to college in January. His father had been the village chemist until only a few years ago then he had suddenly packed up and moved away. Richard had only been in the village to visit some old friends when the accident had happened. Her parents had been very reluctant to talk about it and she still wasn't sure of the full details. Nobody seemed to have an explanation for why he had ventured so far out into the marshes on his own, he must have known how dangerous it was . . . and yet here he was, in this picture with her and Hollis. The figure standing behind him looked very like his father, which was odd, and even odder was that she was sure she had never had her picture taken with Richard Reeve. He wasn't a friend, just another village boy who was about her own age. She had known him well enough to bid him the time of day but that was all. Even stranger was she was quite sure she had never set eyes on Hollis before that night. It just wasn't possible to be in that photograph, it had to be some sort of trick, some elaborate hoax. But why? What purpose could it possibly serve?

Her curiosity rapidly changed into guarded mistrust. What did this American want from her? Why had he turned up out of the blue with a photograph that made it look as though they were friends? She touched the picture with the tip of her index finger and scratched her nail across its surface, searching for a flaw, something that would explain how it had been done. It looked old but that was an easy trick to play, any student of photography could produce that effect with the right chemicals. She looked across at Hollis with suspicion and wondered how he had done it. Where had he got hold of a picture of her and Richard? Not just them, there was also the blurred picture of their parents standing behind them and if she looked closer it seemed to her that she could see a picture of her grandfather standing behind her father. How on earth had he made it look as though they had posed together so naturally?

Hollis watched the suspicion and mistrust cloud her eyes and he leaned forwards across the table, lowering his voice to speak. 'I told you that you wouldn't believe it. Imagine how I felt when I discovered that picture when I went through my grandfather's things last week. My father died only recently and I was sorting out his desk when I found that bundle of old letters and photographs that belonged to my grandfather in the war and that picture was amongst them. Look at what is written on the back.'

Emily turned it over slowly and read the line of scratchy, faded handwriting. 'This must be Dennis and Douglas, the two Englishmen who Merris wrote me about before he disappeared.' It was dated 1970.

She looked back to Hollis as he continued, at the same time offering her a bundle of letters to read. 'Merris was my grandfather's name, he had been stationed somewhere in East Anglia during the war, although none of my family had the slightest idea where the village was or what it was called because of the wartime censorship on servicemen's letters. My grandmother addressed her mail to Merris through a central army mailing address in New York.'

Hollis paused and took a sip from his glass as he glanced out through the raindrops pattering softly against the window pane towards the dark, brooding silhouette of the derelict inn across the green before he continued. 'One night in the February of 1943 Merris suddenly disappeared. It wasn't during a mission over enemy territory or in an air raid during leave in London. He just vanished. The Pentagon investigated the disappearance, of course, but there was a war on, people were getting killed all over the place, and then there were those who were deserting, vanishing into the woodwork just to get out of it – which, of course, they had to consider in his case. Anyway, to cut a long story short, all the investigations were inconclusive, they didn't find a trace of him, even the local police drew a blank. Eventually he was officially listed as missing on active duty and his personal effects were sent home. That was the end of it. By the time I had grown up he was just a couple of faded photographs in an album. And it would have stayed that way if that crazy, impossible picture of you and me with that other guy in the foreground hadn't turned up.'

Hollis paused and looked at Emily. 'That other guy, does he live around here? Could I meet him? Perhaps your grandfather, Dennis, could throw some light on what really happened, tell me why Merris disappeared. I am sure my grandmother would have written and asked him years ago if she'd had an address.'

'They're both dead. Richard died last January, there was an accident on the marshes and he drowned. But my grandfather vanished in the war. I'm sure I remember my father saying something about Richard's grandfather too, I think he disappeared with mine. I wouldn't be at all surprised to find out that all three of them disappeared at the same time.'

Emily hesitated, she couldn't make any sense of the picture. Her head was reeling, full of questions, but she didn't know where to begin. She hadn't ever really given a passing thought to her own grandfather's disappearance, it had happened so many years ago, before she was born. He was just somebody in one of the family albums, a distant figure shrouded in mystery. Nobody ever talked about him, but there had to be a connection with the disappearances and this picture. But how and why? She carefully re-read the line of scratchy handwriting on the back and then slowly turned it over to stare at the faces in the photograph.

She looked up to Hollis and with a frown on her face she asked, 'Why didn't your grandmother make more fuss when he disappeared? Why didn't she send a print of this picture to the authorities and insist that they investigate it properly? Why leave it until now? Anyway didn't the clothes look out of place to her when she looked at this picture?'

Hollis blinked, snapping his attention back to her.

A chilling thought now began to tighten in the pit of his stomach. 'We are in that picture because we have to find out what happened. First our parents were in it and now us. If we don't do it then our children will appear once they're born.' As he spoke the words he knew without a doubt that this was true. 'My grandmother didn't see that picture until 1970 because the roll of film lay forgotten in the bottom of a cardboard box beneath the rest of Merris' things. I think my father or his brother found it in the attic and had it developed. From what I learned when I found it this picture was the only one on the film that came out at all, the others were all blurred and over-exposed. It looked as though the light had gotten into the roll. I don't know how my father felt about seeing himself in the picture, my uncle was reluctant to talk about it. He wanted to burn the photograph.'

Hollis paused and smiled but Emily didn't respond. She traced her fingers around her image. It was ridiculous, it was beginning to give her the creeps. If what he was trying to suggest was true then that picture was changing slowly all the time.

'At first I didn't know what to think either, in fact I still don't. Finding that picture has turned my life upside down. I've put everything on hold back home while I try to get to the bottom of it. I have to find out why it happened, what this is all about. I don't have much to go on after fifty years, just that bundle of old letters and photographs. I didn't even know the name of the village or the airfield but I guessed that the village must be on the edge of the Fens from my grandfather's description and his pictures. I knew it had three pubs, two ponds and a church. I knew he was billeted in a pub with a gallows sign that had a huge, ferocious looking black dog on it and now I know, or at least I'm pretty sure, that it's the derelict building across the green. I have also seen my grandfather's name on the memorial plaque in the church so I know this is the village where the picture was taken.'

Hollis rifled through the old snapshots until he found the one that showed the interior of the snug bar and he put it beside the one Emily was holding. 'I would have liked to have got a look inside that place but it's locked up. It doesn't look as though anyone has been in there for years.'

Emily carefully compared the pictures. 'Yes, you're right, it must be the same place, although I've never actually been in there. It was shut down when I was quite small.'

Emily paused and then added, 'But I think there is a way in. Shirley, who runs the post office, holds the key for the agents just in case anybody is ever interested in buying it and wants to have a look round. It saves them coming all the way out from Norwich. I'm sure she would let us have it if we asked.'

'It would be great to be able to get in there for a couple of hours . . .' Hollis began, then he hesitated as he glanced anxiously around where they were sitting. He had just caught the familiar reek of stagnant decay. He almost knocked his arm against the landlord's leg who had quietly moved away from behind the bar while they were engrossed in their conversation and stood absently wiping a greying dishcloth across an adjacent tabletop, cleaning the same spot and making little effort to disguise his attempt to eavesdrop.

Before Hollis could speak or move the three ghostly, almost transparent, figures began to appear and crowd in around the startled landlord. The air darkened and seemed to fold and melt, wrapping itself into a thickening shroud around him. Gurgling, muttering voices assaulted his ears, drips of slimy marsh water and fragments of glistening weed and broken reed stems fell from the swirling figures to scatter across the table top. There was the briefest impression of blackened, skeletal figures prodding, touching, pushing at him, leaving dirty wet smears of mud on the landlord's clothes and all over his apron. He gave a shriek of terror as he stumbled backwards and lost his balance. He scrambled back onto his feet almost as soon as he fell and fled behind the bar to reach down beneath the pumps for a cudgel in case of trouble. He turned to stare back across the almost empty room, his lips slack and trembling, his face chalky white. But his attackers had vanished. They had been and gone in the blink of an eye.

'What was that? What the hell was that?' he gasped, wiping the back of his hand across his mouth.

Old Walter turned away from the fire and looked blankly at him. 'I told you before that no good would come of having strangers in the village. Nobody listened to me, nobody ever listens to me.'

Emily had tensed as she detected the stench, it had triggered a memory. She was sure she had smelled this before, when she had first entered the bar. Seeing the photograph had been such a shock that it had made her forget those three, strange, ghostly figures that she thought she had glimpsed when she first walked in. Now there was no doubt. They seemed to be materializing right in front of her. She could see their soaking, weed-entangled, rotting clothes, their blackened, decomposing faces and their bony hands. She gasped and gripped at Hollis' hand where it rested on the table cradling his glass, knocking it and almost spilling its contents over the scattered letters and photographs that lay there.

'What in God's name were they?' Emily cried in horror. She tried to stand, sending her chair crashing backwards onto the floor behind her as the three apparitions blurred together and evaporated into thin air.

'Well that's the craziest part of all this, I think they're the ghosts of our grandfathers. They are the ones who started this weird nightmare. I think they tampered with the photograph somehow to try and make my father, and then me, come here and find them. I'm sure that's what they want, they want us to find them. But where would we start, they vanished so long ago.'

Emily was still standing. There had been something about one of those shadowy figures that compelled her to reach out to the adjacent table and pick up a fragment of the wet weed that they had left behind. She held the tiny piece of greenery between her fingertips and turned it over to examine it, but it crumbled at her touch, losing its colour and shape as it dissolved into a slimy globule of woody fibre and mud.

'They can't be ghosts. Ghosts don't leave bits of themselves behind, do they?' She held out her muddy fingers towards Hollis as she waited for an explanation.

Hollis shrugged. 'I don't know. I don't know much about ghosts. These three have been hanging around frightening the hell out of me ever since I got to England. At first they only filled my dreams, or rather my nightmares – they kept chasing me through the marshes and the boat I was in was sinking. Then they would rise up out of the water, gripping the boat, shaking it. I felt a terror of drowning flooding through me. After that they started to appear beside my bed, in the car, they even sat at my table during dinner last night. It was such a shock to see them sitting there I spilt my soup everywhere.'

He paused for a moment to find words for his next thought. 'One thing I do know for certain is they're becoming more physical, more real. They seem to have done this ever since I arrived in Candleford. Not that I've really had much choice about where I go, I can't seem to go anywhere else. I tried to turn back in Thetford Forest and they spun my car off the road, then they somehow killed the ignition so I'm trapped in this cursed place at the moment. They keep on repeating the words, "must find . . . must find . . ." in those gurgling voices of theirs and the only thing I can think they might want me to find is them – well their bodies anyway. Oh, and there's something else, they've given me the distinct impression that they are guarding me, like when they prevented those three lads from attacking me when you were coming in through the door, and just now when they stopped the landlord from listening into our conversation. But why? Do you suppose the unfriendliness around here has something to do with their disappearance during the war? It seems odd but I got the distinct impression that everyone around here is trying to hide something.'

Hollis was suddenly interrupted by the landlord's angry voice. 'I want you two out of here. I don't care who your father is, miss, but I won't have my regulars upset with all these strange goings on. It's just not natural. Now get out, get out now, I'm closing up early. Go on, Walter, be off home now and make sure to lock your door tonight, do you hear me?'

The old man rose unsteadily to his feet and, with the aid of his stick, he hobbled towards the door.

'Come on, we had better do as he says. We're obviously not welcome here any more.' Emily suppressed her anger as she gathered up her bag.

Hollis opened the door for her and waited while the old man went through before letting it swing shut. Walter paused on the top step for a moment and stared at Hollis as he gripped his arm. Raindrops were streaking down his cheeks and forehead and trickling into the crevasses and wrinkles that time had weathered into his skin.

'You be careful, young fella, there's a danger loose in the Fens tonight that will hunt you down if you don't look out.'

Hollis heard his stick tapping on the pavement as he hurried away and he felt a sense of mounting panic. What the hell had he meant? What was behind that veiled warning? He turned up his collar against the rain and slowly went down the steps wondering what on earth he was going to do now. He didn't want to spend the night in his car but it didn't look as though he was going to have much choice.

'Where did you say you were staying?' Emily asked, looking up at him from beneath the magazine she had taken from her car to shield her from the downpour as he walked down the front steps of the Louse and Rag inn. She couldn't just drive away and leave him there after what he had told her and what she had seen in that picture. There were just too many unanswered questions, and he had said something about his car not starting. She couldn't leave him stranded on such a foul night.

A faint, eerie, howling broke through the hazy darkness coming from the direction of the Fens. As they listened it grew louder with each cry.

'Did you hear that? What is it?'

Hollis was alarmed, he suddenly felt very exposed and threatened as he stood out there in the open. He wanted to quicken his stride and run to the car. The howling brought back echoes of his recent nightmares as the memories came flooding to the surface of his consciousness. Images of a huge, black dog with iridescent eyes filled his mind. The thought mesmerized and paralysed him, engulfing him with its darkness. He shuddered, raindrops trickled down the back of his neck and the spell was broken. He ran the last few paces, wrenching open the car door.

'It's a dog, isn't it? It's an enormous devil hound. I know about it, I dream about it!' His voice had become ragged with fear.

'Don't be silly. There are lots of old legends about dogs running loose in the Fens but there's no truth in them. There can't be . . .'

Emily's voice trailed away without conviction as she looked

out across the top of Hollis' car through the rain that was bouncing and drumming on its roof and on into the inky darkness of the marshes. Before tonight she would have laughed at such an idea; myths, legends and ghost stories were things best left for fireside stories, something to tell at Halloween, but already too much had happened to disbelieve and she had been severely shaken. The sound of that howling cry had nudged a string of her half-forgotten, childhood memories awake and now, in one frightening instant, it had made her question all those persistent warnings when her parents had told her never to stray far from the house and never to go anywhere on her own. And she had never, but never, been allowed to go anywhere near the edge of the Fens. She remembered how they had always insisted that she was always safe indoors long before it grew dark and now that she thought back there had always been a sensation of fear in the house. Noises in the darkness had terrified her and made her hide her head beneath the blankets. There were things her parents never talked about, never tried to explain away, but she remembered her mother hurrying to her bedroom on wild, winter nights and staying there, a still, silent silhouette at the moonlit window, watching, staring out across the marshes. On those nights there had always been the steady tread of her father's footsteps in the hall and the room beneath her bedroom as he paced through the house, his shotgun in the crook of his arm. It was almost as though he had been waiting. Waiting for something not quite unknown.

The sound of the front doors slamming on the far side of the green and the hurried footsteps crunching in the gravel made her look quickly around. She could almost hear the low, urgent voices calling to one another and sense the dark shapes crossing the wet grass as they headed towards the church. She was about to ask Hollis again where he was staying the night when she caught that same odour that they had smelt in the pub. She sniffed anxiously, turning her head.

'Hollis, it's back. That reek of decay, you can smell it can't you, it's all around us.'

Hollis spun round at the sound of people hurrying across the green as the strong, stagnant smell filled his nostrils and then grabbed Emily's arm and pointed.

'Look! I told you that I thought those ghosts were guarding me. I think they're protecting both of us now.'

Emily swallowed a startled cry and brought her hand up to her open mouth. Hollis was right, she could just make out the three, transparent figures, their clothes glistening wetly and shimmering in the lights from the Louse and Rag. They were slowly encircling the cars, appearing to glide effortlessly over the ground, in and out of the shadows. Suddenly the lights in the pub went out followed by the coloured light bulbs that were strung beneath the eaves and lastly the spot lamp illuminating the gallows sign. The car park where they were standing was plunged into utter darkness and a door at the back of the pub opened and shut before two people hurried through the yard, whispering and muttering as they cut directly across the wet grass, skirting the pond towards the church and the derelict building standing beside it.

Hollis followed the sound of their voices with his eyes and suddenly whispered, 'Look, there's a light on in one of the upper windows of that derelict inn. No, it's gone, but it was there, did you see it?'

Emily looked up at the dark, empty building just in time to see the faint, flickering light of a candle flame or a lamp move across the middle window before it dimmed and disappeared into the interior of the old building.

'There it is again!' Hollis hissed as another light appeared. 'I've had enough of this. I'm going back home to telephone the police. I'm going to tell them that someone has broken into that derelict building, and I want to ask my father some questions. I want to show him that photograph and see what he makes of it. Quickly, come with me, it isn't far.'

Emily slipped into the driving seat of her car and fired up the engine, pulling away in a noisy cloud of exhaust fumes before Hollis had time to call out. He took a step after her. 'Wait, my car won't start!' He threw his arms up into the air but failed to catch her attention. 'Damn!' he cursed, hoping that she would have the sense to come back for him when she realized he wasn't following her.

He let his hands fall back to his sides. It seemed suddenly very quiet, too quiet, all he could hear was the rain beating on the roof of his useless car. He hunched his shoulders against the weather and was about to get in when that demonic, howling cry split the darkness. It was closer now, it seemed to be almost on top of him. He gasped in fear and scrambled into the car, slamming and locking the doors as quickly as possible. There was something out there in the darkness, some huge, hideous creature and it seemed to be bearing down on him. He could sense it rushing towards the car, every nerve and fibre in his body was crying out against it but there was no way he could escape. He was trapped, helpless. His heart was racing, the blood was pounding in his ears and his breaths were coming in short, strangled gasps. His hands and face were cold with sweat. The tail lights of Emily's car were disappearing around the end of the green. He was all alone.

Suddenly the car filled with the disgusting stench of decay as the three shadowy figures crouched protectively around him. Their strengthening voices were urgent, babbling, and their blackened fingers were pointing, stabbing at the dials on the dashboard. For an instant Hollis just stared and then

158

it dawned on him, they were urging him to try and start the car, they were trying to persuade him to escape. Something heavy struck the side of the vehicle, rocking it violently. The howling cries he had heard were all around him now and it seemed to have grown darker, almost unnaturally darker. Frantically he stabbed the key towards the ignition and twisted it hard. Nothing happened. The car rocked again, more violently this time, and he thought he heard something run across the roof.

'Start, damn you, start!' he shouted, twisting the key again.

The starter motor whirred and caught, and the engine burst into life. Hollis hit the headlight switch and slammed the car into gear, stamping on the accelerator. The rear wheels spun and the car slewed sideways, kicking up a shower of loose stones and gravel before jolting forwards and careering onto the grass. Hollis cursed and wrestled with the steering wheel – they were heading directly towards the pond. He braked hard, reversed back, bumping down off the grass and dislodging whatever it was on the roof. He slammed the gear stick into drive and accelerated away past the post office. One quick glance in the rear-view mirror was enough to tell him that there was nothing following and he looked across to the derelict inn and frowned. As his car had careered towards the pond his lights had illuminated the front of the building, lighting up the upper windows and picking out a row of figures with white faces all looking out, watching him. They had ducked back out of sight as the headlight beam had swept across them but not before he had caught a glimpse of their coloured robes and strange-looking head-dresses.

'What the hell is going on in this Godforsaken place?' he muttered through clenched teeth, having to force himself to slow up as he reached the bend in the road at the end of the green. The tyres squealed on the wet tarmac and he realized that he would drive off the road and into the Fens if he wasn't more careful.

He switched the wipers on to fast speed and peered out, looking for the entrance to Sparrow Hall. He remembered it was not far from the village sign and he didn't want to miss it and risk having to turn around on such a narrow road with those deep dykes and undergrowth on either side.

He found the gateway easily enough and drove up to the house, his headlamps illuminating neat flower beds and shrubs landscaped around a large, imposing Georgian façade. White painted columns flanked wide stone steps that led up to a studded front door that stood wide open. The light from the hall streamed across the drive. The lower windows were all heavily shuttered as if the house was locked up and deserted, and there were no lights in most of the upstairs windows. Emily had been about to drive back into the village to look for him when he arrived.

'You'll never believe what has just happened . . .' he began as he climbed out of his car but he hesitated as a stocky, thick-set figure walked out through the front door and stopped, hands on hips as he looked down at him from the top step.

Even with the light behind him Hollis could see it was the farmer who had so rudely evicted him from the disued airfield earlier in the day, and the large, ferocious looking dog that had accompanied him then now appeared at his side, snarling and baring its teeth, its ears flattened along the side of its head as its hackles began to rise.

8

'CULLODEN, STOP IT, Hollis is a friend. Lie down, there's a good boy.'

Emily laughed as she ran up the steps to stroke the dog's large head. Gradually the dog's snarls subsided into a low, grumbling growl that vibrated in the back of its throat. It lay down, but it kept its head erect with its eyes watching as it followed Hollis' every move.

'Come on, come in out of the rain. Culloden won't hurt you,' she called, turning her attention to her father, hardly noticing the suspicious glare he was directing at the young American.

'Daddy, there's something really strange going on in the village tonight. Somebody's broken into that derelict old pub next to the church. We saw lights going on in the upstairs window. Shouldn't we call the police or something? The villagers were being very hostile in the Louse and Rag, too. The landlord told us to get out and then he shut up early . . .'

Emily paused as she became acutely aware of the glassy stare her father had fixed on Hollis, who was still standing, hesitating, in the pouring rain at the bottom of the steps. She frowned, looking from one to the other. Her father had never reacted like this to anybody she had brought home from school or university before. He was quiet, a very private man, and he could be moody and withdrawn sometimes but she had always put that down to the worries of farming the unpredictable land on the edge of the Fens.

'I'm sorry, Daddy, it was rude of me not to introduce Hollis first, only I was so worried about the people breaking into that old building I quite forgot. This is Hollis Calvin, his grandfather was stationed here during the war –'

'I know, we've already met. He was trespassing on the airfield earlier today. Now what do you want?'

Gregory Skinner interrupted his daughter without taking his eyes off Hollis and spoke in a cold, dismissive tone. She had never known him like this before.

'Daddy, Hollis' grandfather was a friend of your father's. I think they disappeared at about the same time. He's got this photograph, a really strange picture, that he found in his grandfather's things. I really would like you to see it.'

Gregory hesitated, his cold, angry stare collapsing into a frown. 'A photograph? Is that all you've come here to talk about? Why didn't you say so? Why didn't you show it to me earlier?'

His voice was distracted, the name Calvin certainly stirred the dust of his memory but he couldn't, on the spur of the moment, think why.

'Calvin?' he asked, looking hard at the young American. He hadn't meant him any particular malice earlier in the day when he had evicted him from the airfield but he was well aware that strangers were not welcome in Candleford, never had been. Over the years since he had taken over responsibility for the family farm he had developed a gruff, unwelcoming exterior to keep strangers off his property, as much for their own good as his peace of mind. He had long ago given up trying to explain to people that Candleford was a very isolated, insular community because the more he tried to dissuade people from visiting the village the more their curiosity had been aroused. He kept his family very separate and tried not to get involved.

Culloden suddenly leapt to his feet, his hackles raised and back arched. His face was a snarling mask of razor-sharp teeth. All at once the snarl turned into a yelping cry and he shrunk backwards, turning to run back into the house with his tail curved between his hind legs. Gregory's eyes narrowed suspiciously at Hollis. He remembered that he'd had the same effect on the dog earlier when they were on the airfield. He had even had a devil of a job trying to get the dog near where Hollis had stood after the animal had come out of hiding in the undergrowth.

'What have you done to my dog?' he demanded angrily, taking a step forward only to stop and stare as the air around the young American seemed to move and shimmer, swirling and forming into three indistinct, shadowy figures. He didn't have time to really register their existence before they vanished.

'What the Devil?' He frowned in confusion, rubbing his eyes as he doubted what he had seen.

Emily had glimpsed the three figures as they appeared and melted, she had sensed them there in the front drive the moment Hollis had got out of his car. She guessed they would materialize in response to Culloden's snarling bark, and she had been about to warn her father of their presence but had not known how to explain before he had interrupted her.

'Daddy, I was about to tell you. There is a lot more to this than just a photograph.' She touched his arm with a protective gesture and it made him jump. He stared back at her.

'More? What do you mean more?' His voice faded as, far away to the right of the house, a howling cry cut through the night from the direction of the marshes.

Hollis spun round, his shoes crunching on the wet gravel of the drive, his heartbeat quickening as the hairs on the nape of his neck prickled. It was the same, unearthly sound he had heard outside the Louse and Rag and it made him realize that the creature who had made it must have circled around the village and come through the marshes, following his scent, hunting him down.

'Both of you had better get inside. Be quick about it! We'll carry on this discussion in my study.'

Gregory hurried them through the front door. Hollis didn't need asking twice and he followed Emily in, leaving Gregory to pause on the threshold and stare out across the lawns and shrubbery towards the dark, empty marshes as the howling cry broke out again. It was closer now, not far from the old orangery.

'God protect any poor soul caught out there alone tonight,' he muttered under his breath as he slammed the front door and securely locked and bolted it, before following the others and calling out to his wife to come and meet Emily's guest.

The study was not a large room and it was dwarfed by a large partner's desk covered with papers which was positioned beneath a shuttered window. In front of it there was a worn leather armchair and a long coffee table standing on a worn Turkish rug. Farming magazines were scattered across the table partly hiding a shotgun and an open box of cartridges. The walls of the room were hung with dozens of pictures, some of them looked very old and so much in need of cleaning that their subject matter was almost totally obscured. From his brief glance he was able to guess that they were a collection of family portraits.

Hollis' attention was drawn to the door as they heard Emily's mother walking down the corridor. She walked into the room and shut the door behind her. She was a tall, slender woman who moved and looked as though she had stepped from the pages of *Vogue*, her hair didn't show the slightest trace of grey and her high cheekbones and clear

166

blue eyes gave her a classic beauty. But it was her smile that put Hollis instantly at his ease. She gestured to him to sit down and offered him a drink, moving immediately towards the drinks cabinet and pouring out liberal measures of a good, single malt whisky for Hollis, herself and her husband, with Emily choosing to have a soda and lime. Her father quickly dispensed with the introductions. Hollis couldn't help noticing his abruptness, the guarded caution in his voice. It wasn't the same as the blunt, unfriendliness of the villagers but he did get the distinct impression that his visit wasn't exactly welcome. He felt that Emily's father wanted it over and done with as quickly as possible. But why? He was beginning to think that his arrival in Candleford was like a pebble being unexpectedly dropped into a still pool of water. His presence was causing ripples, disturbing something that had been shrouded, something hidden. But what?

'I've never experienced anything so weird in my life. Hollis, show them the picture, tell them about the ghosts – and shouldn't we tell the police about the break-in?' Emily began but was interrupted by her father.

Gregory frowned at his daughter and shook his head. 'First things first, let Hollis tell us what brought him here in the first place – in his own words.'

Hollis shifted uncomfortably in the armchair. 'You're going to think I'm crazy, I know you are. My father died recently and while I was trying to sort out his desk I discovered a bundle of my grandfather's letters and photographs from the war. To cut a long story short I was reading through them when this picture fell out . . .' Hollis paused and took out the picture that showed himself and Emily with Richard in the foreground, glancing at it before silently passing it across. He watched the look of shock and then disbelief cross their faces as they recognized first Emily, then Gregory himself, in the picture before he continued.

'Yes, that's how I felt when I first saw it, it's impossible isn't it. I know I never posed for it and that until tonight I had never met your daughter. I've never travelled to England before or met Richard, who Emily tells me has recently died. Now you tell me – what do you make of it?'

Gregory scowled. The picture was absurd and yet he knew deep inside that this was something more than just a clever fake and he began to ask the same questions, voice the same doubts, that his daughter had over in the pub. As he began to probe Hollis for a motive there was more than doubt and suspicion in his voice, there was anger, a rage boiling up inside him that Hollis couldn't understand.

'Think what you like, I didn't invent that wretched picture. It isn't a trick, well certainly not of my making, and you must know that I haven't got anything to gain by coming all the way over here, disrupting my life like this except to find the answers. I'm as confused as you are and I want to know how the picture got in amongst my grandfather's letters. There isn't an explanation unless you believe in magic or the supernatural, and I don't. Or at least I didn't until I stumbled into this nightmare and now I'm having doubts. Too much has happened since I've been here in England and I'm not sure of anything any more.' Hollis took a shallow breath and pointed at the crumpled pile of old letters and photographs.

'The only clue I had to where that photograph could possibly have originated from was that short note my grandmother wrote on the back of it and a brief paragraph in the last, unfinished letter that my grandfather wrote while he was here before he disappeared. Look for yourself, read through all his letters – an earlier one states that he had become friendly with Dennis Skinner and Douglas Reeve, and the last one says they had their picture taken together in the snug bar of the pub he was billeted in. He wanted his wife, my grandmother, to see what his friends looked like. Go on, read them, then tell me honestly that you wouldn't have wanted to get to the bottom of it if you had been the ones to pick up a photograph of yourself with a group of total strangers in it taken almost thirty years before you were born!'

Hollis paused as he felt his cheeks flush hotly. He hadn't meant to respond like that and he lowered his voice to continue. 'My family didn't have any idea which village or airfield Merris, my grandfather, was stationed at, and I wouldn't have had much chance of finding it from the letters alone. I had been showing these pictures around quite a lot before a blacksmith in Thetford Forest recognized the place as Candleford . . .'

Gregory finished reading through the bundle of correspondence and a quick, cursory glance at the photographs was enough to confirm his worst fears. There was no mistake, the village was definitely Candleford and he didn't have much difficulty picking out his father standing behind him and Richard Reeve in the front even though they were slightly blurred and out of focus. There wasn't much doubt in his mind now, Hollis Calvin's grandfather must have been the American airman his father had befriended. Gregory frowned and rubbed his hand across his forehead. Fragments of suppressed memories were coming back, breaking through to the surface of his thoughts. He looked up, his eyes hardening as his gaze met Hollis'. Now he remembered why the name Calvin had meant something. He suddenly rose to his feet and strode to the far end of his study. His mouth was a bitter, angry, compressed line and his hands were clenched at his sides. He couldn't bear to look at Hollis, he was afraid of the anger, afraid of the rage he had buried inside himself for the past fifty years and he was afraid of what he might do if he didn't take a moment to control himself, to come to terms with the fact that this young man's grandfather had been responsible for the death of his own father. Now the memories were flooding back and time hadn't blunted their edges at all. The fear and terror he had suffered as a child was back. He remembered eavesdropping on their conversations. He hadn't understood much of it then but he had known that the villagers were going to hunt the American down, that they were going to kill his own father if they had to. They would stop at nothing once they had found out that their secret rites had been watched. The memory of those eerie lines of lights moving through the marshes and converging on the village came back in a rush. He could almost hear again the howling of the demon dog growing closer, paralysing him with fear as it stalked its prey. And he could remember all those nights he had spent hidden beneath his blankets knowing that it had killed and devoured his father.

Emily rose and took a step towards him in confusion. What was going on? He hadn't seemed to have taken the slightest interest in what had happened in the Louse and Rag, had ignored the break-in at the old pub next to the church and he hadn't wanted them to phone the police. He certainly wasn't behaving like the father she knew. He seemed to have become even more angry, more upset, after reading the letters than seeing that strange picture. Why? Why was her mother sitting so still, like an alabaster statue, white-faced and tense. The only thing that moved in the room was her mother's hands as they trembled slightly around her whisky glass. She was beginning to wonder how either of them would react when they heard the rest of Hollis' story or saw those ghosts that had been following him around ever since he arrived in England.

'Daddy, you look so angry. What's the matter? What's wrong?' The heavy silence was beginning to hurt her ears.

Gregory turned sharply at the sound of his daughter's voice. She looked so vulnerable in the soft light of his study, he knew his own face must be pale and drawn and he could feel a slight tremor beneath his right eye, a sign of tension that gave little sign of the turmoil that was going on inside him. How could he begin to tell his daughter of what danger she had inadvertently put herself into tonight? How could he explain what she had done by befriending Hollis in front of the villagers and then inviting him back to the house? For the first time since she had been born he regretted shielding her from the truth. He had never imagined after all this time that the past would come back to haunt him, that the same tragedy could possibly re-enact itself. He had been a fool.

The spasm beneath his eye got worse and he pressed the fingers of his right hand against it in an attempt to stop it but it merely aggravated it.

'Wrong? What's wrong?' he replied, his voice tight with anger. 'If you had the slightest idea then you wouldn't need to ask me – we wouldn't be in this predicament. If only you had been more careful who you spoke to in the village! Haven't we told you enough times, warned you about talking to strangers – and to think you brought him home! And he's American – it won't take people long to put two and two together, to work out who he is . . .'

Gregory regretted his outburst almost before its echo had died. He realized he had said too much. Culloden began to growl at Hollis and then thought better of it and slunk into a corner beneath a chair.

'What on earth are you talking about?' Emily began, but Gregory ignored her and looked directly at Hollis who was sitting uncomfortably clutching his pile of letters. He tried to stand up but Gregory frowned and motioned him back. He couldn't let him leave, not without some sort of explanation. The boy had no idea of the danger he was in.

'No ... wait ...' His anger was collapsing into embarrassment – he couldn't possibly hold Hollis responsible for something that had happened years before he was born, it wasn't his fault. But what could he safely tell him? What could he say without peeling back too much of the veneer of apparent normality that concealed the evil that permeated the lives of the villagers? It had clung to them for hundreds of years, isolating them from the surrounding villagers, cutting them off with its poison.

'I'm really sorry, it was most unkind of me to speak about you like that and under other, different, circumstances you would be most welcome here.' He was thinking fast, searching for the words. 'It's really not your fault and you couldn't possibly have known the repercussions your visit will cause, what stirring up the past will do. How could you? There's virtually nothing in these letters to forewarn you. I am sorry for my outburst, it was uncalled for, but it's Emily's safety – my family's safety – that I'm so worried about. You have no idea how difficult it is to protect them living here like this . . .'

He came to an abrupt halt, leaving his sentence unfinished. Beads of sweat prickled his temples, he had already said far too much. He wrung his hands together as if trying to wash the words away and looked down at the patterns on the Turkish rug between his feet as he wished he'd the courage his father had had. He wouldn't have worried about speaking out; he would have told Hollis the truth about the Lanterns, about the terrifying hold they had over the local community. He would have told him the truth about his grandfather's fate without a moment's hesitation. But perhaps if his father had been more careful about airing his views he would be alive today. Gregory shivered. It wasn't easy to escape from the spectral shadow that had clouded his life, he had spent too long as a prisoner of his own silence to throw it off in one reckless breath.

'Daddy, you have to tell us! What are you so afraid of? What is this all about?' Emily's voice cut through his indecision making him jump as he looked up.

Was she right? Had he stayed silent for too long? But where was he to begin? He directed his gaze towards Hollis and took a deep breath. 'Your grandfather got himself involved in something he didn't understand while he was stationed here during the war. I know because I overheard my father discussing it with him in the kitchen shortly before they both disappeared. It was . . .' Gregory's voice faltered, the words dried on the tip of his tongue. 'I'm sorry . . . I'm sorry, I can't tell you any more . . .' he continued quickly. 'I dare not. But my advice to you is to get away . . . go as fast as you can and go as far as possible.'

Gregory stopped and pulled out his handkerchief to mop at the sweat trickling down his forehead and the back of his neck. Now he really had said too much, but at least it might save Hollis' life if he acted quickly enough. Gregory glanced anxiously around him towards the shuttered window, listening, half-expecting to hear the demon dog howling in the garden outside as it searched for a way into the house. He looked at the gun lying on the table with the box of shells beside it and he wished he had taken the precaution to load it earlier in the evening.

'Oh, sure, thanks for warning me, Mr Skinner.' Hollis smiled thinly. 'But I'm afraid it's come too late to be of much use. I'm trapped here whether I like it or not, trapped by the ghosts of your father, Douglas Reeve and my grandfather. I

173

don't think there's a chance in hell of escaping until I've found out what happened to them, until I've discovered what those Lanterns did to them!'

'No – don't ever utter their name!' Gregory cried, putting his hands over his ears.

Emily's mother gasped and half-rose, staring at Hollis in horror. Her face was deathly-white as her glass slipped from her fingers and the remains of her drink spilled down her dress. Hollis could have laughed at the shock and terrified expressions that spread across their faces, only there wasn't anything the least bit funny in the effect those few words had had.

Emily ran to her mother and grasped her hands, pulling her down onto the couch and putting her arms around her protectively. She looked up in bewilderment, first at Hollis and then her father. 'For goodness sake, what's going on around here? What are you all so frightened of?'

Gregory recovered and gripped the back of the Chesterfield for support. 'Wait! Just be quiet!' he said dismissively as he concentrated his attention towards Hollis. 'How on earth did you find out about . . .' He hesitated, swallowing as he lowered his voice. The word did not come easily from his tongue. 'About the Lanterns?'

'I haven't found out anything yet.' Hollis shrugged. 'But it wasn't difficult putting two and two together and realizing that they must have had something to do with those sudden disappearances during the war. Remember, there are mentions of them in the letters – Merris described how he had accidentally stumbled into the wrong room on his way to bed one night. He thought it was some sort of fancy dress party and he described their clothes and the head-dresses they were wearing. But it was your father and Douglas Reeve who called them the Lanterns. They made it pretty clear

174

to Merris that they weren't very fond of them. On its own I wouldn't have given that another thought but as I was pulling away from the Louse and Rag to follow Emily here tonight my headlamps lit up the front of that derelict old inn across the pond where Merris was billeted. That same old building where Emily and I saw lights in the upstairs windows. There was a crowd of people in one of the upper rooms, they were staring out at me and they were dressed in exactly the same robes and head-dresses that my grandfather described in his letter. They all ducked back out of sight as my headlamp beam swept across them but not before I'd got a pretty good look. But who are these Lanterns? Why are you so frightened of them?'

'I think it's time you told both of them everything, Gregory,' Sheila intervened in a small, tense voice.

'No, no, that's not necessary, and it would be most unwise and far too dangerous.' Gregory shook his head. 'But what's all this nonsense about my father's ghost? I've never heard such rubbish.'

'That's what I've been trying to tell you about ever since I got home tonight,' Emily interrupted, finally getting her father's attention. 'It wasn't only because of that photograph that I brought Hollis back here with me, although heaven knows seeing it gave me quite a shock. It was the ghosts – I've seen them, they're real, if real's the right word, and I've never smelt anything like them before in my life. A terrible odour of decay invades the air around them whenever they appear. They're nothing like ghosts you read about, they appeared in the pub and frightened the landlord, then I caught a glimpse of them circling our cars outside in the car park. And then, just now, when Hollis pulled up in front of the house and got out of his car they were with him. I'm sure Culloden must have seen them, you saw the way he howled and ran back indoors. I'm surprised you didn't see them.'

She paused and lifted her head and sniffed, looking quickly around the room. 'Wait! That smell, they're here! It's getting stronger – can you smell it?'

'Don't be silly, girl, this situation is bad enough without you letting your imagination run riot. Ghosts indeed!' Gregory snapped as the broken veins in his cheeks flushed with renewed anger. He had to keep a tight grip on the situation, he had to suppress any further talk about the Lanterns and stop it from getting completely out of control.

But the stench of decay was getting stronger, it was tickling his nostrils and catching at the back of his throat; but it was impossible, he refused to subscribe to this hysteria. 'This has gone far enough!' he began as three shadowy figures began to materialize around the chair where the young American was sitting.

Culloden howled and vanished to the furthest corner of the room. Sheila screamed, her eyes wide with terror, and she threw up her hands as if to ward them off. Her head suddenly slumped forwards as she collapsed into unconsciousness and fell against Emily who gently laid her back on the couch. Emily turned towards them, her own heartbeat quickening. There was something so vile about their appearance but she had to look. Her eyes were drawn irresistibly towards their strengthening forms by the sound of the soft patter of mud and water as it cascaded on to the floor. She looked from their rotting clothes to the tangle of weed and broken reeds wound about their bodies but her gaze stopped when she reached her father. He was standing completely rigid, staring open-mouthed towards Hollis' chair, his face was stretched into a chalky white mask, his lips were trembling slightly as though he were trying to speak but the words were stuck in his throat. Nothing came out except for a few strangled gasps and a thin string of saliva that dribbled unnoticed from the corner of his mouth.

But it wasn't the look of terror at the sudden shock of seeing the apparitions that Emily had expected to see mirrored in his face, it was something quite different and it made her catch her breath. She wondered what dark secrets he had been hiding all these years. His eyes were full of guilt, full of the terror of being found out. His eyes were focusing on just one of the figures, the one who had struck a hidden chord in her memory earlier in the evening when they had appeared in the pub.

'Father!' Gregory gasped. There was no mistaking that familiar figure even through the mess of tangled weeds and with its blackened, decomposing skin and bones; it couldn't be anyone else. Even the walk, everything about the way it moved as it came silently towards him, reaching out with skeletal, dripping fingers and leaving behind a trail of mud and slimy water on the floor. It was his father.

Panic suddenly freed his tongue. 'No, no, please, don't come any closer. I'm sorry, I never meant to hide the truth, I was always intending to tell but I was so afraid . . . so afraid.'

Gregory stumbled backwards, raising his hands in a futile, placatory gesture, but there was no escape. He reached the wall and pressed himself hard against it, his whole body quivering in fear. 'I couldn't do anything – who would have listened?' He wept as wet, bony fingers touched and caressed him, tracing the outline of his face.

The cold, dead touch made him shiver and he felt dizzy, sick with revulsion. His knees began to buckle but before he could sink down to the floor those same dead fingers gripped his with such an urgency they held him upright and sharpened his consciousness. A gurgling, drowned voice called out his name. The voice of his father dead for the last fifty years reached inside his head, cutting deep into the core of his guilt and despair.

'Gregory, open your eyes. Look at me, open your eyes! Open them now!'

The voice was so compelling, so demanding, filled with the echoes of a lost childhood, of those short, carefree days before his father vanished. Days that were unstained by the dark knowledge of the Lanterns and what he had guessed they had done. He was unable to resist and his eyelids opened, but the sight that met him made him gasp, taking his breath away. The blackened, decaying face of his father was only inches from his own, so close that straggles of wet weed and matted hair hung down and brushed against his cheeks. He gagged and retched, overpowered by the stench of putrefaction. He felt numb with shock as he saw the shrivelled skin and grey-black layers of muscle and sinew exposed so clearly, the ruinous mouth and the persistent dribble of slimy black water that seeped from the corners of his eyes and the withered remains of his ears. He spoke but the words sounded so far away. All sense of feeling was vanishing and the room was beginning to spin, everything was swimming in and out of focus. Faintly, from the enfolding blanket of darkness, he heard the voice again.

'Gregory, listen to me, it wasn't your fault, you were only a child. Your silence saved your life then but now you must tell the truth. Tell them about the Lanterns. Gregory, do you hear me? Tell the truth, the truth . . .'

The figure of Dennis Skinner began to fade and Gregory staggered as he clutched at the empty air in front of him. The other two figures melted but not before the taller one had reached out a tentative hand towards Hollis. Words hung in the air as they left – 'You must find . . . must find . . . we cannot rest until you find . . .'

Then they were gone leaving only the mud and water on the floor. But the odour of stagnant decay seemed to linger even more strongly as it hung damply in the room.

Sheila stirred on the couch and cried out as she sat bolt upright, the long, elegant fingers of her right hand were on her mouth as she grasped Emily for support and searched the room with frightened eyes.

'Where are they? Where are those three figures? Did you see them? You did see them, didn't you?' She stared down at the puddles of slimy water and the fragments of weed and mud on the floor close to Hollis' feet and her frown deepened as she followed the trail of wet footprints to where her husband stood. He seemed deaf to her as he kept rubbing at a streak of mud on his cheek and staring at his fingers.

'Gregory!' she called out in a louder, demanding voice making him blink as he looked at her. 'Tell me, what has been going on? I don't understand, a moment ago I swear I saw three figures, awful looking creatures, but now they have gone. Where did all that mess come from?'

'They were ghosts, ghosts of Dennis Skinner, Merris Calvin and Douglas Reeve,' Hollis answered quietly, looking across at her. 'Your husband had just refused to tell us anything about the Lanterns and they appeared.'

'What did the ghost say to you, Daddy?' Emily asked in a frightened whisper. This time their materialization had been so terrifyingly real that it had taken all her self-control not to scream, and she had nearly fainted when it had crossed the room and grabbed hold of her father, almost lifting him off his feet. Soaking the floor with mud and broken fragments of weed, it had made weird, gurgling noises, as if it was trying to talk. It was almost as if it was trying to make her father understand something, and it had visibly affected him.

'Truth – he wanted the truth . . .' Gregory muttered bleakly, wiping away the last of the drying mud from his cheek with the back of his hand and crossing to the empty leather armchair opposite the Chesterfield and sinking wearily into it.

'The truth,' he repeated under his breath looking nervously around the room. He sensed they were still there even though he could see nothing; he knew they were there, hovering, waiting to reappear the second he deviated from the truth. But where was he to begin? There had been so many lies, so many denials over the years that the truth had been corrupted almost past recognition.

'Hollis was right, Sheila, they have come back to haunt us. The ghosts are the shades of my father, Douglas Reeve and Merris Calvin. They all disappeared during the war at the same time, so they must have been together – they are the people you saw a few moments ago, they are the ones who created all this mess – we all saw them . . .'

Gregory swallowed and shivered, feeling an urgency in the cold, damp atmosphere that was pushing him to get on with it. 'It won't be easy to understand but I think my father is demanding that I tell Emily and Hollis about the Lanterns. It seems I must tell them everything, but where shall I begin?' He paused and stared down at the black, crumbly grains of mud that clung to the back of his hand. It was making his skin itch and he rubbed distractedly at it with his thumb.

'Why don't you start by telling us who the Lanterns are and what they do?' Hollis prompted him softly.

Gregory looked across at his wife and she nodded, urging him to tell them everything.

'You have to understand – we are not a part of them, we don't belong to the Lanterns and we never have.' He lowered his voice and looked directly at his daughter. 'It's not been easy all these years living in their shadow, especially after what happened to my father. I grew up always looking over my shoulder, seeing those lines of lights travelling across the marsh and hearing the beast howling in the night. All I could do was hide and wait. I listened in the dark too terrified to move lest it sensed me, and then the chanting voices of the Lanterns would stop outside the gates. My father was right, my silence saved my life. If those Lanterns had the slightest idea of how much I had overheard at the kitchen door I would have become their victim. I would have vanished as mysteriously as my father and they would have ensured my silence for ever. You see, they are an ancient, magical cult steeped in black ritual and their power and hold over the village is through silence. Nobody dares to speak openly about them, it brings ill luck and the demon dog hunts to death whoever breaks the silence. Fear keeps the best secrets.'

Gregory stopped and mopped at his forehead with his crumpled handkerchief. He felt as reckless as a skater gliding out over thin ice and he was waiting for it to crack beneath the weight of his indiscretion, and then the cold, murky waters of all that secrecy would swallow him up.

'That beast, the one you just mentioned, was it the same creature I heard when I got out of my car in front of the house? What sort of animal is it? What has it got to do with the Lanterns?'

Gregory looked across at Hollis with his eyebrows raised in surprise. 'Of course you don't know, how could you unless you had researched the history of the Fens. What you heard was the cry of Black Shuck.'

He paused and swallowed, glancing fearfully at the shuttered windows with the handkerchief crushed hard against his mouth. Logic, reason and a veneer of education told him

181

the creature couldn't possibly exist outside myth and legend but he had grown up with its shadow cast over him and was surrounded by the secret cult of the Lanterns who worshipped it. 'It . . . it's the demon dog of the Fens,' he choked out in a small whisper. 'It is the spectral hound of hell who has haunted these meres and marshes for over a thousand years. According to legends the first nomadic tribes settled and built their crude mud huts on the higher ground around the Fens and began to cultivate the land – and they were unaware of the beast that lurked in that vast expanse of wilderness. At first the creature was no more than a rumour, a story like so many others that was brought back by the intrepid travellers and explorers who ventured deep into the marshes. At that time it didn't have a name, it was no more than a silent, benign shadow, a canine shape glimpsed in the uncertain light of the camp fire, or a soft rustle of reeds and a splash – too loud to be a fish in the muddy, swampy channel on a still night. Then it was just watchful eyes in the firelight that blinked and vanished if anybody approached. It was elusive, secretive and hidden. But the one thing all these early stories had in common was their sense of uneasiness, the sense of being persistently stalked. And even then there were many tales of travellers who vanished mysteriously while they were deep in the Fens and large paw prints were found around the last place where they were seen.'

Gregory frowned and looked darkly at Hollis and Emily as he fiddled with his handkerchief. 'Myths, legends – or reality? I'm not trying to say that the beast is real and I'm not trying to frighten you, I'm just trying to sketch in some of the background so you know what all this is about. Believe what you want but to those early settlers the beast became very real and the further they encroached into its domain the more real it became. It wasn't just a shadow any more, it wasn't just something half-seen, it became a huge, powerful creature the size of a calf with saucer-sized eyes that glowed in the dark. They heard its howling voice in the wind on wild, stormy nights and they would find its paw prints everywhere in the soft mud around their houses. Then the beast began to terrorize those small village communities in random attacks. It would drag off anyone caught in the open after dark, especially lonely travellers who hadn't reached a safe haven or children playing close to the edge of the marsh as twilight fell.

'The villagers tried hunting it to no avail, so they built strong wattle fences and burnt torches throughout the dark winter months when the creature's attacks seemed to be at their most frequent. But nothing would keep it out and a great fear of the beast grew up throughout the Fens. I know you're going to say that this is ridiculous and that something like that couldn't exist beyond the imagination but try and imagine the ignorance and the isolation of those early communities scattered throughout the marshes. To them this creature was very real and they couldn't just pack up and go somewhere else, life was hard enough without having to start again. Necessity drove those early settlers to find a way of living with their fear. They had no other choice but to make the spectral beast a part of their lives, to absorb its savagery. They gave it a name and invested it with magical, almost supernatural, powers. Cults grew that worshipped it and they attempted, through their rituals, to harness its power. With the passage of time these rituals became the foundation of the myths and legends of Black Shuck, the demon dog of the Fens that we know of today. "Black" because its coat was as black as death's shroud, I suppose, and because it always hunted at night, and "Shuck" came from the Anglo Saxon word "Scuccs" – it means demon. The modern world with its television and ease of access has mostly shrunk the fear and influence that the hound held over the people of the Fens and pushed it back into its proper place, but not here, not in Candleford. The Lanterns have seen to that. They worship Black Shuck, they've been doing it around here since the Dark Ages, and they still hold this village in a remorseless grip of fear.'

Gregory paused and mopped at his forehead again. The room seemed so silent, it was as if the walls were listening.

'But how? What do they do that's so terrible? Why doesn't somebody stop them – inform the authorities or something?' Hollis asked.

Gregory laughed harshly. 'How do you inform the authorities about something that doesn't exist? The moment anybody comes here they disappear. The cult is so secret that nobody knows who is a member of it and who isn't – and nobody is prepared to tell. But you ask what they do that is so terrible? Why they murder people, Hollis. They lure them out into the marshes with those lines of lights and perform some sort of ancient, pagan sacrifice to their Demon Dog. That is what I overheard my father talking about in the kitchen just before he vanished. It has something to do with the old belief that strangers who stay in the village beyond two sunsets are a bad omen, they believe their presence here wakes the creature and sends it prowling restlessly until a sacrifice is made. But you'll find it difficult to prove anything, the people around here clam up if you start asking questions. But you will have already experienced that, won't you. The marshes are a very dangerous place, it's all too easy for accidents to happen.'

'Murder? You mean the village people like old Walter – Charles in the shop . . .?' Emily's voice faltered into a gasp of horror as she stared, lips trembling in horror.

'Many of them are involved with the Lanterns and now you see why we've been so protective of you, why we sent you away to school and why we've done our best to keep you out of village life.' Gregory's face was grim as he continued. 'But we have no idea who is involved, nobody talks of it and that's part of the strength of the fear, not knowing who it is safe to talk to. My guess is that there's more than a dozen of them who aren't involved but I'm not about to try and find out who they are. It wouldn't serve any purpose except to warn the Lanterns of my curiosity, and if I should accidentally ask the wrong person . . . Anyway, I couldn't do anything to stop their evil rituals, nobody could, and I should know, I've been convinced that they were the cause of my father's disappearance for most of my life. I used to blame the American, your grandfather, for stirring things up, but on reflection I can see there was more to it. In fact I distinctly remember overhearing my father telling the other two he was on the verge of exposing them, he said they were an evil stain on the community. He knew who they were too, but of course he vanished before he could do anything. But some time in that conversation I remember he warned Merris to be on his guard. He told him that on no account was he to watch the procession of lights from his window. He said they would weave a hypnotic spell over him and lure him to his death and that he had to get out of the inn and get as far away as he possibly could from Candleford, even if it meant deserting his unit. I'm sure they filled the car with all the spare petrol from the farm and they were going into the village to collect him on the night they all disappeared. So you be careful, both of you, I'll repeat that warning my father gave Merris all those years ago – get away from here, go tomorrow morning and get as far away as you can before night falls. Remember, the Lanterns are a very dangerous cult, there's no knowing the extent of their evil powers. They have very long memories. I don't want anything to happen to either of you.'

185

Hollis smiled and shook his head. 'You're forgetting, Mr Skinner, I can't go anywhere. I'm trapped here whether I like it or not but . . .' he paused as he sifted through the pictures. 'Something's just occurred to me. Remember that ghost of my grandfather and how he kept repeating "must find must find"?' He lay the pictures down and put aside the one of himself with Emily and Richard. 'Look at it, I don't think there's any coincidence about me being here. That picture isn't a fluke. Now I've listened to you tonight I've put two and two together and I believe that everything that's happened to me was deliberate. It has forced me to find the remains of my grandfather, your father, and Douglas Reeve. We have to lay them to rest. I don't think they necessarily worked it out to happen just the way it has but at the time they knew there wasn't anybody who could do it. You were only a boy of five, Douglas' son couldn't have been much older and my father was only about the same age. Somehow they used the roll of undeveloped film and projected the future onto it. Remember that roll of film wasn't developed until after all three of us were born.'

Hollis laughed suddenly, 'It's not only the Lanterns who have long memories. I think they bit off rather more than they bargained for when they lured my grandfather and his two friends to their deaths. I reckon they've been prepared to spend the rest of eternity getting even!'

'But that's crazy.' Emily frowned. 'Even if it's all true and they lured you here with that photograph it won't do any good, you'll never find their bodies. It's been fifty years since they disappeared – where would you start to look? There are miles and miles of bottomless mud, water and reeds all overgrown out there in the Fens. It would take years even with a properly co-ordinated search party and then you would barely scratch the surface. In fact your boat would probably glide right over them, the water's all dark and peaty so you would never see them. Remember, nobody who lives around here is likely to want to help you, not after what my father's just told us about the villagers.'

Emily shivered and fell silent. The room suddenly felt cold and cheerless and the doubt and confusion in Hollis' face made her add, 'You don't have to believe me, I'll fly you over the Fens tomorrow and you can see for yourself.'

'I'm afraid Emily's right, your chances of finding those bodies would be more than a million to one,' Gregory said in agreement.

He sniffed as he imagined he caught the smell of the marshes again, but he was wrong and he noisily blew his nose in his handkerchief. 'You see, Hollis, the marshes swallow up anything that falls or is dumped into them. Everything vanishes without a trace, sometimes for thousands of years, and then suddenly one day, for no apparent reason, they reappear. They just pop back up to the surface, blackened and shrivelled but perfectly preserved, even the clothes. You would be amazed at the condition of some of the early settlers we have found floating on the surface.'

'No, wait! Did you say perfectly preserved, even their clothes?' Hollis asked, his interest sharpening.

'Why, yes, that's right, there's something in the peat and water. I think the state of preservation depends on how deep they are. The sediment acts as a pickling agent. It's enabled the archaeologists to find out so much about the earliest settlements – but why do you ask?'

'Because those three figures that keep appearing don't look very well preserved to me, in fact quite the opposite, they're decaying and their clothes are rotting and falling off their bodies. But they must be submerged somewhere in the marshes because of all that mud and slime, water and tangled weed that pours off them whenever they appear. Could they be lying just beneath the surface trapped in the weeds?' Hollis paused and reached down to touch one of the drying pools of water on the floor close to his chair.

'But there's something else about them that's been bothering me – this power they have to keep me here, to prevent me escaping. Emily said earlier in the pub that they didn't act like ghosts and she's right. They're much more real than ghosts, more physical. It's almost as if they're not really ghosts at all but some strong presence, almost material. I remember reading that there are various magical cults scattered all over the world that are believed to have strange, bizarre powers; voodoo magic has its living dead, vampirism reaches beyond the grave, witch doctors in the African continent can kill just by looking at somebody. I wouldn't have given any of that stuff more than a moment of curious thought before I found that photograph and got drawn into this nightmare, but it's set me thinking: what if the Lanterns do have some dark magical power only it's backfired? What if they murdered those three because they thought they knew too much but instead of silencing them they just lay out there in the marshes with their souls trapped in some sort of limbo half-life between the living and the dead? I know what you're thinking but it's no more far-fetched than the story of Black Shuck, is it? I don't think they'll stop haunting me until their bodies are buried in consecrated ground. And if *that* sounds crazy then wait and listen to this, when I first arrived in England I had this recurring dream of being in a sinking boat in a narrow channel between banks of tall reeds. These figures were always there in the boat with me or in the water around it and the sense of drowning – the fear – was overwhelming. You don't suppose that's what happened to them, do you? You don't think they were taken out in a boat and murdered? Would the Lanterns have done that? Does anything I've said help to narrow the search?'

Gregory thought for a moment and then shook his head. 'There are so many channels but yes, I suppose it's possible, it might shorten a search by a year or two if one was ever made.'

'I've often wondered how those lines of lights appeared to move so effortlessly across the marshes but of course I've never dared to watch them for very long, I was far too frightened especially after all the warnings you gave me. I never wanted to pry much because I know how much it upsets you to talk about the Lanterns, dear, but how do they travel in such straight lines? I know there are a few paths that lead out into the marshes but they really aren't that straight, are they?'

Sheila's voice made them turn in her direction.

'You know I've never really questioned it before either,' Gregory answered in surprise. 'I suppose it's because I grew up believing that the Lanterns had this terrible power and their lights gliding in effortless straight lines through the misty darkness was all a part of it, but Sheila's right, they couldn't possibly do it by using the footpaths. But they could if they used shallow-bottomed boats. There is a whole network of dykes, ditches and drainage channels that lead out into the Wash, most of them are controlled by sluices and pumps to maintain their levels but a few of them are tidal. Just imagine it, after all these years of imagining that they had some special power, that they could just change direction at any moment and head straight towards me bringing Black Shuck to Sparrow Hall . . . But now I know they couldn't because none of those channels lead directly here!'

'I don't think that finding out they probably used boats makes them any less dangerous, Daddy,' Emily warned.

'No, but it gives us somewhere to start,' Hollis interrupted quietly. 'Can you remember exactly what happened after your father and Douglas Reeve left the house to collect Merris the night they all disappeared? Did you see the lights in the marshes then?'

Gregory lowered his head, concentrating, pressing the palms of his hands hard against his temples. He was thinking, reaching back to try to catch those childhood memories. The room seemed to dim around him as the memories swelled.

'Yes, I remember . . .' he began. 'It had been one of those bitterly cold, dark February days with a raw, wet wind coming in straight from the North Sea driving squalls of sleet and snow horizontally across the marshes. I remember there was a lot of activity in the barn, a lot of coming and going I didn't understand – oh, yes, there was a smell of petrol where some had been spilt near the car – whenever I stop at a petrol station even now it reminds me of that day. I knew something was going on and I eventually got sent to my room for pestering my father with my questions. I suspect now it was his way of protecting me, the less I knew the safer I'd be. Anyway it was pitch black outside by four-thirty and I must have got into bed and fallen asleep because at around seven, maybe eight o'clock the sound of raised voices in the kitchen below my room woke me up. I crept downstairs past the sitting room where my mother was listening to the war news on the wireless and I listened at the kitchen door. There was a heated argument going on. Douglas Reeve was trying to get my father to postpone going back to the Black Shuck to collect your grandfather, Merris. He was calling him all sorts of things – stupid, a reckless idiot – and telling him it was madness to go in there now, especially after dark. It seemed that they had just found out for sure it was where the Lanterns held their ceremonies. He kept on repeating, "I'm sure they know we're on to them," and, "It's far too dangerous, the place will be full of them." I also heard him tell my father "you never know what magic they'll weave to trap us if they suspect we've come to help Merris escape."

'But my father only laughed at him and then I distinctly remember him saying, "The Lanterns don't have any real power. All that magic and dancing around in fancy dress is all hocus pocus, a lot of nonsense set up to frighten people and control them." But he still kept on insisting that Merris was in real danger because he had stumbled on the truth about them and the sooner they got him away from there and the village the safer he'd be. They both believed that the Lanterns would stop at nothing to silence him, to make an example of him to everyone else. A lot of other things were said that I didn't understand and they were still arguing as they went out to the car, but my father was adamant that they must collect Merris and get him away from the Black Shuck before something happened to him. The last I saw of my father and Douglas Reeve was when they got into the car and drove off towards the village. I had a sort of funny feeling, a premonition if you like, that I knew something bad was going to happen to them but there was nothing I could do. I couldn't stop them going. I remember my mother crying in the days that followed and the awful emptiness that my father's disappearance caused. The car was found some months later in a back street in Kings Lynn, it had been stripped of everything, even the seats.'

Gregory looked up and there were tears misting his eyes. He blinked and rubbed them away with the back of his hand but a teardrop escaped to trickle down his cheek.

'The lights?' Hollis prompted gently. 'Did you see the lights that night?'

'Oh, yes, yes I did, only it was much later. Something woke me up, a noise outside, voices – I think they came from the marshes. I remember being afraid but I managed to look out of the window and caught a brief glimpse of the lights moving away from the village. They seemed to float, shimmer and suddenly vanish beneath a thick blanket of fog that was silently rolling across the marshes from the direction of the Wash.'

'That must have meant they were using one of the drains or channels going in a north-easterly direction. I wonder, do you think we'd be able to find it on the Ordnance Survey map?' Emily suggested.

'The map will show most of the larger channels, but there are probably dozens going in that direction, they would all join up with the main, Middle Level Drain. Why? Are you thinking of flying over that part of the marsh? Remember the reed beds have become very dense and overgrown there since they stopped cutting reeds for thatch years ago. You won't stand much chance of seeing anything – remember, it's been fifty years . . .' Gregory left the sentence unfinished.

'I wish I could get a look inside that derelict old pub, it's the last place we know they were together before they disappeared,' Hollis murmured, thinking out loud.

'Shirley's got the key, in the post office. I wonder if she would mind if we borrowed it?' Emily answered.

'No!' Her father's voice was louder and sharper than a pistol shot. 'Emily, I absolutely forbid it, it's much too dangerous. It's one thing giving Hollis a short flight over the marshes, you're a very good pilot, but I don't want you getting involved any more than that. The Lanterns will kill you. I don't want you going into that place!'

Emily frowned and reached forwards, picking up the photograph of herself with Hollis and Richard, taking a last look before holding it out towards her father. 'I am already involved whether you like it or not, Daddy. I might not have known about it before tonight but I am a part of that indelible image and always have been, at least from the moment I was born. I can't walk away from it, I can't escape any more than Hollis can.'

'Emily, I have always been afraid that something like this was going to happen.' Her mother's voice was small and tight with fear and she felt her hand grip her arm. 'I know there's nothing we can do to stop you but please, please promise me you'll be careful.'

'Mother, of course . . .' she began but fell silent as a howling cry echoed through the house and the stagnant odour of the marshes filled the room.

Gregory leapt to his feet and ran to the table, his fingers fumbling with a box of cartridges, spilling them across the desk top as he quickly loaded his gun, snapping it shut before spinning round to face the shuttered window. The atmosphere thickened and the three shadowy figures appeared, their hands raised in gestures of defiance.

Hollis sat perfectly still, his fingers gripping the worn leather arms of the chair, his heart beating fast. His blood was pumping and the hairs on the nape of his neck prickled. Dennis Skinner may have thought the Lanterns and all those stories of Black Shuck were a lot of nonsense but whatever was making that howling sound outside seemed very real to him.

Something heavy struck the window followed by the sound of claws, or fingernails, being raked across the glass, scrabbling, as if they were trying to find a way in. The sound made Hollis shudder and set his teeth on edge. Emily and her mother were sitting huddled together on the sofa, their hands pressed over their ears in an attempt to shut it out. Culloden, who had been hiding beneath a chair in the far corner of the room ran towards the window, snarling and barking, his hackles ridged up along his back. The window shook violently and

193

small fragments of plaster broke loose around the frame as puffs of dirt and dust billowed out of the shutters' hinges. Hollis was paralysed with fear, another attack like that and whatever creature it was would break in, one bound and it would be on top of him. His senses were screaming at him, telling him to get up and run for his life.

Gregory was cursing through gritted teeth. 'Come on, come on, you ugly bastard. I've told them all about you, I'm not running away any more!'

He threw the gun butt up against his shoulder and snapped off the safety catch but before he could take aim or his trembling fingers could tighten on the trigger, the three ghostly figures moved between him and the window, blocking his line of fire. Their gurgling voices rose in anger as they glided across the room towards the window. Culloden looked around, his snarls turning to yelps of fear as he fled back to hide under the chair. The three figures passed over the spot where he had once stood, merging together into one dark, shadowy mass. Then they vanished, melting through the shutters, leaving nothing behind but a few fragments of weed and streaks of mud.

The assault on the window stopped abruptly. The howling cry became a yelp and seemed to disappear into the rainy darkness. Gregory was the first to move. He let out a low sigh of relief and flicked the safety catch back on as he slowly lowered his gun to rest in the crook of his arm. One by one the others began to recover from the sudden shock of the attack and shakily stood up. Hollis walked across to the window and crouched down, touching the dust and broken fragments of plaster that had fallen to the floor beneath the window.

'Now you can see why we are so against you getting involved, Emily. It hasn't taken those Lanterns any time at all to work out why Hollis is here, they've sent out their creature to kill him. The beast has never actually come to this house before, not in all the years since my father disappeared, but I've heard it often enough. It's been out there in the marshes, hunting its prey but it's never come here before. The sight of it would probably have been enough to frighten us all to death if it had got in.'

There was a grimness and a real fear in Gregory's voice as he lay his gun down on top of the desk and pushed it away from him. 'I don't know why I've bothered to carry that gun around all this time – you can't kill phantoms, can you!'

'You don't believe your father was right then when he said that Black Shuck wasn't real?' Hollis asked, glancing up. There had been something about that attack that didn't quite add up. 'You think the Lanterns have the magical powers to make him attack anybody they want, don't you?'

'Yes, yes, of course I do. Didn't you see what just happened? God only knows why it stopped, it could have come straight through that window. How else would it have known where you were if the Lanterns hadn't sent it? They saw you with Emily, they saw you follow her back here. Too many people have vanished mysteriously over the years, including my father, for me not to take them seriously.'

'Wait a minute, Daddy, let Hollis speak, I'm curious. What are you trying to get at?' she said, turning towards him.

'I'm not really sure . . .' He frowned, quickly climbing to his feet and brushing away the fine layer of dust and plaster from his fingertips. 'There's no doubt that something large hurled itself at that window – but what was it? From what your father has told us tonight I am sure that the Lanterns would stop at nothing, even murder, to keep the village under their power but something is not quite right.'

Hollis paused, glancing down and stroking Culloden on

195

the head. For some reason the dog had become very friendly. 'There was something about that attack that doesn't add up. Surely if this creature, this Black Shuck or whatever you call it, is really some sort of phantom, a ghostly demon of the marshes, then ordinary glass, bricks and mortar wouldn't keep it out. Remember these other ghosts that have been haunting me, they seem to be able to appear and disappear at will, they pass right through anything they want to, so why didn't that creature just charge straight through the wall or window? What stopped it? And there's another thing, Culloden wasn't frightened was he, but ever since I've arrived here he's been hiding from these three ghosts, he is terrified of them. I wonder why he wasn't afraid of this one? Obviously he couldn't have thought it was a phantom, or perhaps it's because he doesn't know the myths!'

'Are you doubting what I have told you?' Gregory replied angrily, his face darkening. 'I haven't the slightest idea why the creature didn't behave as you expected it to – perhaps there are thousands of ways for ghosts or demons to behave, but I've lived here long enough to know what it was – and after the way it nearly tore that window frame away from the wall I am inclined to believe all those old stories. You just watch out both of you!'

'Yes, yes, of course we will and I wasn't doubting for a moment what you have told us.' Hollis was quick to apologize, it was easy to see from Gregory's response that it would be pointless to try to argue a rational approach to explain away whatever had hurled itself at that window, his fear of the beast of the Fens and the Lanterns who worshipped it was too far ingrained for that. Hollis glanced down at his watch. It was getting late and he needed to find somewhere to stay.

Emily saw him look at his watch and suddenly realized

his predicament. 'It will be all right for Hollis to stay here tonight, won't it? There isn't anywhere in the village.'

'Why yes, of course it will, we have plenty of room,' her mother replied looking directly across at Gregory.

Her father frowned but nodded his head reluctantly. 'Yes, you'll have to stay here now, especially after . . .' He paused to look fearfully around the room. They were still here, he could sense those three ghosts. Hollis was right, there was no escape. Instinctively he reached for his gun, gaining a small comfort from the touch of the polished wooden stock and the cold metal barrels.

'I can't stop you from doing whatever you intend, I would much rather you leave the past alone, but most of all I want you both to be careful. I don't want you disappearing – I don't want history repeating itself not after all this time. I couldn't bear it if we lost Emily as well.'

Gregory fell silent and grasped a handful of loose cartridges to stuff them into his pocket before striding across towards the door to check on all the outer doors and windows. He paused with his hand on the door handle and looked back. 'I don't suppose it will do any good but take Culloden with you.'

Hollis smiled as Emily's father pulled the door shut behind him, perhaps he had listened to what he had to say after all.

9

THE MORNING SKY WAS a cold, flat, egg-shell blue without a cloud in sight. A raw, blustery wind stirred up the fallen leaves and sent them skating across the surface of the pond towards Hollis, who was waiting and keeping a firm hold on Culloden's lead just out of sight of the post office while Emily tried to procure the key to the derelict old inn. The wind tugged at his slacks and found a way into every gap in his clothing making him shiver as he wished he had brought a pair of gloves with him.

'Sit! Sit, boy, quiet,' he muttered, looking slowly around the village green.

It looked exactly the same as the day before, even the same fishermen were back in their places around the higher pond sitting statue-still, waiting for the fish to bite. To the casual eye it was a timeless, pretty place, full of peace and tranquillity, only he knew it wasn't like that – it couldn't be, not after what he had learned the night before. The stirring net curtains, the half-glimpsed figures looking out of their cottage windows, they were not reflecting a mild curiosity at his presence, not today, today they had taken on a much more sinister meaning. The bell on the door of the post office jingled noisily making him turn and look across. His face broke into a smile as Emily reappeared.

'Got it!' she whispered, slipping her arm through his and hurrying him away across the wet grass towards the church. 'Don't look back or give Shirley anything to be suspicious about. Make it look as though we are just going to visit the church – she doesn't know I've taken the key!' Emily grinned conspiratorially, patting the bulge in the pocket of her Barbour.

'What? You stole it?' Hollis cried out in shock.

'No – I've just . . . sort of . . . borrowed it,' she replied. 'Just as I was about to ask her for the key I remembered what my father said last night about nobody being really sure who is and who isn't involved with these Lanterns. Shirley has always been such a nice person but you never know, do you? On the spur of the moment I told her that I was expecting a really important package from college but that I had forgotten to get Culloden indoors when the postman was due to call so he may have left it with her. She wasn't happy but she still went back to check – just as I guessed she would. It didn't take a moment to slip round the counter and take the key from its hook before she got back.'

'But what if she misses it? Surely enough people saw us together last night for them to put two and two together and warn the Lanterns.'

'It's you who wanted to get inside that tumbledown old building – not me!' Emily replied, her eyes flashing with anger.

'Yes, yes, I know, I'm sorry, it's just that I don't want to get you into trouble. I've got this strange feeling too, it's as if everybody's watching us this morning.'

'Damn!' he said, as he tripped up entering the churchyard and let Culloden slip the lead through his fingers.

'Here boy, stay close,' Emily called after the dog as he bounded away amongst the headstones. 'Culloden – come here!' she hissed, catching a glimpse of him as he emerged from the undergrowth, head down, scenting the ground between the graves.

202

Hollis watched him for a moment and then ran after him, stopping and crouching down to see where he had been sniffing the ground.

'What are you looking for?' Emily asked, hurrying up to him after she had caught the dog.

'I'm not sure, it's just that Culloden seemed to be very interested in something around here,' he replied, slowly standing up.

'It's nothing, probably just one of the village dogs he can smell, perhaps it's a bitch in season. Come on, people will begin to think you're acting suspiciously if you spend all morning crawling around the graveyard on your hands and knees. We can get into the back yard of the Black Shuck if we go through a disused gate on the far side of the churchyard. Here, follow me.'

Hollis closed the back door of the empty building softly behind him and slid home the top bolt just in case anybody had seen them enter and decided to follow. He walked through into the main bar and stood perfectly still in the shuttered interior waiting for his eyes to grow accustomed to the gloom. Thin rays of dusty sunlight streamed through the cracks in the shutters and a fly buzzed at one of the windows. The sunlight was picking out the iridescent colours on its wings where it hung suspended in a shroud of cobwebs. Emily sneezed and almost tripped over a pile of broken chairs that were stacked in the centre of the room as Culloden pulled hard on his lead. The dog growled, his ears pricked, and then he sniffed at the floor and tried to get to the half-open door into the hall where the stairs led up to the first floor.

'It's a wonder he can smell anything in here, it's so damp and musty – and it feels so cold,' Emily muttered, shivering and making the dog come to heel.

'It's much smaller and dingier than I imagined, and it feels so forlorn, so empty,' Hollis replied, moving slowly through the rooms on the ground floor, pausing to examine a faded picture that still hung on the wall. He wiped his hand across the dirty glass in the frame and kicked at the broken shards of a beer glass where it lay amongst a litter of old newspapers in the corner of the hall. 'This must be the snug bar – the place where that photograph was taken.'

He stopped just inside the small, low-beamed room on the other side of the hall, his heart was beating faster as he took the picture from his pocket. He sensed Emily was standing beside him, silently looking at the huge, empty, fire-blackened inglenook, its dog-grate choked with long-dead ashes. All that was left of the old-fashioned pots and pans and the bric-a-brac from the shelves and walls was a rusty kettle that lay on its side, half-buried in rubbish, and a bent, brass poker in the hearth with the remains of a corn dolly that had been left, forgotten, on one of the shelves. The room felt cold and empty.

Hollis sighed and pushed the picture back into his pocket. He had imagined that finding the room would be significant somehow, full of atmosphere, but there was nothing, not even a whisper to break the still, silent air – nothing to stir up the echoes of the long-dead past. Whatever it was he had hoped to find there it wasn't lying dormant in that derelict old inn. Even the three ghosts seemed to have deserted him at that moment.

'There's nothing here, let's get going,' he muttered, turning and walking out into the gloomy hallway.

Emily took a last look around the snug bar and shrugged. It was difficult to imagine it full of noise and people with the smell of hops and tobacco mingling with the woodsmoke from the fire. 'Come on, Culloden,' she murmured, following Hollis out.

The dog padded along beside her and then suddenly stopped

and growled before leaping up the stairs. 'Hollis – wait! Hollis, come back, I think we had better take a look upstairs – something must be up there, look at Culloden!'

Hollis ran back and watched as she slipped the lead to let the dog bound up the stairs, scenting each tread before he disappeared around a twist in the stairs. They heard him running along a corridor above their heads. Hollis glanced quickly around and picked up the leg of a broken bar stool, gripping it like a club before he followed the dog.

'Be careful – and keep close to me,' he whispered as he climbed the stairs, cautiously peering along the upper corridor as he followed the noise that Culloden was making.

Eventually they came to a large room above the snug that faced out on to the village green. 'This must be the room I saw those people in last night, they were dressed up in robes and strange head-dresses. I can still smell incense or perfume or something, can you?'

Hollis looked out of the window, ducking quickly back when he saw old Walter slowly climbing the steps of the Louse and Rag across the pond. He was so engrossed in his thoughts that Emily had to touch his arm to get his attention.

'People have been in here recently, look at the footprints in the dust, and from the way Culloden's behaving I'd say there was a bitch with them.'

Hollis watched the dog sniffing the dirty floor and run around in circles, leaving an erratic trail of paw prints in the dust. 'Culloden, come here!' he called, taking a step towards him, but it was already too late, any recognizable prints that had been there had been scuffed out by Culloden. Sighing he let the dog continue and looked carefully around the room. It was completely bare of furniture and, unlike the room downstairs, it seemed used somehow. On one wall was a high shelf and a row of ornate lanterns. He went across and stood on tip-toe to have a closer look: there were more than two dozen and they all looked as though they had been used recently.

Emily walked across to the fireplace. 'There are two large cupboards set into this wall. Come here, look, there are padlocks on the doors.' She paused and asked slowly, 'You don't suppose the Lanterns keep their robes and things in there, do you?'

'Well it shouldn't be very difficult to break into them, and there's really only one way to find out. Keep the dog with you.'

Hollis ran down into the snug bar and retrieved the bent poker from the hearth of the inglenook. He took a deep breath and glanced anxiously around the empty room as he pushed the poker down behind the hasp of the first padlock. Emily gripped onto Culloden's collar as Hollis gave the poker a brutal pull. There was the sound of splintering wood and the four small screws securing the hasp to the door tore free. The hinges creaked and the door swung open to reveal shelves piled high with brightly coloured robes and frightening, leering, primitive masks carved in wood and moulded with reeds and paper – some of them looked very old. Hollis quickly used the poker on the other hasp and pulled open the door to reveal more robes and head-dresses all neatly laid out on the shelves with boxes of candles and small, oblong squares of some dark, pungent incense. The three incense burners looked similar to the ones he remembered seeing in a church procession back home. A quick look round only proved that what they had discovered didn't really amount to very much, except to confirm what Emily's father had said about the Black Shuck being the Lanterns' meeting place. They had found the robes to confirm this but there wasn't anything there to incriminate anybody by name, just a load of paraphernalia and ceremonial bits and pieces.

'Wait – wait a minute – what's this?' Hollis cried suddenly as he rummaged through the back of a shelf in the first cupboard and found an inner cubbyhole partly concealed by a loose piece of plywood. He quickly cleared the shelf and pulled out everything, scattering it all over the floor as he pulled aside the piece of wood and reached inside to feel the handle of a large wooden box. It was so heavy that he needed to use both hands to lift it out and he carefully put it down in front of them. They stared at it as Hollis fiddled with the small, spring-loaded, brass catch that secured its lid. It snapped open quite unexpectedly and slowly he lifted the lid, gingerly pulling aside the heavy piece of black velvet that concealed the contents.

'Books! It's full of books!' he sighed, an edge of disappointment in his voice as he picked up the top, leather-bound volume and opened it. He gave it no more than a cursory glance before passing it across to Emily.

'It's very old, it's been hand-written, Latin I think, or very early English.' She paused and frowned as she concentrated on remembering the little Latin she had learned at school. *La Clavicule de Salomon* was scrawled in a spidery script across the title page, below it was a crude drawing of demons dancing in a circle and carrying lamps. With them was an enormous, black, four-legged beast with huge, saucer-shaped eyes.

'I think this is a book of spells,' she said, looking up as Hollis passed her another, slightly smaller, volume that was also hand-written. The title page was written with bolder letters – *Le Grimoire du Pape Honorius* and underneath, in a different hand someone had scrawled: 'Our black book of secrets – read and grow powerful. Lanterns, Lanterns burn so bright, succour the beast with your guiding light.' Inside it was filled with crude, hand-written spells and a mass of symbols and drawings that she couldn't begin to decipher. She shivered and shut the book quickly. There was something so evil, so dark and foreboding contained in those pages.

'This one's different, it's more like a ledger, there is a number stamped on the front of it, it's a three I think. It's called *The Book of Scucc's Dead*. There are names and dates, strange symbols scratched down the margins, some of them come from the 1700s ...' He fell silent as he began leafing through the pages, running his finger down the seemingly endless list of names. Suddenly he stopped, the colour draining from his face.

'Emily – listen to what I've found!' he hissed, his lips trembling. 'Dennis Skinner, February 15th 1943. Douglas Reeve, February 15th 1943. Merris Calvin, February 15th 1943. And there are more, dozens more after them. Listen to this last one – Richard Reeve, January 21st 1995. There are plenty of blank pages after that one still waiting to be filled in.'

He looked up at her. 'You know what this is, don't you?' His voice was barely a whisper by now. 'This must be the Lanterns' record of everybody they have ever killed – I mean "sacrificed" to the Demon Dog!'

Emily stood up quickly, letting the other book of spells fall open onto the floor. 'They'll kill us for sure now that we've seen all this!' She went cold at the horror of what the villagers – people she knew and had grown up with – were involved in. 'Come on, we've got to get out of here, escape while we still can. There's no way we can disguise those broken locks, they're bound to find out that it was us. Somebody's sure to have seen us on the green when we went over to the church.' Emily started to back away towards the door.

'No wait! I think this box has a false bottom – listen, it

rattles. There must be something else hidden, something they really want to keep well out of sight.' Hollis' voice stopped her in the doorway as he prodded the sharp end of the poker at the inside of the box. The thin, plywood, false bottom suddenly gave way, breaking into two pieces. Hollis pulled them both out.

'Now what do we have here?' he murmured, staring down at a selection of daggers and an old flintlock pistol. In amongst them there was a heavy, oblong object that had been securely wrapped in an oil-soaked cloth and he carefully lifted it out. The oil had impregnated the wooden bottom of the box, coating it with a dark stain.

'It smells of machine oil,' he said, rubbing the thumb and forefinger of his left hand together and sniffing them before he began to unwrap the parcel.

'It's a gun, and there are eight bullets. I don't know much about guns but it looks like one of those you see in war movies,' he said, laying it out with its ammunition on the cloth.

'But why would the Lanterns need a gun or any of these other weapons? What purpose could they serve?' Emily asked, retracing her steps to look down at it.

'I don't know, it certainly doesn't look as though any of them have been used for a long time, although they obviously wanted to keep them very well hidden. Perhaps they use them to kill their victims when Black Shuck isn't very hungry, who knows?'

'That isn't very funny, Hollis! Let's get out of here, this place is beginning to give me the creeps.'

Hollis hesitated. 'Don't you think we should put most of this stuff back – they might not realize . . .'

'No, what's the point, they'll know it was us whatever you do. Let's just get out of here, get as far away as possible from this wretched place.'

'But I can't do that, you know I can't, not until I've found those bodies.' Hollis reached for the gun, checking the chambers were empty before slipping it into his coat pocket along with the handful of bullets. He picked up the ledger and rubbed his sleeve across the front of it before wrapping it in one of the ceremonial robes and then thrust them both inside his coat and buttoned it up. He picked up the second spellbook from where it had fallen open on the floor and closed it before holding it up for Emily to take.

'We can't take it all with us, but we must keep the book. Here, hide it under your coat, we'll keep these for evidence; at least they'll prove that the Lanterns used this place for their meetings. Now, if you can really fly a plane and you meant what you said about helping me search the Fens – let's get going!'

Hollis stood in the entrance of the vast metal-fabricated barn that acted as a hangar as well as a farm machinery and grain store and looked at the two light aircraft that Emily's father owned. The wind had dropped to a chilly breeze and the afternoon sun didn't seem to have any warmth as he turned up his collar and thrust his hands deep into his pockets. He touched the revolver that he had left in his pocket as he watched Emily check over the Cessna 150 and climb up the gantry ladder onto the wing to pump fuel into the aircraft's tanks.

'Okay, I'm nearly done. Can you come over here and help me pull the plane out?' she called, brushing a stray strand of hair from her eyes and leaving a faint streak of grease on her forehead.

She stowed the ladder and removed the wheel chocks and showed him where to grip the propeller. The aircraft was much lighter than he had imagined it would be and the wings rocked and trembled in the light wind as it rolled easily over the concrete hardstanding outside the barn and onto the old taxi way. 'I must be mad!' he muttered to himself. For a moment he had misgivings about flying over the vast expanse of mud and water of the Fens in something that seemed so small and fragile.

'Hop in, it's perfectly safe, I've done this lots of times. I was flying my father's planes before I could drive a car. He bought me this one for my twenty-first birthday. It's beautiful, isn't it?' Emily laughed at his apprehension as she climbed up into her seat and pulled the door shut.

'Yes, sure, it's great, but it's a little small, isn't it? You must admit it looks pretty puny against the ones I'm used to travelling in,' he replied uncertainly, as he climbed into the seat beside her and pulled his door shut, taking a moment to work out the buckling system of his seat-belt.

'Yes, it may be small but it's much more fun flying in one of these, you'll see.' She grinned, returning her attention to completing her instrument pre-flight check.

She glanced outside and called out 'start prop' as she fired up the engine. The propeller swung slowly over then the engine roared into life making the small plane vibrate as the propeller became a shimmering arc in front of them. Emily switched off all the electrics except the magnetos and set the throttle to a quarter of an inch while she held the revs at 12,000 to check both magnetos before increasing to 18,000 rpm. She idled back and cast her eyes quickly over the instruments for any tell-tale red lights before she pushed the throttle forwards and let off the brakes. The plane began to roll slowly forwards.

'Wait! I've just had an idea,' she cried, bringing the plane to a stop and shutting off the engine before she jumped out. 'Don't touch anything!' she called back to Hollis as she ran back into the hangar.

211

Hollis shifted in his seat to try and get more comfortable and he felt the plane rock slightly. The movement sharpened his misgivings but before he had time to reconsider flying over the Fens Emily reappeared carrying two, bright red, plastic, spherical objects. They were larger than footballs and both had orange, reflective beacons on top with small drag anchors attached to short lengths of cable fixed to the bottom.

'I just remembered that my father did some aerial surveying for the Ministry of Defence a couple of years ago and they never did come back to collect these marker buoys. If we see anything we can drop them and mark the spot.'

She passed them up to Hollis who stowed them in the space beside their seats and then she scrambled up, pulling the door shut behind her. She searched quickly through the map pouch beside her and passed him a couple of large-scale maps of the section of the marshes she intended to fly over. They opened the one that showed the Middle Level Drain.

'We'll fly north, north-east and keep crossing and re-crossing all the dykes and channels that flow into the Middle Level Drain from the north of the village first. We'll try to follow them on the map and mark them off as we fly over them.' She gave him a red felt pen from the pouch.

Restarting the engine she taxied onto the runway, set the brakes and ran the engines up to full power; she took a last, quick look around and then released the brakes. The Cessna quickly accelerated along the runway and the nose lifted, the rumble of wheels vanished abruptly and they were airborne. Hollis felt his stomach sink for a moment as they lifted off the ground and banked away across the village towards the marshes. The afternoon sun glinted on the dark, peaty water of the dykes and channels and the tall reeds threw waving shadows as they flew over them. There was a power and a strange beauty in the wild landscape that was slipping effortlessly away beneath them. Hollis turned towards Emily and was about to raise his voice to make himself heard above the roar of the engine when he caught sight of a shadowy, indistinct figure out of the corner of his eye. He snapped his head round and his breath caught in his throat as he smelt that faint but familiar odour of decay. The three ghosts were crowding into the space behind him and before he could move or warn Emily, the shorter of the figures, Dennis Skinner, reached forwards and gripped her shoulder with his wet, withered fingers and pointed past her, showering her with mud and water. His voice gurgled urgently.

'East, east, we lie much further east . . .'

Emily shuddered and flinched instinctively away from the dead touch, accidentally pushing the control stick forwards. The plane dived, vibrating violently as it picked up speed.

'Get back, you crazy bastard, get back!' Hollis shouted in panic.

The apparition shrank back away from Emily as the sound of the engine reached screaming pitch and the tall reeds and murky waters of the marsh rushed up towards them. Emily grappled with the controls and managed to pull the plane out of the dive with moments to spare and they skimmed over the top of the reeds. The colour had drained from her face and her eyes reflected the sudden shock of that ghostly touch.

'What are you trying to do – get us both killed? What good will that do you, who's going to find you then?' Hollis shouted at the three figures as his panic turned into anger. Gradually he recovered his composure and lowered his voice. 'Pull another stunt like that, touch either one of us again, and we'll go back to the airfield and let you rot out here for eternity. Have you got that?'

'No . . . no . . . wait, Hollis, don't scare them away, we need their help. The chances of finding their bodies without

213

it are pretty remote. I'm sorry if I reacted like that a moment ago but it was the shock.' She paused, glancing around, a tentative smile on her face. 'It was the shock of having my grandfather suddenly right there behind me – touching me. I want to find their bodies now I know about them, I want to put their souls at rest as much as you do. There was a moment last night when we were listening to my father talking about the three of them before they disappeared when I was really proud of my grandfather. It must have taken a lot of courage to stand up against those Lanterns.'

'Yes, it must have, I don't think I could have done it,' Hollis agreed as he watched the three figures take on more solid forms in the back of the plane. 'Okay, you can help us by telling us when we're getting close – but remember, no touching!' he insisted, but in a softer voice, trying not to look too closely at their wretched, decomposing bodies but instead returning his attention to the map and the watery wilderness slipping past so effortlessly six hundred feet beneath them.

'If you look out there to the right you'll see why you couldn't have searched the marshes any other way,' Emily called out over the roar of the engine as she banked the aircraft and took a more easterly direction and headed directly towards the Middle Level Drain, crossing a wide area of stagnant meres and treacherous stretches of liquid mud and tangled undergrowth that it would have been impossible to negotiate either on foot or in a boat.

'You're right.' He nodded, looking down and feeling a shiver of apprehension go through him. If they had engine failure now . . . if something happened . . .

'But then, if you think about it, if we can't get there then the Lanterns can't either, unless they really do have supernatural powers, so there would be no point looking there anyway!'

Emily smiled across at him and pointed down as they passed

over a narrow channel. 'You're right, but how would you know what it was like beyond the bank of that channel if you were in a boat? You wouldn't be able to see through the reeds and undergrowth, would you?'

Hollis nodded in silence as he watched the wildness gradually change. Now they were flying over dense reed beds intersected by a maze of dykes and drains that all seemed to be heading in the direction of a wide river that dissected the marshy landscape in an unnaturally straight line, vanishing towards the distant glimmer of the sea in the Wash.

'That's the Middle Level Drain, everything drains into it from miles around, the Fens are tidal here.' She held the aircraft on the same course for a few moments, looking down at the beds of reeds, and then banked steeply around and flew back over it a few hundred yards further north, repeating the search pattern and gradually working their way towards the Wash, covering a large, roughly oblong, area of about a quarter of a mile on either side of the Middle Level Drain.

After they had been flying for about forty minutes Hollis asked, 'Why do the bottom of some of these reeds look darker all of a sudden? And I think I can see mud banks in some of the channels.'

'It's because the tide is going out. A lot of this part of the Fens is salt marsh,' she replied, altering her course slightly to overfly one of the larger, more obvious, channels.

Hollis returned his attention to searching the marsh below, but the noise of the engine and the constant vibration from the plane as they covered the seemingly endless rush of reeds and water only a few hundred feet below them was beginning to give him a headache. A feeling of hopelessness was creeping over him. Perhaps Emily's father had been right after all, they were wasting their time in a fruitless search.

'Another ten minutes and we'll have to go back, we're running low on fuel,' Emily warned him.

Her voice broke into his thoughts and made him blink and glance around. Their three ghostly passengers were being very quiet; he saw them silently crowding against the windows just behind him, their heads staring down at each watery channel they crossed.

'It's hopeless, isn't it?' he muttered, addressing them with an edge of impatience in his voice. 'We're no closer to finding your bodies now than we were when we took off!'

Merris turned slowly towards him, and the look of sheer despair etched into his wasted, shrunken face made Hollis wish he had kept his mouth shut. 'I'm sorry . . .' he began, then the other figures suddenly became very agitated, gesticulating towards a densely overgrown channel about a hundred yards from where it joined the Middle Level Drain.

'We are there . . . over there!' he cried, water and mud gurgling from his mouth.

Emily throttled back and put the nose down as she banked sharply to the right, following the figures' wild pointing. The noise of the engine seemed to fade and Hollis imagined he could hear the rush of the wind humming over the wings and fuselage as they descended in a steep arc. He slid the window back and stuck his head out, craning his neck to look down. The slipstream tore at his hair and made his eyes water as he searched the dense mass of reeds with the glistening mud and tangled roots that hedged in the narrow channel. Moorhens and water rail, disturbed by the noise and shadow of the aircraft skimming so low over the top of the reeds, scattered across the dark surface of the water to vanish amongst the undergrowth.

'Can you see anything?' Emily shouted over the roar of the engine as she pushed the throttle forwards and climbed away. The three figures began wailing and pointing frantically.

'I think they're trying to tell us that we have to go further back in this channel,' Hollis cried.

Emily climbed away and made a wide turn to take the plane back over the Middle Level Drain, flying it directly along the channel. 'I hope you realize that I'm going to lose my licence if anybody sees me flying this low,' she muttered grimly as she put the aircraft into a shallow dive.

'Look really hard because I haven't got enough fuel left to do this more than once or twice,' she warned him as he stuck his head back out of the window, blinking and forcing his eyes to stay open.

The sunlight sparkled on the sluggish ripples in the narrow channel and the tall, waving reeds on its banks with their glistening roots were a forest of light and shadow as they flashed past beneath him. They were flying so low he felt he could almost reach out and touch them when he saw it. It went past so quickly that he could have missed it with a blink. It was a long, dark shape overhung by reeds, half-buried by mud and covered with reed roots.

'I've seen it! It's down there! It's there, we've just flown over it. Go back!' he shouted, his voice almost drowned out by the noise of the engine as Emily climbed to circle the spot. The voices of the three ghosts reached a crescendo of excitement behind them. Emily peered down and saw what looked like the dark outline of a boat on the edge of the channel. It was almost completely hidden by reeds and partly submerged in the mud. She was sure nobody would ever have seen it if they hadn't been looking for it.

'We'll drop one of those marker buoys.'

She levelled out the aircraft and headed back towards the Middle Level Drain. 'Try and aim to anchor it in the mouth

217

of the channel, it's the only way we'll ever be able to find it again when we come back at the next low tide – then we'll come back in a boat along the Middle Level Drain with the authorities and collect their bodies.'

'Yeah, sure,' Hollis shouted back, twisting around in his seat to reach for the buoy, but he hesitated for a second as he hunted the small, cramped space behind the seats, realizing that the three ghostly figures had gone. They had vanished in silence, taking that stagnant odour of decay with them.

'You'll have to force the door open if you want to throw it out. Are you ready? The mouth of the channel is coming up any moment now . . .'

Hollis barely had time to sense the enormous feeling of release that flooded the cramped cockpit of the aircraft, or to hear the sigh of relief that disappeared into the roar of the engine, before Emily's voice galvanized him into action. He grasped the buoy and pulled it into his lap; with his left hand he undid the door catch and forced the door open with his shoulder, pushing hard against the slipstream. He leaned out as far as he dared. Ahead the broad, muddy waters of the Middle Level Drain were catching the sunlight. He dropped the marker buoy and watched it curve away in a lazy arc beneath them to land with a splash amongst the reeds a yard or two inside the channel. The current seized it and it began to drift out into the drain but the drag anchor sank into the mud and roots beneath the surface of the water in channel and it stopped, tilting slightly against the tug of the current before bobbing up and down in the water.

Hollis let out a sigh of relief and sank back in his seat as the plane climbed away across the Fens and headed back towards the airfield. 'We've done it! We actually found them! We –' Hollis' voice faltered and his laughter turned to anxiety when the roar of the engine faltered and missed a beat.

Emily cursed and tapped at the fuel gauge as she climbed, trying to gain as much height as possible. 'Come on, come on, don't cut out on me now!' she whispered. Her whole concentration focused on coaxing her plane home as she watched the altimeter climb. In the distance she could just see the tall tower of the village church; beyond it was the airfield with its bright, green roof of her father's hangar and the grey-white, concrete runway and the slightly darker strip of taxi way where the bombers used to queue up for take-off during the war. There was a chance they would make it, the village was no more than a mile and a half away, if only she could gain enough height, if only the engine would keep going for just another few, precious seconds. The needle on the fuel gauge had dropped below empty, the altimeter was touching 950 feet.

'Come on! Come on!' she coaxed.

Hollis swallowed, he felt sick and terrified. All he could do was sit there and watch helplessly as the marshes slipped away beneath them. His hands were clenched tightly into fists, his jaws were clamped together so tightly his head ached. He could see the distant roofs of the village, but it looked too far away. The tall reed beds they were flying over had given way to thick clumps of undergrowth: low, twisted blackthorns and banks of weeds and nettles that grew around stagnant pools of mud. There were now deep, well-cut ditches beneath them with sluices that forced back the wilderness. Looking out to his left he realized that they were following an old track of some sort. It looked almost completely overgrown and it led directly towards the back of the church. He caught sight of a movement beneath the trees, a fleeting shadow – something was running through the undergrowth. He pressed his face against the window and looked down. There was an enormous, black dog. It broke cover and veered off the track, plunging through the undergrowth, running scared probably, frightened by the noise of the plane. He followed it and caught sight of the remains of a broken roof and walls of a small stone hut partially hidden by blackthorn and elderflower bushes.

'Black Shuck!' he hissed, turning towards Emily in the moment the engine cut out.

'Damn!' Emily muttered, her voice tight with concentration in the sudden silence; she barely registered that Hollis had said something about a dog, she had her hands full now if she was going to get the plane down safely. 'I'm going straight in, I'm going to try and land on the taxi way so prepare yourself for anything.'

She didn't look round, she knew it couldn't be more than half a mile, probably a lot less, and she had enough height to get over the village. She just hoped it would be enough to get them onto the airfield, but the approaching roofs and chimney pots looked so high, so solid, as she put the nose of the Cessna down to keep her air speed hovering around 80 knots. She knew if she let it drop below 70 knots they would stall and then the plane would fall out of the sky.

'Hold tight!' she hissed, glancing at the altimeter as it unwound and holding the aircraft in a shallow dive across the rooftops. There wasn't going to be any room for error and she was not going to have a second chance.

Hollis gripped the edges of his seat, holding his breath as he watched the village lift up to meet them. He saw the startled face of a fisherman as he looked up to see them crossing over the second pond just before they flew over the roof of the derelict old inn beside the church. He caught a glimpse of some figures in the backyard of the building, three, maybe four, and the back door was standing wide open. The next instant they were skimming over small fields, hedges and clumps of bushes.

'Jesus Christ!' he gasped as the rusting boundary fences of the airfield rushed towards them, then he screwed his eyes tightly shut and waited for the crash as the wheels sank into the rows of sugar beet and their plane was pulled over. Then he felt a light bump followed by a dozen or so more as the plane landed on the taxi way and its wheels trundled over the tussocks of grass that grew in the concrete before it slowed and came to a stop. He let out his breath in a long sigh of relief and looked around at Emily – she was grinning.

'There! I told you it would be much more fun flying in one of these little planes, didn't I!' She was smiling as she checked everything was switched off before she opened her door and climbed out, but the sheer relief at being back on the ground in one piece was obvious in her voice.

'Oh yes, sure it was, but don't ever ask me to do it again. I'll stick with USAir if it's okay with you. There was a moment back there when I thought we weren't going to make it!' Hollis grumbled as they walked back towards the house.

'I had my doubts too, but I promise to save enough fuel to land next time, don't worry,' she laughed.

Hollis stopped her and looked at her for a moment. A lot of the reckless spirit of her grandfather, and his courage, had rubbed off onto her; he had really grown to admire her in the last twenty-four hours. 'Okay, if there ever is a next time I want a parachute!' he replied, feeling a grin spreading across his face. 'But right now we had better get on the telephone and inform the authorities about finding those bodies. And I'll need to inform the American Embassy, officially Merris Calvin is still missing on active service.'

10

HOLLIS STOOD, his ear pressed to the receiver, as he waited for the switchboard operator to connect him to the right extension at the Embassy. The phone line crackled. 'Yes, that's right, I want to report finding the body of my grandfather, Lieutenant Merris Calvin, Army number 733726. He was officially reported missing in East Anglia in February 1943. Yes, that's right, we have found his body and the bodies of Dennis Skinner and Douglas Reeve, two of his friends who disappeared at the same time. They are in a boat partly submerged in the marshes close to the Middle Level Drain. Yes, the police in Kings Lynn have been informed. They are sending down a team to try and retrieve them tomorrow at low tide. Yes, sure, that's right, Candleford – Sparrow Hall, you can't miss it.'

Hollis replaced the receiver and smiled at Emily and her mother. 'They're sending someone up here first thing in the morning.'

'Well, if they do manage to recover those bodies from the marsh tomorrow your father will have to make the arrangements to get them a proper burial in the churchyard, won't he, Emily dear? Do you think Douglas Reeve still has any relatives living around here? It's been such a long time . . .' Sheila smiled and turned to Hollis before Emily had time to answer.

'Of course you'll want to take your grandfather's body home and have him laid to rest amongst his own family, won't you?'

Hollis shrugged and shook his head. There was something

nagging at the back of his mind, something important but the hair-raising landing had driven it completely out of his head. 'I don't know what to do for the best,' he admitted, walking slowly across to the window and looking out. 'Merris has been laying out there in the mud and weeds at the bottom of that boat for so long perhaps it would be better to bury him here side by side with his two best friends. I'm sure that's what both he and my father would have wanted after all this time.'

Emily suddenly laughed. 'The Lanterns certainly aren't going to relish the fact that we have found them, not after they have lain hidden out there in the marshes for all those years. I'll bet there's one hell of a commotion when they discover we've broken into those cupboards and found their robes and things too!'

'Emily — they already know!' Hollis cried, interrupting her. 'I saw a group of villagers milling about in the yard at the back of the building — the back door was wide open, I saw it as we flew over it. And there's something else . . .' He paused and stood on tiptoe, looking down at the mass of paw prints that spoiled the flower beds outside the study window. 'There's no demon dog, well there is but it's no phantom, no ghost, nothing like your father described last night. I'm not saying there isn't any substance to those old legends, after what's been happening to me recently I am convinced that ghosts really do exist, but I'm beginning to think that the dog we heard howling in the marshes when we left the Louse and Rag last night and who later hurled itself against this window is real. Do you remember when I called out "Black Shuck" when we were flying back towards the village just as the engine cut out?'

Emily quickly nodded, impatient for him to continue.

'Well I caught a glimpse of a dog, a huge, black brute running along that overgrown track. It was heading towards

226

the village when it suddenly veered off, plunging through the undergrowth and hurrying towards a ruined hut that was partially hidden in a dense clump of thorn bushes. There definitely wasn't anyone with the dog and it made me wonder, what if the Lanterns keep their own dog hidden away out there in the marshes and use it to look like Black Shuck? It would be much more reliable than conjuring up a phantom, wouldn't it? They could use the beast to terrify people whenever they wanted and they could keep the belief in all those myths and legends going indefinitely. Fear is a very powerful persuader – a great way to control people.'

'But that's crazy! There are dozens of dogs who live in the village – it could have been any one of them, loads of them go for a wander in the marshes – Culloden's always getting out. Perhaps if you saw him running through the bushes you would think it was Black Shuck!' Emily exclaimed.

'Perhaps,' Hollis answered grimly. 'But there's only one way to find out. I'm going to try and capture the one I saw. If I'm wrong and you can identify who it belongs to then I'll return it to the owner. But if I'm right . . .' Hollis fell silent as he reached for his coat and pulled it on.

'Wait!' Emily called out after him. 'If you're right then you think the Lanterns are going to bring it here tonight, don't you? And if you're right it won't be coming just to frighten us this time, will it?'

Hollis nodded bleakly, his hand was on the door handle. 'I don't think your father was far off the mark last night when he was worried about the Lanterns putting two and two together and working out why I'm here. They know your family aren't a part of the organization so who else but us would have broken into those cupboards and stolen their secrets? Remember they've murdered before and by now they know that *we* know about them – they'll have to murder us too if they want to stay hidden. We've got all the evidence right here and catching that dog might do no good at all, but then it just might throw them completely off balance. It might make them hesitate just long enough for the police to get here in the morning. At least doing something is better than just sitting here waiting for it to get dark – just waiting for them to arrive.'

'But it's very dangerous out there in the marshes. Won't you wait until Gregory gets back? I'm sure he won't be long, then you can take Culloden with you.' Sheila tried to stop them leaving the house but Hollis shook his head.

'There isn't time, we have to go now before it gets dark.'

'Please be careful both of you . . .' Sheila called out after them as Emily led the way across the fields at the back of the house towards the church as they followed the overgrown track that led out into the marshes.

'Are you sure we haven't passed the place where you thought you saw the hut? We seem to have come a long way out into the marshes and it's beginning to get dark. I would hate to meet some of those Lanterns out here, we might get lost!' Emily called out anxiously to Hollis who was forcing a way through the waist high weeds and nettles. She had to keep stopping and shielding her face with her arm to protect herself from the sharp thorns and trails of creepers that hung down from the branches that overhung the path. She was beginning to regret rushing out so hastily – she was hot in her heavy coat and swarms of insects were buzzing angrily around her head, even the ground beneath her feet began to feel boggy and she kept sinking up to her ankles into the soft, glutinous, evil-smelling mud.

Hollis suddenly stopped as he reached an area of the path that was clear of undergrowth. Away to his left he could see the dense clump of bushes that hid the hut. He was about to turn and tell Emily to keep her voice down when he heard a noise from the direction of the hidden shed, a low-pitched growling sound that set the hairs on his scalp prickling. He looked quickly around for something to defend them with, grabbing at a dead branch in desperation but it crumbled away to nothing in his hand.

'What was that?' Emily hissed, catching up with him and gripping his arm.

The undergrowth rustled and broke apart as an enormous, unkempt mastiff emerged onto the path less than twenty feet in front of them. It snarled, baring its fangs menacingly, strings of saliva hung down from its gaping jaws and flecked its black muzzle. Its staring eyes were bright yellow and seemed to grow larger as it bounded forwards. The snarl deepened and became a blood-curdling howl. It was the most savage, terrifying creature that Hollis had ever seen and he staggered backwards in an effort to get away from it but in doing so he knocked into Emily and sent them both sprawling onto the ground as the dog launched itself, leaping high into the air. Emily's scream was drowned out by a sudden, deafening explosion that echoed through the undergrowth from about a yard behind where they lay. The huge beast seemed to stop abruptly in mid-air, almost hovering above them for a second, before the howl became a choking yelp and its body jerked and convulsed as it crashed to the ground to fall dead at their feet. Hollis turned his head and looked up to see Emily's father standing, white-faced, a few paces behind them, the smoking gun gripped in his trembling hands as he stared down at the dog.

'Daddy, thank God you came. How did you know where we were?' Emily cried, scrambling to her feet and running to him.

Slowly he lowered the gun to put his arms around his daughter as Culloden ran past them growling to sniff at the dead dog.

'Your mother told me where you were. She told me what Hollis had said about seeing that dog as you came into land and showed me those books and the revolver that you took from the old inn. Suddenly it all seemed to make sense. I had caught glimpses of that creature myself dozens of times but I had always assumed that it had to be the beast of the legends. I never for one moment thought it may be a real dog!'

Gregory gave a dry, shallow laugh and helped Hollis to his feet. 'Mind you, when the creature leapt at you then there was a moment when I thought I might be too terrified to pull the trigger. All those old fears, all those old phantoms from my childhood seemed to well up. I've never been so frightened!'

Hollis grinned uncertainly and brushed at the thick mud on his jeans. 'Well I'm glad you're a better shot than I am!'

Culloden suddenly barked and ran towards the hidden hut and the others followed, forcing their way through the thick undergrowth into the open doorway. Emily took one look inside and retreated. 'I think I'm going to be sick,' she gasped, holding her stomach.

Hollis took a deep breath and stepped in over the threshold. A wave of nausea overwhelmed him at the sight that met his eyes. The rough earth floor was littered with dog faeces and gnawed bones and there were vile, bloated scraps of rotting meat. Everywhere he looked there were heavy iron rings and hooks set into the crumbling brickwork with loops of rusty broken chains. The stench of decay and filth was almost unbearable but it was the sight of the wretched remnants of another dog lying where it had died, still chained to the back wall that made Hollis retch. The white glint of its backbone was clearly visible where it had erupted through the rotting, dried-out carcass and it showed with a ghostly glow in the gloomy shadows.

'Come away, Hollis,' Gregory urged, quietly taking his arm

230

and leading him out to where Emily stood, pale and shaken from what she had glimpsed inside the hut.

'Hollis was right,' Gregory continued, steeling himself to look back. 'The Lanterns must have been keeping dogs chained up in here in the most awful conditions for a very long time and using them to frighten people. It is no wonder that the people who reported what they thought was the demon dog said it was such a ferocious creature – after this sort of torture and inhuman treatment the poor animals must have been driven wild with despair.'

Gregory frowned and caught sight of Culloden sniffing at a piece of rotting meat. 'Culloden, come here boy, don't touch that stuff. Heel, boy.' He put the dog on a lead and passed it over to Emily. 'Come on, let's get back to the house, there's nothing more we can do here.'

'But we can't just leave that poor dog lying there. Shouldn't we get it off the track and cover it up with something? It's not the poor creature's fault the Lanterns turned it into a wild animal.'

'No, we have to leave it exactly where it is so that the authorities can see it and everything else just as we found it when they come tomorrow morning,' Gregory insisted.

'I'll bet the dog will be gone and the hut will have been cleaned out by tomorrow morning. Come to think of it everything we disturbed in that old pub will have vanished as well. Remember you told us last night that if anybody starts asking questions about the Lanterns and if it looks as though the authorities may be about to start an investigation into their activities then they all melt away into thin air . . .' The other two stared at Hollis as he spoke.

'Damn! I wish I had brought a camera with me!' Emily exclaimed.

'There's no time to go and get one, anyway it wouldn't

make any difference,' her father replied softly, glancing up at the darkening sky. 'All a set of photographs would prove is that somebody has been keeping dogs out here in the marshes in terribly cruel conditions. We haven't got any names have we, there aren't any names in those books you took from the Lanterns' meeting place and we don't have anything that would point the finger conclusively at anyone. Come on, let's get back to the house, I'm worried about Sheila being there all on her own.'

Hollis took a last look back at the dog where it lay in the centre of the track and then glanced up to the ridge of the steep pantiled roof of the old inn where it loomed ominously above the trees.

'Yes, we'd better hurry, I reckon those Lanterns are sure to pay us a visit once it gets dark. They'll be after those things we took from the inn this afternoon.'

'Hadn't we better call the police?'

'We'll ring the moment we get back, but I doubt they'll be much help tonight. The nearest police station is miles away at Black Ferry – we'll probably have suffered the same fate as Merris, Douglas and my father before they get here . . .' Gregory paused, looking thoughtfully at Hollis. 'The people from the Embassy should be here at first light so all we have to do is hold out until morning. Are you any good with a gun, Hollis?' he asked, grimly reloading the shotgun as he led the way back to Sparrow Hall.

'Sure, I've squeezed a few off in the shooting range at college, but I've never actually shot at anybody.'

'There's a first time for everything.'

Calling the police proved impossible. On their return they found that not only had the telephone lines been cut but also the main power supply to the hall had been disrupted. Gregory was considering driving across to the farm office on the edge

232

of the airfield, which ran on a separate supply, but Sheila was against it. She warned him that she had caught a glimpse of two or three suspicious characters hanging about near the entrance to the drive just before they had got back.

'Well, there's nobody out there now, why don't we make a dash for it before it gets dark. We could spend the night in the pub near Cockley Cley. We'd be safe enough there, wouldn't we?'

Gregory looked at Hollis and then shook his head. 'You don't know these Lanterns, Hollis. Believe me, you might not be able to see them but if Sheila says they're out there, then they'll be hiding in the undergrowth, probably waiting for us to do just what you've suggested. Don't forget they're pretty good at creating accidents, and the road we'd have to take runs too close – far too close – to the marshes for my liking. No, we'll be safer here. Sheila, you and Emily organize all the oil lamps and candles you can find and take Culloden with you while Hollis and I see what we can do about barricading the doors and windows. I think we are in for a long night.'

Hollis peered out of the study window in the soft, flickering light for a moment before closing the shutters and bolting them. He saw that it had started to rain again. The thickening dusk was rapidly drawing in around the hall, blotting out the flat, desolate marshes and emphasizing the building's isolated position. Somewhere beyond the garden wall an eerie howl suddenly broke the silence and Hollis felt an icy shiver run up his spine. Behind him he heard Gregory swear under his breath as he fumbled and dropped a box of cartridges, spilling the contents out across his desk.

'Damn those Lanterns. They must have kept another one of those dogs hidden up somewhere in the marshes. Quickly, bolt those last two shutters and help me load these guns. I seem to be all fingers and thumbs.'

As Hollis swung the shutters closed he saw lights, dozens of them, appearing amongst the garden shrubbery and hooded figures carrying lanterns began to emerge from the darkness to cross the lawn towards them.

'Jesus Christ! I never imagined there'd be so many.'

Hollis stepped back instinctively and grabbed the heavy iron bar to pull across the shutters. But then he hesitated, holding the shutters open a crack to watch as three familiar shadowy figures began to materialize on the edge of the lawn and stand between the approaching Lanterns and the hall.

'Gregory, it looks as though more than half the village are surrounding us. We'll never be able to keep them all out. What are we to do?' Sheila's frightened voice called out from the upstairs landing where she and Emily were watching the ugly crowd advancing across the lawn towards the house.

'Hollis, for goodness sake close that shutter! Bolt it down and then come over here and help me load.'

There was a note of panic in Gregory's voice so Hollis turned and hurried across the study. The doors of the gun cabinet had been flung wide open and the desk was littered with his collection of shotguns, two small-bore rifles and a revolver.

'I don't think those Lanterns are going to have things all their own way.' Hollis grinned as he quickly pushed two cartridges into the chambers of the gun and snapped it shut.

'What did you say?' Gregory frowned, stuffing a handful of ammunition into his pocket and gathering up as many of the guns as he could carry before making for the open door into the hall.

Before Hollis could answer shouts erupted from the steps of the house, along with the sound of breaking glass and a heavy object being hammered against the front door. Then he heard screams and the sounds stopped abruptly.

'Quick – upstairs – we'll be able to cover the hall from the first landing and fire on them from the windows as they come across the lawn.'

As Hollis grabbed the rest of the guns and ammunition he suddenly remembered the photograph that had drawn him all the way to Candleford. 'Emily, get your camera! Take as many pictures of the Lanterns as you can.'

The flash from the camera almost blinded Hollis as he took up a position next to Gregory at the open window. Below them, dozens of hooded figures who only moments before had been advancing menacingly on the house were now hesitating and beginning to draw back.

'Something's down there,' Sheila whispered, moving closer to her husband. 'Something has frightened them and they're beginning to scatter.'

'I'll make them scatter, all right,' he hissed through clenched teeth as he threw a double-barrelled shotgun up against his shoulder.

All those years of living in fear of the Lanterns, all those times he kept silent when he should have spoken out, all those instances when he should have done something but did nothing boiled up inside him, breaking through to the surface as he closed his finger around the trigger. At that moment he was consumed by a lifetime of anger and he fully intended to take his revenge. He was not afraid any more. He looked down the barrels, centring the gun on the landlord of the Louse and Rag. There was no mistaking him despite the mask he wore, and he was ordering the others forward so he had to be one of the ringleaders. As Gregory's finger gradually tightened three ghostly figures appeared in his line of fire and he saw the spectre of his father and his two friends closing in around the landlord. Gregory froze and lowered the gun. He watched as the fat man stumbled backwards, choking and gasping for breath as the long-dead, muddy fingers clawed at his face and tore away his disguise. On either side of him panic spread through the mob and they began fighting one another as they tried to run back to their cars, but as each one moved blackened bony fingers reached out to strip away their disguises.

'While I was closing the shutters I thought I saw them. I had a feeling they wouldn't let any harm come to us tonight,' Hollis called out. 'Keep taking pictures, Emily. We should have enough evidence to show the police when they get here. When we've finished that cult should never bother us again.'

Gregory looked grim. 'And just for good measure I think we should show them that we are armed, just in case they think about coming back again before morning.'

He raised the gun to his shoulder again but before he could fire Sheila grabbed his arm. 'No, wait. Killing them won't solve anything, Gregory. It won't bring back your father, or anybody else, so please don't do something you might regret for the rest of your life.'

Gregory laughed as he pulled himself free from her restraining hand. 'I'm not going to do anything as silly as that – well, not now, not unless they really do break into my house. I'm just going to fire a couple of warning shots over their heads to make sure they don't even think about coming back.'

'They'd be fools to try with the ghosts of Candleford watching over us. Look down there, you can just see them in the light of that abandoned lantern, they're guarding the entrance to the drive.'

As the others followed Hollis' gaze they could all just make out the three shadowy figures ranged across the entrance to Sparrow Hall. And they knew that they would sleep safely – and soundly – in Candleford tonight.

236

11

HOLLIS SHIVERED in the dull grey wreath tails of mist that hung across the water and he pulled his coat collar up higher around his ears, bracing himself against the slight motion of the motor launch as it chugged slowly along the Middle Level Drain, pushing out a dirty white bow wave that washed in lazily amongst the roots of the tall reed beds that lined the muddy banks on either side. The mist seemed to shroud everything in a damp, clinging silence, even subduing the voices of the policemen who were helping the team of divers to check over their equipment and the two officials from the American Embassy who stood slightly apart from the others in the stern beside the body bags.

'Those bodies had better be where we said they were.' Emily's whisper barely escaped from where she sat wrapped up against the cold, watching for the marker buoy they had dropped in the mouth of the channel when they had seen the dark shape of the boat lying, half-submerged amongst the reeds. She knew it couldn't be much further, her main worry was that during the attack on the hall some of the Lanterns might have come out in the night and removed it.

'They will be there, don't worry,' Hollis whispered back, glancing over his shoulder to where her father was deep in conversation with the police inspector who was in charge of the recovery operation. He could hear Gregory telling him what he knew about the Lanterns and trying to explain why they had been searching over the marshes the previous day without the reasons sounding too absurd.

'It's there – look, ahead of us to the right! I can see the marker buoy we dropped to mark the channel!' Emily suddenly cried, jumping to her feet and clutching at Hollis' shoulder to keep her balance as the boat changed direction, swinging in towards the bank and sending a colony of ducks flying noisily into the air.

'The channel – I can't see it – where's it gone?' Hollis hissed under his breath as he quickly stood up to search along the endless line of reeds, looking on either side for the bright red buoy bobbing up and down in the water. Surely the Lanterns hadn't moved it during the night, they would never find the channel if they had.

The helmsman slowed the engine and studied the reeds and swirls of currents that would indicate the flow of the hidden drain and then he nudged the bow of the boat to the left of the buoy and cut a path through the seemingly impenetrable mass of reeds to reveal the entrance to the channel. The shallow keel bumped and scraped on the mud and roots that had silted up the mouth and it suddenly became very dark as the reeds closed in on either side, brushing against the gunwales and showering them with icy drops of water.

'I don't know how far you're planning to go searching in here for them bodies but these old channels can be very treacherous if they're not dredged regularly and this one doesn't look as though it's been touched for years. In fact I doubt whether anyone's been in here since they stopped cutting reed for thatch. I wouldn't want to be trying to get us out against the tide when it turns,' the helmsman warned, thrusting a long boat hook in amongst the mass of tangled roots that were grasping at them from beneath the water to hold them steady against the ebbing current.

'Exactly how far away is this boat?' asked the inspector, looking from Hollis to Emily.

'It's only a few yards into the channel on the . . .' Hollis paused and turned to face the Middle Level Drain that was now completely hidden by the reeds behind the stern of the boat. It was difficult to get his bearings, they were completely hemmed in by the tall reeds and he had only seen the boat for a few moments from the air. They had been circling so which side of the channel would it be on? He closed his eyes and tried to forget the circle of expectant faces intimidating him as they waited impatiently for an answer. He could see they weren't wholly convinced that they had really seen anything. Slowly Hollis lifted his left hand, the one he had used to shield his eyes from the sun as he had looked down the channel.

'It was on the right – yes, I'm sure it was, the channel widens out and the boat is lying tilted slightly onto its side, buried quite deeply in the mud. I am sure it wasn't very far ahead of us now.'

The inspector turned, undecided, to the helmsman. 'How long do we have before the tide turns?'

The helmsman glanced over the stern of the boat and spat into the water, watching the globule of spittle float away sluggishly amongst the reeds. 'About an hour, maybe an hour and a half, but it wouldn't be safe to stay in here any longer than that.'

'Go ahead slowly, but keep an eye on the tide,' the inspector instructed.

The boat shuddered and the bow nosed through the reeds that choked and overhung the channel.

'It's here!' Hollis whispered, gripping Emily's hand as they emerged through the reeds into a wider part of the channel. 'This is exactly the same as the place in my nightmares. I saw the figures rise out of the water in front of me from that dense

241

mass of reeds, it must have been high tide when the boat was submerged . . .'

He suddenly stopped talking as one of the policemen at the front of the boat shouted to the helmsman to stop. They had seen the dark outline of something lying in the mud of the right-hand bank. The boatman stopped the engine and let the boat glide across the narrow channel to bump softly against the rotting timbers of the wreck. Two of the divers jumped into the water and secured the two craft together with ropes while other members of the forensic team began to set up pumps to suck out the mud and water that had completely filled the old craft.

'There isn't anything visible. I thought you said you saw them lying in the boat? I hope you haven't brought us out here on some wild goose chase!' Gregory frowned. It wasn't that he didn't want to believe them only he could imagine the repercussions there would be if the boat was empty, the new strength it would give to the Lanterns. Anxiously he watched the generator being started and the pumps begin to suck a steady stream of thick, muddy water and silt from the boat.

'I know they are in that boat. Yes look . . .' Hollis swallowed and stared as the tops of three, weed-entangled, blackened heads were beginning to appear as the level of glutinous mud inside the boat gradually subsided.

Emily clutched at her father's arm and turned away with tears in her eyes. 'Daddy, I can't look,' she whispered. Seeing the ghosts appear in the Louse and Rag and in her father's study had been so different. No matter how revolting their appearance had been, or how disgusting they had smelled, they had been real, almost, even if they had been animated purely by the strength of their determination to be found. But this was different, seeing them dredged up out of the mud and debris that had accumulated in that boat over the years, washed in and out with each tide, filled her with a great sadness. They looked so pitiful, so small and shrivelled as they sat shrunken and huddled together, their clothes no more than slimy rags that clung to their wasted, blackened bodies.

The forensic team worked fast setting up a hoist and in less than ten minutes they had transferred the bodies onto the deck of the motor launch and Hollis sighed as he blinked away the tears that had begun to fill his eyes. A great wave of relief was flooding through him. He had done it! He had achieved the impossible, he had found the three bodies. He was about to turn to Emily and tell her how glad he was it was all over when one of the forensic officers who was putting the bodies into the black bags called them over.

'From the look of it all three of them were murdered, possibly before they were put into the boat.'

He pointed down to a neat, round hole in the centre of each forehead. The officer paused and glanced up at the inspector to ask, 'Do we have enough time to dredge the bottom of the boat to look for the murder weapon, Sir?'

'I think you may already have it,' Hollis answered flatly, making them all stare at him.

It didn't take too much imagination to piece together the events of that awful February night over fifty years ago when Dennis Skinner and Douglas Reeve had driven to the Black Shuck Inn to collect his grandfather. 'They were probably killed on the night they disappeared with that revolver we gave to you along with those books and robe we took from the derelict inn in Candleford. They were probably murdered in the very room we found them in, although I doubt we could ever prove it or find who did it after all this time.'

Hollis smiled as he turned away. It didn't matter now

243

anyway, the important thing was that they had found the bodies and they could give them a proper burial.

'We had better start back, I don't want to be caught by the tide,' the helmsman warned, keeping a wary eye on the three body bags that were oozing a thin trail of muddy water across the deck.

'Yes,' Hollis murmured to himself, 'there's nothing more for us here, we've found what we came for.'

EPILOGUE

THE FUNERAL HAD TAKEN PLACE two days before. It had been a solemn, serious affair with a military guard of honour sent from the American Embassy. Hollis was glad it was all over and he could stand alone in the churchyard beside his grandfather's grave. He had a small bunch of flowers clutched in his hand ready to lay upon the mound of smooth, dark earth; he wanted to say a final, personal goodbye before he drove down to Gatwick to catch the late afternoon flight home.

It was a cold, dull, gunmetal-grey morning with a restless wind that ruffled through the dead leaves sending them scurrying along the ground and which pulled the low rain clouds across the sky. It began to rain, staining the surrounding headstones with long, dirty wet streaks. Hollis shivered and pulled up his coat collar. It was time to try to get back to normal, to get back to the life he had so abruptly curtailed when he had chased down the origins of that weird photograph that he had found amongst his grandfather's letters. Emily's family had made him very welcome and they had pressed him to stay as long as he wanted, even some of the villagers had seemed to warm towards him, but he was getting homesick. He felt a peculiar sort of loss now the persistent haunting had stopped and, in an odd way, he missed those three ghostly figures. They had left a void in his life that he knew would take some time to fill. He smiled and pulled the photograph out of his pocket, gently rubbing his fingers across the faded surface as he stared at the tiny thing that had started it all. At least he would always have this impossible, indelible image to remind him of these strange events, even if he would never know how the three of them had managed to alter the undeveloped roll of film in Merris' camera. Had they, he wondered, somehow managed to turn the Lanterns' magic against them in those last, desperate moments as the gun was pressed against their foreheads?

Hollis sighed and was about to slip the photograph back into his pocket before the rain spoiled it when a faint ripple of movement caught his eye. It was no more than when a small pebble has been dropped into a still pond but it was enough to catch his attention. The picture was changing, metamorphosing as he watched. He and Emily were fading, in fact the whole group of figures was melting away and in their place his grandfather and his two friends appeared. Not as drowned, weed-covered figures in sodden, rotting rags but as they had been on the day that the photograph had been taken. They were standing with their arms linked in front of the enormous fireplace at the old inn, and there was a slight smile on the face of each one of them as they gazed at him out of the picture. Hollis smiled back and carefully put the old photograph back into his pocket. Ghosts, magic, myths and legends. He knew now, for sure, that there was some truth in all of them; even though they had managed to dispel the lie about the frequent sightings of Black Shuck in the area around Candleford, proving it to be the work of the Lanterns. Emily's father had been right when he had said that they would vanish from sight, and all that could be hoped for is that they would never reappear. He glanced down at his watch; it was time to go.

He crouched down to lay the flowers on the grave – and froze. There were paw prints in the wet soil, enormous paw prints. They had trampled down the wet grass and left marks over the other two graves before vanishing into the undergrowth beyond the gate that he now knew led out into the Fens.

He straightened up quickly as the sound of rustling in the thick bushes beyond the gate caught his attention. As he stood up he caught a glimpse of a large, dark shape, the shape of a black dog with bright, yellow eyes watching him, moving closer. He stumbled backwards and turned to run for the car. Too much had happened in the last few days to stand there and doubt what he saw. The words of old Maurice, the domino player, came rushing back to him, they were shouting inside his head: 'Beware Black Shuck. Never, never look back at him across your shoulder, and never stop or turn around. Beware if the black dog is on your heels.'